SATANTA'S WOMAN

Other Five Star Titles
by Cynthia Haseloff:

The Chains of Sarai Stone
Man Without Medicine
The Kiowa Verdict

SATANTA'S WOMAN

A Western Story

CYNTHIA HASELOFF

Five Star
Unity, Maine

Copyright © 1998 by Cynthia Haseloff

Five Star Western
Published in conjunction with Golden West Literary Agency.

November 1998

First Edition

Five Star Standard Print Western Series.

The text of this edition is unabridged.

Set in 11 pt. Plantin by Minnie B. Raven.

Printed in the United States on permanent paper.

Library of Congress Cataloging in Publication Data

Haseloff, Cynthia.
  Satanta's woman : a Western story / by Cynthia Haseloff.
  — 1st ed.
      p.   cm.
    "Five star western" — Verso t.p.
    ISBN 0-7862-1335-3 (hc : alk. paper)
    1. Satanta, Kiowa Chief, ca. 1815–1878 — Fiction.
2. Kiowa Indians — Fiction.   3. Indians of North
America — West (U.S.) — Fiction.   I. Title.
  [PS3558.A72294S28   1998]
    813′.54—dc21   98-29040

W
HASELOFF,
Cynthia

The author wishes to thank Robert Kincaid for finding and sharing the book, KIOWA VOICES. The author also wishes to acknowledge permission from the Texas Christian University Press to quote Kiowa songs from this book, KIOWA VOICES, VOLUME I (1981) by Maurice Boyd.

Prologue

Huntsville, Texas 1878

The light steps echoed softly over the cold tiles of the empty church. There was no warmth in the high-ceilinged room. Not even a candle burned on the altar.

Father Molinari heard the bell of the confessional. It was his firm belief that someone always came when he was eating. He had, therefore, learned to push his food quickly into his mouth and chew once or twice before swallowing and stuffing more food into the orifice. He now finished chewing his last bite of lunch and washed it swiftly down with the red wine. He caught up his vestment from the wooden peg near the door and began trudging up the flight of stairs and down the hall toward the confessional box where someone waited. Over the years he had heard all the confessions there were. He was sure of that. As he often said, there was nothing new under the sun. Of course not, he agreed with himself again. The sins are all old. Only the sinners change. He burped softly and brushed the crumbs from his round belly before seating the cloth around his shoulders and settling it into place. He opened the door, moved into the seat, assumed the comfortable and fatherly position he had perfected over the years.

"What is it you wish to confess, my child?" he asked.

No response came from the other side of the louver. *Oh, dear,* thought Father Molinari, *it's going to be like that. Why can't people just say I did it, whatever it was, and get on with their confession? This one is going to take time.* And if his feet were not so cold against the bare floor, he might doze off.

"Speak up," he said more abruptly than he intended. "Delaying never got the job done."

"Father, forgive me, for I have sinned," the low but clear woman's voice began, then stopped.

Molinari settled back in his chair and crossed his hands over his full stomach. "Yes, yes," he encouraged quietly as he waited.

She began again with the same words. "Father, forgive me, for I have sinned. I have lived as the wife of a man not my husband. I have been Satanta's woman."

The round little priest sat up. "The Kiowa chief?"

"Yes," she said.

"You were his prisoner," the priest explained to himself as well as to the woman.

"I was his woman," the low voice said again.

"There is no condemnation for a woman under the duress of such circumstances, unless. . . ." The priest's words trailed off as he considered the extraordinary thought that a civilized white woman might have a relationship with a savage.

"Unless what?"

"Unless you lusted after the savage?"

"And what is lust, Father?"

"Lust . . . ," he started, "lust is an inordinate desire or appetite for something or someone. It is pleasure in the flesh."

"Pleasure in the flesh is wrong, Father?"

"Do not play with me," the man answered. "If you were raised in the Church, you know that pleasure in the flesh is wrong . . . *concupiscentia carnis* . . . lust of the flesh."

"Even in marriage?"

"In marriage some pleasure is acceptable, a reward for children," he affirmed. "But you said he was not your husband. You could not have been married to this man . . . not in any meaningful way, not in any way the Church recognizes."

8

"No," the woman's voice confirmed his point. "Not in anyway the Church recognizes."

Father Molinari settled back, his point made, the battle won. "And do you repent of this egregious sin?" He waited patiently for this woman to answer. He looked at his foot turning blue on the cold, shadowed floor. He squinched the toes several times to restore the circulation. *Well, well?* he thought to himself. *Can this take so much thought?* He drummed his fingers impatiently over his lunch. Then, his fleshy pink ears caught the sound of the door of the confessional closing softly as it released the confessor.

"The devil!" swore Father Molinari. "Ruined my lunch and, then. . . ." *And then what?* he thought with uncharacteristic doubt. *And then turned away from God's forgiveness bestowed by the Church?* A thought dangled. *Could anyone turn away from the overpowering forgiveness and generosity of God?* And worse still came another thought. *Could any human institution presume to dispense the unmerited favor and reconciliation inherent in the defining love of God?* The thoughts were too deep, too contentious for the priest. Perhaps he could yet get a short nap.

Adrianne Chastain blinked in the blinding brightness of the December noon. The interior darkness of the church had left her vulnerable to the natural light. Even the black veil over her face and throat did not protect her in the first moments.

She stood on the steps of the church, looking around at the small square of the town's buildings. She had never been in Huntsville before, had no reason to be there, no business in the south Texas prison town. The weather for December was warmer than in the northern counties from which she had come. Huntsville was more like the deep south, like Louisiana where she had lived. *It must have suffocated him,* she thought.

Chapter One

October 13, 1864

Susan Doogan nursed the baby at her breast contentedly as the black woman, Mary Johnson, pushed an iron pan of cornbread into the cook stove. "Ain't she pretty?" she asked.

"She's right handsome, Susan. Most babies is pretty. Then they grow up and turn into reg'lar ol' people." Mary talked without looking around. Finally, she wiped her hands on her apron and leaned over the chair where the mother and baby sat. "But that one, she is a pretty baby." She reached to the floor and lifted the two-year-old Millie into her arms. " 'Specially compared to this ugly thing here." Mary nuzzled Millie and carried the giggling child with her to the back door. "Nice for October. Oh, oh, Susan, here comes your mama. Looks like she's in a fizz over them horses. Seems like one of the men could have stayed to help with the work around this place. Your mama's a workin' fool, but she could use some help like other folks."

"They had to get the winter goods and the wood from the sawmill for the new rooms Mama's buildin'. Mama'll be just fine," the young Susan said, closing her blouse and coming to stand beside Mary and the toddler. "She ain't happy, unless she's plumb worked out. That's how Mama judges the day . . . if she ain't exhausted, she must have not done enough."

"You just as bad, you'self. You shore are the prime child of Adrianne Chastain. Both of you bitin' off more than you can chew most of the time. Just look at her." Mary grinned. "That

10

white woman's got another basket full of eggs. Like we ain't got but eighty dozen now."

"She's used to sellin' 'em, Mary."

"They ain't no soldiers at the fort no more. The folks that's left all got chickens from the ones she give away."

Susan's voice was serious. "You think she's forgiven me?"

"Sure she forgive you. Ain't she told you often enough? You just done what you thought was best fer her and fer Joe Carter. Them faints of hers was comin' too often. All that dyin' and buryin' and marryin' and money-changin' was just too much at the same time, even fer your ma. She got a heart like ever'body else. You done right, and she knows it, too."

Lottie Doogan, Susan's five-year-old, shouldered in between the two women at the door. "What you lookin' at?"

"Your grandmother, child. The livin', breathin' force of this here place, maybe the *whooole* world." Mary spoke softly, jiggling the toddler before turning back to her kitchen and setting the child down beside her sister. "You all go out an' set up the dinner plates on the table in the arbor. Be a nice day to eat outside. Pretty soon gonna be too cold."

"Ain't she something?" queried Susan, still standing at the door.

"Who?" asked the black woman.

"Mama."

Mary pursed her lips slightly and, coming again beside Susan, observed the woman advancing toward the cook house. Adrianne Chastain, mother and grandmother, looked fit and well, little more than older sister to her daughter. Not a large woman, she securely held the reins of the cattle and freight empire left by her husband's father. There was no slack in her. She knew every task that must be done and how to do it because she had done most of them herself over the years. Yet a smile came easily to her oval face. When she pushed, she

11

pushed softly and never beyond reason. The freight hands and cowboys said, working for Mrs. Chastain was just like working for a man, except mostly the language was better. They meant it as a compliment. Her blue eyes were shaded by the broad-brimmed hat she wore. Wisps of hair escaped the braided knot at her neck. A man's work shirt was stuffed into her skirt and held in by a wide belt at her narrow waist. Dusty boots pushed the riding skirt ahead of her, cutting a wake across the short dry grass. She soundly patted the genuinely ugly brindle bulldog that ran out from the porch toward her.

"She's gonna check them sheets as she goes by," wagered Mary.

"Sure she is and test the line," agreed Susan. "I'll put the baby down, check Joe Carter, and help you finish dinner. I ain't tired."

"It's done, and you is." Mary spoke softly to herself, then louder to Susan. "Don't let your ma hear all them *ain'ts*. She don't want you to be no ignorant talker."

Adrianne stopped briefly at the long clothesline strung out from the cook house to poles set deep and pounded into the ground. Although the lines were long enough for the big washes required by the inn and headquarters for a dozen cowboys and freighters besides the family, they were taut. Her free hand caught the line and tried it. No line at Mrs. Chastain's ever dragged hard-scrubbed, clean clothes on the dirty ground. She didn't like clothes thrown over a fence to dry, either.

"You got those spots out, Mary," Adrianne said as she came onto the porch and tossed her hat by the brim on the washstand. She sat the egg basket beside it, caught up Millie, and led Lottie by the hand into the kitchen. "The hens are laying again. What you got there, baby?" She sat down in the

12

rocker, dropped her booted heel on a small stool, and took the piece of colored paper Lottie offered her.

"Ain't you somethin'?" whispered Mary.

"Sure, she's somethin', she's my darlin' Lottie," said the smiling, uncomprehending woman, as she pushed back the child's hair with one hand and her own with the other.

Francis — called Francc — Peveler once said that in Young County, Texas, he had come to the end of the world and then took one more step. There was nothing, he said, north of the Texans but the North Star. France was wrong. North of the border county — and, indeed, to its west and south — lay Comancheria. And within this vast, rolling buffalo country lived the Kiowas and Comanches and their allies. The white people had not, as it seemed, entered an uninhabited land. They had merely entered the anteroom, the pantry of a great house in which the owners were occupied elsewhere in the regular rounds of their lives and would come again to this well-stocked room.

And even as Peveler thought these thoughts and spoke them aloud at Red Bluff on the Canadian River — to the north-northwest — the Comanches and Kiowas gathered to punish and evict the trespassers. Little Buffalo, an ambitious Comanche, summoned them, armed with a strategy to drive down in force on the unprotected frontier, kill the people, burn their homes, take their goods, their cattle and horses, their women and children, everything. He had scouted the country several times before going to the fires of the different bands, seeking men to follow him on his raid. He told them where the people lived and drew their houses in the sand along the creek with his quirt. Knowing the principal soldiers had gone away to fight other white men in the East, they listened. They would ride out of the northwest down a tributary of the

13

Brazos, cross its quicksand bottom going south, and turn again west into the farmsteads below the river. The Kiowas and Comanches knew the land well. It had been theirs before these whites had begun to plant their buildings and crops on it, before their cattle and horses had grazed away at the buffalo grass.

The valley of the Brazos had first begun to draw the Texans when Fort Belknap had been built in the summer of 1851. As its thatched *jacales,* tents, and tarpaulins gave way to sandstone buildings, settlers had come. Around the Army they had felt safe and had hoped to make a home or a business prosper in relation to the fort and its needs. There was corn to plant and beef to grow for the government. There were contracts to get, services to offer. And in addition to the Army's needs, there was the business and work created by the nearby Brazos Indian Reserves.

The Does had come with others drawn to the opportunity. They had bought and claimed land sixteen miles west of the fort and south of the river. Two miles down Elm Creek — a stream that paralleled the Brazos, falling off from the northwest, turning slowly north, and emptying at its eastern end into the southeastern flow of the river — the family had built their home.

The Doe place was larger than most. They established their headquarters as the Doe Trading House, an inn and store within easy proximity to the fort, but supplying the neighbors with the necessities that precluded a longer trip to Belknap. Travelers heading west to the gold fields, and later drovers on the Western Cattle Trail, could find good food, clean beds, and a square deal there. For liquor and staples there was a sutler's store to the southeast.

The headquarters compound consisted of the main, two-story frame house and its outlying cook house and laun-

14

dry. The first floor was used for the family's commercial enterprises — the small store, the office for the freight company, and the rooms for travelers. Upstairs were the family rooms. Scattered around the place were all the buildings required for a self-sufficient household on the frontier — large barns and corrals, smokehouses, chicken houses and hog pens, one-pen cabins for the hired hands and their families, if they had one, and a blacksmith shop for the resident repair of wagons. Animal structures were attached to several of the cabins to protect horses or oxen from casual theft by Indians.

From these premises, the Does' ox-drawn *bois d'arc* freight wagons moved onto the dusty or muddy roads of Texas. From them, Adrianne supplied the store at Belknap with eighty to a hundred dozen eggs a week, with fifty-pound sides of bacon, as well as all the hickory work shirts and ladies dresses she could sew together at fifty cents apiece. To assist Mrs. Doe in the heavy operations of the headquarters was the smith, Bill Miller. A strong man of many skills he served as carpenter for the building of additional structures and teamster when Carter Doe needed an extra driver.

Fort Belknap and the Indian reservations were abandoned in the late 'Fifties. Many families moved on to greener or safer pastures. In the first months of the Civil War, the fort provided a base for the weak and inferior Texas border cavalry — a token protection for the local inhabitants. All told by 1864, there were not more than fifty or sixty white people left on both sides of the river. Determined to stay, they established "forts" of their own. Fort Murrah lay north of the river for the protection of families on that side. A hundred feet square with a stout, picket stockade and cabins inside, it presented a fair protection — if the outlying settlers could get there. South of the river Fort Bragg offered little more than the log walls of George Bragg's cabin and shooting slots for stalwart men.

By the fall of 1864 at the Doe Trading House, most of the hirelings were gone — gone to fight their brothers in the East, gone to take their families to safety, gone to other work, unneeded now on the withering frontier. Adrianne and her daughter had so few travelers to care for that their rooms were given over to the ranch foreman, Britt Johnson, his wife, Mary, and their children. They, like their neighbors, were drawing into the central buildings.

Little Buffalo considered the marks in the dust again. Each cabin along Elm Creek was marked there. Today seven hundred Kiowa and Comanche warriors waited for his signal to move out into the land. According to the plan, they would ride down along the sides of California Creek, cross the Brazos at a ford, and then be upon the settlers in their strung-out homesteads. One by one the tribesmen would take, loot, and burn each house down the creek, then swing out farther west and turn north, moving swiftly without stopping for their separate home camps — some to the Pease River, some beyond the three forks of the Red. He looked into the eyes of the men around him. The young leaders waited as horses at the beginning of a race, contained but ready, eager, knowing what lay ahead. He touched the burning brand in his hand to a pile of firewood in several places and waited for the tinder to flare and catch before tossing in the whole burning stick. Turning back to the other men, he raised his naked arm streaked with paint, holding the costly repeating rifle. *"Ahe!"* he shouted and gathered the reins of his horse and swung quickly atop.

"Ahe!" cried the others, also taking to their horses.

Only one remained studying the map left in the dirt. Satanta smiled as he touched a homestead with his lance point. "You are mine," he said. "I claim you."

16

★ ★ ★ ★ ★

France Peveler spoke to the black man, Seth, holding the lines of the horse team loosely. "What think, Seth? What you havin' for your lunch at Fort Murrah?"

"What e'r they got, sir?" the other said, knowing his limited choices. Seth did not belong to France, but to his brother. He had been lent for the occasion of going to Weatherford to get in the winter supplies. But still, he was careful with his master's brother. "Mister France, you see that smoke rising over yonder?"

"Nothing, Seth," the younger man assured him. "Just some cowboy roasting coffee for his lunch, maybe branding something."

"Awful lot of smoke goin' mighty high up fer a campfire," observed the black man, looking at the youth who rode his horse beside the wagon. He turned back and spat over the opposite side. "Might be Injuns."

"It's too late in the year for Indians. They come in the spring and summer. Winter's almost here. It is nothing, Seth." The white man concluded the topic. "I think I'll have some apple pie. Ruby May always has a fresh apple pie. Her husband must be a happy man . . . Ruby May and apple pie, too."

Seth popped the reins lightly at a horsefly on the off-gelding's back. But his eyes returned to the column of smoke. Under his breath he muttered: "Too late fer Injuns. How them damn' Injuns know it's too late?"

Peveler and his wagon entered the picket walls of Fort Murrah. The young man looked with satisfaction at this informal fort, the best effort of the local settlers who had not pulled out with the Army and the others too afraid of Indians to stay. He had helped build it. Late in the summer, the men had gotten together, dug a trench around the few buildings, dropped

17

sharpened logs upright into it, tamped them down secure against their enemies. If the outlying families got there or to the Bragg place on the other side of the Brazos which was also well fortified, they could make a fight — if they got there.

"Hey, Peveler, what's the smoke?" called out Jerome Barnes from the doorway of his house.

"Just a cook fire," answered the lanky youth. "Ruby May got any lunch ready? Any apple pie?"

"Sure. Light and come in," offered the other man. "They're feedin' around back, Seth. Get you some grub, too." The black man tied up and ducked around to the back of the cabin. "You hear any shootin'?" queried Barnes.

"Naw," shrugged off France Peveler, going toward the door, Ruby May, and the apple pie.

Barnes lingered at the door, listening. "I swear I heard shootin'." He turned slowly and followed Peveler inside.

"Good God A'mighty," swore Peter Harmonson.

"What is it, Pa?" Perry Harmonson lifted his eyes from the tangled brush, where the cattle sometimes hid, to look into his father's ashen face.

"It's by-God Indians," the elder Harmonson exclaimed, putting spur to his horse. "Fergit the calves. It's by-God a *bunch* of Indians."

Perry glanced over his shoulder and wheeled after his father. "Shoot fire!" An arrow whistled past his head. "Ride, Pa!" he yelled as the other man slowed. "They ain't goin' to get us like they did James. Ma would never stand for it."

He came alongside his father. They drove their horses down the side of shallow California Creek and clattered across. Laying whip to the horses, they tried to gain ground as the Indians slowed for the creek.

"Yhah! Yhah!"

18

"Get to that thicket up yonder," gasped Peter Harmonson. "The bastards'll think twice 'fore they come in after us. We can hurt 'em from there."

It was a horse race then — the Harmonsons and the Indians. Sometimes one gained, sometimes the other, as they ran over the prairie, driving toward the thicket on Rabbit Creek. Perry's horse pitched and coughed as an arrow pierced it broadside. The man felt the horse give beneath him. He applied his quirt mercilessly, pushing the dying animal toward the thicket. "You might as well die up there as back here," he choked. "Come on, Dandy, just a little bit more, and I'll let you be."

The horse collapsed just as the elder Harmonson hit the thicket. Perry threw his leg over the saddle and ran toward his father. He slid into the dry creekbed on the seat of his pants, flaying his hands on the rocks. Without noticing the pain, he leaped to his feet and followed the older man into the dense thicket. The two men fell on their bellies and waited the few seconds before the Indians came after them.

"Your ma'll sure as hell be mad, if I get you killed," said Peter Harmonson.

"She won't like it much if you get killed, either," answered the son.

"Then, by-God, Son, we won't do 'er. We'll just kill the hell out of them damned Indians, if it's all right with you." The older man twisted a smile into his leathery face.

"It's all right with me, Pa," nodded the son.

"You got him?" asked Peter Harmonson, as the first brave ventured into the creekbed.

"I got him, Pa." Young Harmonson sighted carefully, then squeezed off his shot, hitting the buck squarely in the crotch.

"What's the matter with you?" protested his father, holding his rifle ready for the next man.

19

"I'm a mite nervous," said the younger Harmonson.

"Well, his nuts is a helluva long ways from his heart, Perry. Shootin' like that will get you killed."

Two Indians caught their fallen comrade and drew him toward cover. Father and son rose together and fired into them. They fell. The elder man quickly levered his rifle and put another round into the wounded man's heart. "Hate to see a fella suffer. Fall back now, Son." The men inched their way back into the dense underbrush and lay down, listening. "Quiet," spat out Pa Harmonson.

"I ain't said nothing," the younger man commented.

"Then lay still." Both men lay motionless. "Shit," said Harmonson. "It's my own heart is making all the noise."

Young Perry Harmonson smiled slightly. The war ponies danced outside the thicket — neighing, belching that funny noise when an Indian kicked too hard. The warriors shouted to each other. The Harmonsons listened hard with their ears open and their faces to the ground. Even then they did not understand the words. But no one came down into the creek after the three dead men.

"They was young ones that come in after us," whispered Pa Harmonson. "And they ain't gettin' any older. Reckon them outside is thinking about it. Ain't nothing in here but trouble for 'em." Striking off his hat, he rubbed his balding scalp briskly. "Ain't but one good scalp, neither."

Perry Harmonson turned his head about, listening to the Indians beyond the brush. "Look, Pa, your horse. They ain't got your horse. He's stayed with us, Pa. Good old horse."

The older man glanced toward the horse. "Slither over there and catch up his reins, if you can. But be careful for your ma's sake." Perry glanced back, meeting his father's eyes. The father grinned. "Myself, I aim to whip your ass for missin' your first shot, when we get home."

As the Indians pulled away from the creekbed and followed their comrades toward the Brazos, Perry Harmonson's hand caught the ends of the rope reins of his father's grazing pony. The horse jerked its head up and backed, but Harmonson held fast.

"Get on," instructed Pa Harmonson quietly from behind. The son sprang into the saddle, kicking loose the left stirrup for his father to mount. Both men studied the land around them carefully. Pa turned about, holding his rifle at the ready. It was a long way, two miles, to Fort Murrah — all open ground. To get cut off out there in the open would mean death to the pair. The horse must carry both their weights and still make it. Gently, Peter Harmonson placed his foot in the stirrup and eased in behind the cantle. "Take 'er on out, Son."

Chapter Two

The double-mounted horse broke the prairie with ears laid flat against its head. Both riders bent low against his back. His sides heaved, and the breath blew hard in his lungs as he galloped toward Fort Murrah. No hoof beats followed. No war cries. No flight of arrows. Within sight of the fort, father and son straightened and eased up on the pounding horse. At last, they trotted easily through the open gates.

France Peveler and Jerome Barnes emerged from the cabin with wood-sliver picks stuck between their teeth. Peveler rubbed his belly contentedly, stroking the settling apple pie. Seeing the ragged Harmonsons, Barnes exclaimed: "By Christmas! I did hear shots!"

"Then why in the hell didn't you come help us, Jerome?" asked Peter Harmonson.

"I wasn't sure," Barnes hesitantly admitted.

"You should 'ave checked," said young Perry. "The country's alive with Indians out there. Thick as fleas."

"It's too late in the year for Indians," pronounced France Peveler.

Perry Harmonson caught him full in the apple pie with his clinched fist. Peveler moaned on the ground. "It ain't too late for Indians, France."

"Well, what are we goin' to do?" asked Barnes, considering the prone figure of his dinner companion.

"Close the damn' gate first," muttered Pa Harmonson, loosening the cinch on his sweat-covered horse. "Young Will, come here and walk this animal, and water him when he's

22

cool. Perry, you and France get up on the roof there with that spyglass of Barnes's and see if anybody's headin' in. We'll need to open for 'em or go out and get 'em. Where's the horse herd, Jerome?"

A blank look came over Barnes's face. "They're grazing off to the north, Mister Harmonson."

"You reckon we ought to make some arrangement to get 'em inside the walls 'fore the Indians find 'em?"

Perry had already scaled the roof and lay on it, waiting for France and the telescope. "They're drivin' off the horses, Pa."

"Don't you worry about the horses, Jerome." Peter Harmonson threw his arm over Jerome Barnes's shoulders. "The matter has been taken out of your hands." In the crowd gathered around the elder Harmonson was his grateful wife. "Now, Missus, you and the women get everything that'll hold water or milk and get it filled up. Churns, everything, but slop jars. Time to boil some lead, boys."

Crossing the Brazos and plunging into the mouth of Elm Creek, the young men forgot their prey left behind in the thicket. The abundance of opportunity the afternoon offered drew their thoughts away from their dead companions. They quickly turned their attention to the promised success that lay ahead down the creek. They spotted the settler, Joel Meirs, hiding in the trees. Like yipping hounds, they surrounded him and bayed him from cover into the open.

"*Ahe!* This one is mine," shouted Head Of A Wolf. He began indolently to chase the old man, letting him run as the others watched. Running, Meirs glanced back at the warrior who had slowed to a walk behind him. Beyond the Kiowas, he saw the trees he had left. As he turned again, he focused on the trees ahead, far up the creekbank. He ran harder just to run, knowing that his death was certain. Head Of A Wolf set his long wooden lance in the crook of his arm and squeezed the pony into a trot, and then into a lazy canter. He lowered the sparkling point and drove it in up to the wood through the white man's body before stopping the pony and letting the dead man run off the steel. Meirs coughed blood, caught at the blood surging from the chest wound, and fell dead. Sliding quickly to the ground, Head Of A Wolf pulled Meirs's head back by the hair and swiftly sliced away the scalp in the one swift movement his father had shown him. Head Of A Wolf had counted first coup on the raid, a great honor. Several of the young men jumped to the ground to count additional coups and to mutilate the body of their enemy. Other young men were around the brave now, watching, admiring, awaiting his lead. Laughing, Head Of A Wolf tossed the bloody scalp at a fellow warrior before remounting his horse. The warriors then began tossing the scalp back and forth among themselves before Head Of A Wolf recaptured it in mid-air, secured it, and pushed farther down the creek. Exhilaration showed on the young men's faces as they followed. It was as the chiefs had said. The raid would provide glory and scalps for the men brave enough to take them.

Satanta already had glory. Today his thoughts were on other things — cattle and horses and captives, especially one. These things were necessary to trade to the New Mexicans for the repeating rifles the People needed. Still the seasoned warrior enjoyed the splash of the water against his naked, paint-striped legs as he broke into the Brazos. He knew how the young men out ahead felt. They were too young, too needy of personal glory, too stimulated by the blood to wait for the real fighting. The older men knew themselves and did not waste their efforts too soon.

"Heyah," said Satanta to his riding companion, Aperian Crow. "The young men are eager as we once were."

24

"They are exhausting their horses too soon," observed Aperian Crow, who rode beside Satanta. "They are frenzied."

Frenzied, crazed with the hunger for glory and the ease of killing a man, thought Satanta. They were free now; no longer did they hold the horses and cook for the warriors and wait with the metallic taste of glory in their mouths. No longer merely the sons of great men hearing the stories of their fathers, they were themselves real men of the People. They were making their own stories to tell around the winter fires as they looked into the soft eyes of the young women who would crawl beneath their teepee covers and into their buffalo robes to be loved as hungrily as they had killed the white men.

Thomas Hamby, his son, Thornton, home on a medical furlough from the war back East, and Doc Wilson had spent the morning branding calves not far from the house. The others had gone in to eat, leaving their horses tied and saddled out front. After tying up but before going in, Thomas walked back to the overlook, back to view again the place where they had seen smoke rising. He stood on the creekbank that dropped away six or eight feet into the water, considering the scene before him. Surely his eyes could not be seeing what they saw. Up toward the crossing, a hundred men, not soldiers, but naked men with feathers and paint, were entering, galloping across the quicksand bed, and emerging from the red water of the Brazos. He saw the eight or ten leaders circling something. *What?* he thought. Then Thomas Hamby turned and ran toward the cabin. *Joel Meirs. They were killing Joel Meirs in the bottomland.* "Indians! Indians!" he yelled as he ran. Thornton, his son, appeared at the door. "Get the women and children out!" Thomas was waving his arms. Young Hamby heard and began to push his mother and little ones through the door toward the secret hiding place in the

25

rocky creekbank. Doc Wilson was by his side, his wife and children following the others.

Thomas Hamby panted to a rest at the cabin door. Leaning, heaving from his run, he gasped out the simple plan. "It's come. It's sure enough come. There must be . . . God A'mighty, I never seen so many Indians. We got to do what we decided. Doc, take your horse and ride down the creek and warn the others. Let's see, there is. . . ." Hamby was gasping, grasping for the names in his excitement.

"William Bragg and Judge Williams. The men are gone, so you'll need to help the women to cover," filled in Thornton Hamby, as his father fought to recover himself.

"For God's sake, Doc, see the women don't stop to take nothing," spluttered the elder Hamby.

"Shall I stay and fight with 'em," queried the agitated messenger.

"No," said the seasoned soldier, Thornton Hamby. "We'll need you to make a stand at George Bragg's place. All of us this side of the river agreed we'd fort up there. Pa and I will delay the Indians as long as we can to give you time. We'll meet you and the other men there. Just see the women and kids are hid and ride like hell."

Wilson nodded and caught up the reins of his horse. Throwing himself into the saddle, he cut the turn hard and dug his spurs into the horse's sides. The gelding jumped off in a full gallop.

Thornton Hamby said: "Take it easy, Pa. They ain't here yet. We'll need our guns and fixin's 'fore we ride out. They ain't all in a pack yet, are they?"

Thornton's question caused his father to pause and think. "No, they are strung out some . . . a few out front, the rest following up slower."

"Good," said Thornton. "That'll give us some time."

26

Father and son entered the cabin and took down guns and boxes of cartridges from the wall shelf. Thornton set his dusty hat, as his father wiped the tobacco juice from his whiskered face with the back of his hand. "Reckon we're set," he said, looking into the pale eyes of his father. "I'm going to ride back down to the point and get off a few rounds to slow 'em down some."

"I'll check your ma," said the older man.

"We'll have to time things pretty close, Pa," Thornton stated coolly. "I mean, we'll have to wait long enough for the bucks to see and follow us, and go slow enough so we can draw them off from the women."

"You're the soldier. I'll follow your lead." Thomas Hamby cleared his throat. "I could spit cotton, my mouth's so dry. I ain't never seen Indians like this, like an army."

The men mounted. Thornton wheeled off toward the overlook. He sat still on the horse, letting the Indians see him. "Up here, you bastards," he whispered. Raising his rifle, he placed a round into the horse of the first rider. Thornton watched it stumble and falter. The other riders drew off, turning their ponies away out of range, circling to talk. He fired again but expected the miss as dust kicked up fifty feet in front of the braves. The Indians waited, figuring a way to flank his gun.

Thomas Hamby pulled up beside his son. "Ma and the kids are hid good. I piled brush out front of the cave. What's goin' on here?"

"They are thinking," the young soldier explained. "They are thinking about riding up the hill into my gun. They are thinking they might be the one to die. When we turn our backs, they'll come like a pack of hell hounds. You ready, Pa?"

"Sure I am," said Thomas Hamby. "Ready as I'll ever be."

"We'll ride back as far as the barn and wait for 'em to clear this hill. When we see 'em top out, ride like hell, Pa. It's a long way to George Bragg's place." The young Confederate soldier raised his rifle, beckoning to the Indians. "Come on, you bastards. Come and get me!"

Doc Wilson was screaming before he reached the home of William Bragg, George's oldest son. Mrs. Bragg came to the door, wiping her hands dry from washing the lunch dishes. Behind her, her oldest daughter held the baby in her arms. Wilson danced his horse in front of the door. "Indians! You got to get to hiding." Wilson tried to dismount the whirling horse as the family dog darted away from its feet.

"Well, don't kill us with that horse," Mrs. Bragg said, backing away into the house. More concerned about the wild man and faunching horse than the Indians, she continued: "We know where to go and what to do. You go on now and warn somebody else."

"I'm suppose to help you to hiding," protested Wilson.

The woman crossed her arms over the bib of her apron. "I don't need your help, Mister Wilson, and you're holdin' up my plans with yer talkin'. Go on now, and let us do what must be done." Wilson opened his mouth, but closed it again. "Go on now," encouraged the steady little woman.

"It's a fate worse than death for a woman to be caught by Indians . . . and you got a daughter and baby to think about," Wilson said, trying to scare sense into her.

"It ain't no pleasant fate being talked to death, neither," she threw back at him.

Wilson shook his head and rode west again.

"Come, Clara, bring the baby," the frontier mother said calmly, as she gathered her chicks and headed them toward safety.

28

Mrs. William Bragg and her brood had disappeared long before Thornton and Thomas Hamby burned through the farm yard with the Indians coming fast behind them.

Thornton reined in briefly and looked inside the open cabin door from horseback. "They're gone," he affirmed. The men rested their ponies as they waited for their pursuers in the protection of the settler's buildings. "Couple of rounds here at the cabin, then we'll fall back to the barn. That'll give Doc more time at the Williams' place. After that, Pa, it's just a long run for the Bragg fort."

"Don't you reckon them Indian ponies is gettin' tuckered by now," asked the elder Hamby.

Thornton nodded. "I'm countin' on it," he said to himself.

Chapter Three

Adrianne Chastain moved through the downstairs room, looking for the children. Joe Carter and Jule, Mary and Britt Johnson's eldest son, were spread out on the floor, intently moving tin soldiers in an imaginary battle. Farther away, the smaller Johnson children, Chuckie and Cherry, squatted on their feet, watching.

"Time to eat," said Adrianne, leaning with both hands together against the door jamb.

"We're busy," answered Joe Carter.

Adrianne observed the frail boy, her son. Food was nothing to him. At thirteen, he was still a child — fair and fragile, living mostly in the fantasies of his mind. He pushed soldiers about, not looking at her. The Johnson children wanted to go, but were held by comradeship and the white boy's obstinacy. "Jule, take the little ones and get your dinner." Jule Johnson was quickly on his feet, leading the others out of the room. "You must think of others, Joe Carter. They were hungry, even if you are not."

"I own this floor of the house. It's mine by the will, and they are niggers and must do as I choose." The boy looked defiantly into his mother's face.

Adrianne sighed. "Did Charlie Morehouse tell you that?"

The boy nodded. "Charlie's my administrator, not you. I listen to Charlie."

"Well, your beloved Charlie never missed a meal," the woman said, turning away. To herself she added softly: "Especially not one at my expense." Then louder: "Come to dinner,

30

Son. Everyone is waiting on you." As she left the room, she heard the boy adjust a soldier and slowly rise to his feet.

Adrianne tried to conceal her concern over the boy from him. He was bright and quick to pick up things. Perhaps his physical frailty had made him so. She had fought not to make an invalid of him, restraining herself from hovering over him, encouraging anything that drew him into activity and fresh air without exhausting him.

But she had failed with Joe Carter Doe, as she had with his father. She had not minded so much with Alexander Doe, her husband. They had never matched really. It had all been arranged by their fathers when she was fourteen and he thirty. Her father had huge debts; Carter Doe, his friend, redeemed them. In a sense, with that act, he bought Adrianne for his son. But Alex had another love, many other loves. Adrianne knew nothing, accepted everything that was expected of her. Some eight years after Susan was born, when their second offspring, a male child, was conceived and born, their relations were over. Now the boy, too, was rejecting her. Pushing her aside for Charlie Morehouse, the greatest thief in Young County, diminished only by the greed of his brothers.

After the ambush murders of Alex and Carter Doe, the estate and Adrianne had fallen into the hands of the Morehouse brothers. Carter had tried to avoid legal complications of his family's business by buying Adrianne's share on his deathbed. In his dying testament, he named a trusted old friend as executor and plainly stated that he did not want the will probated through the courts. He did not foresee that his friend would die. The vultures then would not let it be as he wished. Three of the Morehouse brothers by turns had milked the estate — selling the cattle, setting arbitrary prices for them, taking whatever they wanted as payment for their services. Adrianne could not resist the Morehouse brothers in the beginning. Her grief and shock were too great. Her physical seizures had taken her strength, the confusion her clarity. Even Susan, counseled by the oldest brother, Conner Morehouse, had seen that her mother was not herself and asked the judge not to grant Adrianne guardianship of the boy, Joe Carter. But Susan had understood little of the Morehouse brothers and their schemes. To her, they had been fine, up-standing men concerned only for the children's welfare. As men in a man's world, the girl thought, they were better able to care for the bereft family than their ill and unfocused mother. And who could say that Susan herself was thinking clearly after the murder of her own husband and the hasty marriage of her mother to Chastain?

Yes, there had been the foolish marriages. The idiocy of them haunted Adrianne. She herself could not believe that she had been widowed and married three times within fourteen months. There was no reason, no excuse. She was simply out of her mind — deceived by the false hope of restoring stability to her household. Certainly the marriages had not enlarged her in her children's minds and hearts. She could not accept and certainly could not make them understand that she was lost without her father-in-law, Carter Doe. They had been great friends, allies against the world. He gave her a place and an opportunity not generally given to women by making her his partner. Handling the ox teams and hired drivers, always away with Alexander picking up and delivering the commodi-ties the frontier and the Army paid so well for, Carter ran the freight company. He left Adrianne to tend to the business af-fairs and run the trading-house inn. And in return for his trust and her capable management, in his deep fairness, he gave Adrianne half of all, including the increase of the cattle he ran on the preëmpted Brazos lands. Adrianne ran the Elm Creek place. She did business as a man, buying and selling with

32

Conner Morehouse at his store in Belknap, renting more land and cattle pens from him in return for a fifth of the increase of her cattle and his washing and ironing. After Carter Doe's death, there was a void in her. There was no one to talk with about things. And there was another emptiness. She had never been loved, and that hunger and need also drew on her. When the sweet-talking Army officer, Chastain, pursued her, she easily succumbed to him, too naïve in such matters to realize that he was larking a rich widow. But she was too needy emotionally for Chastain. And she had too many problems. His love for her was not deeply rooted. He was a pleasant, happy-times fellow. When his Army unit pulled out of Fort Belknap, both of them knew he should not stay. Sent away with his pockets full, he was killed somewhere back East, fighting his fellow countrymen.

Then there was Sprague — the best cowhand and foreman a woman could want. Morehouse had found him, sent him over to help her. She should have known then, but coveted the astute cowman. And Sprague had wooed her in his shy, awkward way, as he talked to her of her ranching interests. They were married, had to marry because Adrianne needed his help so desperately. He never came to her bed, but quickly took control of her property, linking it closely with Morehouse's interests. Adrianne saw it clearly at last. This marriage, too, had been arranged to bring not only her son's property, but hers, under the Belknap storekeeper's control. She told Sprague to leave. For appearance's sake and to protect the county from marauding Kiowas, he joined a ranger company. On one outing, he was killed. Adrianne made no pretense at mourning. She had been duped. She had been a willing fool. She took the name Chastain again.

From that point, the woman began to rebuild her life and to fight for her son and his property. She actually borrowed money from Morehouse to buy the estate cattle he was selling. This time, with Susan's understanding and help, she openly confronted Charlie Morehouse. She went back to the court, showing that, in sequence, the brothers Morehouse, appointed by the court as administrators and guardians of her son, had taken the estate from being the largest taxpayer in the county down to owing less than three hundred dollars. They had stripped it of everything except the land and a few cattle. The ultimate abuse was that, in return for branding her son's few remaining calves, Charlie Morehouse, the last surviving brother, had taken as payment the coveted racehorse stud, Redbuck. The horse had been the deathbed gift of Carter Doe to his grandson. After five years, falling and rising at last, Adrianne was appointed guardian of her son, Joe Carter. But Charlie had won his heart and corrupted it toward his mother. And the court continued to believe a man should administer the boy's property, if not his person.

Lieutenant Nate Carson of Bourland's Border Regiment sat slouched in his saddle, rocking over the rolling land. "I don't see no Indians, Snodgrass. Why didn't you and Yates just go on into Belknap, instead of coming back for reinforcements against some phantom Indians. God A'mighty, our lunch ain't barely settled and you're draggin' us off on a wild goose chase."

Snodgrass did not reply to the officer. He just set his jaw firmly. Then, rising in his stirrups suddenly, he pointed. "Over there. Two of 'em."

"Two damned Indians, Snodgrass. Two," grudged Lieutenant Carson. He raised his hand perfunctorily and threw it forward. "Go get 'em, boys!" The border unit streaked past as Carson and Snodgrass brought up the rear.

Fifteen men altogether gave chase over the prairie as the

Indians galloped away. The soldiers were not a proud unit. The frontiersmen had little use for them. They were a presence only. The fighting men had gone East with Hood and Bragg and Lee. These men wanted to avoid glory and, most especially, the hazards associated with it. They just wanted to take it easy, ride out on a cold trail now and then, and stay well away from the action. Chasing two running Indians was to their liking. It flushed their cheeks and made the blood pump a little like a good 'coon hunt.

The soldiers rode in a good bunch after the two Kiowas, not trying to flank them or cut them off, just chasing them. Lieutenant Carson with Snodgrass at his side worked his way forward as they rode. He opened his mouth to shout out the command to spread out as the two Indian riders disappeared over the crest of a hill. "Don't lose 'em, ye idiots," he muttered, spurring ahead. Carson topped the hill a moment before the men. He met them coming back, turning his blowing horse into Snodgrass's gelding. Carson fumbled for his pistol. "Fire and fall back," he screamed, getting off an undirected round himself, then riding away like hell. It did not take the others long to obey. At the bottom of the hill three hundred warriors of the Kiowa and Comanche nations waited for them to enter the trap.

"Two damned Indians," quipped Snodgrass, as he caught up with his fleeing commander.

"Shut up!" barked Nate Carson. "We can make it to the McCoy place." He pulled off toward the right, leading the soldiers toward a frail hope of safety. Making the turn, he could see the field behind him. Jones, Neathery, Blue had gone down and were overrun by the savages who jumped from their ponies to finish the grisly work of killing and scalping. The surviving men rode on, getting every ounce of strength and speed from their horses. Carson looked for

Snodgrass at his side, but the saddle was empty. His horse plunged on unladen. The lieutenant remarked the arrows protruding from the fleeing animal and glanced down at his own to see that here, too, the Indians had found their target. He reined up on the small knoll above the McCoy cabin and let his men ride past, wondering where he had lost Snodgrass. A cluster of the enemy disclosed the place where the soldier had fallen. As the lieutenant watched, the forelegs buckled on Brison's horse. The rider went over his head. Soldier Fields slowed beside him. Offering his hand, he jerked the fallen man up behind him. And they rode flat out over the McCoy knoll. Buckingham's horse started to pitch when an arrow struck it. He threw his rider and sped on with the empty saddle.

"Dear God in heaven! They are killing us one by one!" exclaimed the officer, spurring toward the cabin.

In the yard, Mrs. McCoy was yelling and pointing off toward Boggy Creek. The men were not stopping to listen, but streaking on toward the vaguely distant shape of Fort Murrah. Carson slowed beside the woman.

"My husband is out there, down by the creek," she shouted. "Help him."

"I can't help your husband, ma'am. Give me your hand," said the lieutenant. Catching the woman's hand and forearm, he swung her behind him as another soldier lifted the woman with her. *"Yhah!"* shouted Carson and slapped his reins against the horse's neck. He felt the lurch and jerk as Mrs. McCoy caught hold of him, nearly pulling him from the saddle.

Riding two together put him and the other soldiers behind the fleeing troopers. Ahead of him the fragile fort drew him forward. Behind him the raiders pushed him on. The horses around him now seemed to move incredibly slowly.

36

Each hoof strike hovered, moved slowly forward before again catching the ground and throwing it leisurely backward. The *huff-huff* of his animal's labored breathing blotted out all other sound as it came to Carson's ears. The fort. The fort. To reach the fort.

Chapter Four

France Peveler stood up on the roof beside Perry Harmonson. "Look, soldiers!" He pointed.

Perry brought up the telescope in the direction of the coming soldiers. "Oh, shit!"

"What is it?"

"Behind them . . . hundreds of Indians," whistled Perry. He handed the telescope back to Peveler and slid to the edge of the roof. He looked down into the baked hardpan of the fort yard at the men below. "Pa, open the gates right now! There's soldiers coming this way in front of a hundred redskins. They've got Missus Isaac McCoy and Betty Morris up behind them."

Men lurched out from the group and lifted the heavy log bar securing the double gate. Other men, including Peter Harmonson, leaped onto their saddled horses and thundered out onto the flat with pistols ready. Dashing out to meet the incoming riders, they let the exhausted soldiers pass through them. In minutes, they formed a rear guard around the last riders carrying the McCoy women.

The pursuit slowed with the arrival of new fighters on the hill ahead. None of the raiders wished to ride into the guns of the fort. Their leaders considered the matter. Finally, the Indians turned away, heading back toward the abandoned farm and its plunder.

In the fort yard the women slid from the horses into the arms of the strong men who waited. Their sisters quickly gathered around them and began to hear the story. From the roof,

France Peveler yelled out: "They are killing Isaac McCoy and his son right now!"

"Shut up," said Perry Harmonson, shoving Peveler roughly. "His women folk are below. You want them to hear you?"

Peveler looked briefly puzzled, then returned to viewing the unfolding scene. "Well, they are a-killing them," he affirmed his earlier statement more quietly. He watched intently, caught by the horror, drawn to witness it. "Jesus Christ!" France handed the brass telescope to Harmonson and sat down with his head on his knees.

South of the Brazos, there were three houses and a couple of barns and other outbuildings at the Bragg place — Fort Bragg. The Foster house was a hundred yards to the north, and the Vines' about seventy-five yards to the west. The main house was a *jacal* made of logs stuck upright in a trench, fastened together, chinked between with mud and grass, and topped with a dirt roof. It had been converted into a fort with the addition of a small log stockade that ran out from one side of the house around a big tree in the bare yard and on to the other side of the house. The door was thus protected. Old man Bragg was determined not to be killed sitting on his porch. There was enough room in the yard so that Mrs. Bragg could come out the front door and do her laundry under the shade of the tree. A stile over the wall near the tree allowed for the daily comings and goings of the occupants. The only opening in the other three sides of the house was one small window.

Thornton Hamby raced across the flat land, laying over his horse's neck. He no longer tried to delay the Indians yelping at his rear. The final race had come. He had no more time to waste. His father was ahead, slapping reins against his already flying horse's sides. The Bragg place was only yards ahead.

Thomas Hamby skidded to a stop at the stile, fell off with his weapons and ammunition, and scrambled up and over the fence crossing. Thornton scampered up behind him. Neither man attempted to keep his horse, but each let them flee away before the coming raiders. Neither man looked back. The open front door of the house was the only thing either saw or wanted to see.

Doc Wilson stood inside, yelling. "Come on! Come on! Get inside!"

Thornton drew up at the door. "Where are all the men?"

"We're it," said old man George Bragg. "Everybody else is gone or didn't make it in."

As Thornton's eyes adjusted to the *jacal*'s interior, he saw that there were five women, all with small children. "Gracella," he said to one, "you women load every gun and then get under the bed. Chances are you won't get a shot under there. I'll take that little window. The rest of you will cover the door. Don't let any of 'em inside the yard."

Thornton strolled leisurely to the window and leaned his shoulder against the wall.

"Here they come." He whipped his rifle to his shoulder and fired.

Outside a column of Comanche and Kiowa braves began their death circle around the cabin. Riding at full speed, they dropped from view behind their ponies' necks as they approached the rifleman at the window. Swiftly around and around the cabin they went, looking for its vulnerability. Hamby fired, knocking a man from his horse. His companions reached down with studied skill and lifted him up behind them as they sped away. Hamby continued to fire whenever he had a target. Two more shots found their marks.

"*Aaaggg!*" yelped Doc Wilson, falling back from the open door. His stunned eyes sought the other men's faces. "Tom, they've killed me." He staggered back in front of the door.

"For God's sake get out of the door, Doc," said Thomas Hamby, motioning to his friend while trying to maintain his own position. "Lay down. I can't see the yard."

But Wilson was no longer concerned with the others' cautions. He grasped the arrow embedded in his chest and jerked, crying out in pain. He fell hard onto the floor.

The other men heard the deep gurgle of his last breath.

George Bragg was so intent on the scene unfolding with Doc Wilson that he had forgotten the unguarded door. "One's over the wall," he gasped, and spun away with the impact of an arrow. He staggered, looking out into the yard. "He's behind the tree."

"Get back, George. Let me get a shot at him," yelled Thomas Hamby as an arrow cut across his shirt sleeve. "Shit!" He fired, trying to keep the warrior behind the tree, while he looked at his arm.

George moved away from the door and sat on the bed. Slowly, he drew his feet up and lay back on the quilt. "Damn," yelped Thomas Hamby again. "That damn' Indian got me again."

At the window, Thornton Hamby levered off another round, then glanced into the room. Outside the Indians were pulling back. The guns had proved too costly. They withdrew out of rifle range.

"Damnation," spluttered Thomas Hamby. He fired two shots in rapid succession at the Kiowa who had creased him. "Can you get a shot at him, Thornton? That booger's behind that tree, taking his shots at will."

Thornton closed and barred the window. He lifted his father from the floor, pulling him away from the open door. "They've gone to parlay. They are too smart to ride at us head on again."

41

"I can still shoot, Son," whispered Thomas Hamby. "But that 'un behind the tree is still there. With him picking us off from there, the others can come over pretty soon."

One of the women emerged from beneath the bed and checked old man Bragg. Leaning onto the coverlet, she patted his hands. "You'll be fine, Papa. Them damn' Indians ain't goin' to kill us." She straightened and looked about the room. Doc Wilson lay on the floor, dead. Thomas Hamby had been hit twice and rested against the wall beneath the window. Only Thornton Hamby was left to carry on the fight. "Thornton, I'll load so you can keep firing," she said to the man, kneeling to reload. She quickly began the work beside him.

"Stay away from the door, Gracella," he said. "Pa, can you handle the window?"

"You bet," said his father, lifting himself stiffly from his position against the wall. He leaned against the logs and began to lift the bar, but stopped. "Do you hear that?"

Thornton and Gracella paused, listening. The clear bright notes of a bugle played over their ears. "Cavalry?" Thornton questioned himself. "Hell, no, ain't no cavalry. Here they come again, Pa."

This time the Indians circling the cabin were more careful, aimed not at a direct attack, but at drawing the attention of the occupants from the main assault. Thomas Hamby occasionally got off a shot. The ground beyond the window was becoming red with Kiowa blood. Meanwhile, Thornton Hamby carried on the game of cat and mouse with the sniper in the yard.

Running to him with recharged guns, Gracella caught his arm. "They are diggin' over there. I can hear the pick against the side of the cabin."

"Get up, George," shouted Thornton. "Take a gun and dig out a shooting hole on the south wall. You've got to shoot

42

those diggers 'fore they get in."

"I'm dying," said the old man.

"You can't die," continued Hamby, still studying the yard. He popped a shot at the well-covered sniper. "Come on, George. There's women and children in here. We all need you to get up, make a hole, and stop the digging."

"Oh, leave a man to die in peace," the old frontiersman whispered.

Gracella pressed another gun into Thornton's hand and disappeared. "Come on, Pa," she said. "I'll help you." She pulled George Bragg slowly from the bed toward the wall. He leaned dissolutely against it and dug weakly with the bowie knife she had given him.

"Ye gods, I'm weak," he observed.

Gracella drew him down into a chair and took the knife. She dug furiously until she had a hole angled toward the Indians digging outside. She bent and observed the scene before her through the small aperture. Drawing a pistol from her waist, she set it on the lip of the opening and exploded a round toward the men. Quickly she brought her eye down to see what she had accomplished. "Yah, I got one in the eye, Thornton."

Blood gushed from the face of one of the Kiowas. His hand covered his eye as he yelled something to the others who were clustered around him. Gracella placed another shot, sending the diggers scurrying away from view of her shooting port. Old George drew his chair toward the hole and took the gun. "Go help Thornton, Gracella. I can handle this here hole."

Thornton Hamby leaned intently on the sights of the big bore rifle braced against the door. In the yard, the sniper raised up to see what was happening against the south wall. Thornton's bullet nailed him, nearly cutting him in half, sending his body flying spread-eagled back onto the stile.

Satanta observed the mayhem from a distance. The young men were fighting well, but the marksmen within the fort were taking a heavy toll. Adjusting the bugle tied around his shoulder, he glanced at the sky. The October light was already failing and the most profitable target along the creek remained. Beside him Aperian Crow shifted on his pony.

"Little Buffalo is wasting time and men here," noted Aperian Crow. "I am satisfied with fighting. I think I am going home now. My men have many things and many deeds to tell." The Kiowa warrior was one of the ten elite fighters of the tribe — the honored men of the *Koitsenko*. If he was ready to go home, the raid was nearing its end.

"There is one more place," said Satanta. "It is the richest one, with many horses and cattle. I am going on to that place."

"There will be many guns, if it is a rich place," noted the *Koitsenko* warrior.

"Perhaps. But there is no wall. And mostly there are only women there. The men go away on wagons or out to tend cattle."

"There is no honor in fighting women," said Aperian Crow.

Satanta smiled. "We will not fight them. We will rob them and take them captive. A rich place will pay a rich ransom for its women and children and buy many guns for the Kiowas."

"Do you know these children?" asked Aperian Crow.

"I have seen them," Satanta answered.

"Are any very young?"

"There are two young girls," Satanta said.

Aperian Crow nodded.

"We will move on from here," Satanta shouted to the men who rode with him. As they trotted away from the guns of Thornton Hamby, Satanta knew exactly where he was going and what he wanted. The time had come to take it.

44

Chapter Five

Adrianne Chastain closed the ledger and stretched. She listened intently for a moment to the world around her. Somewhere in the house the children were laughing. The air was growing cooler. A chill ran over her body, and she rose to close the window beyond the desk. She paused again, listening, searching for something different in the landscape. She walked quickly to the back of the house and out the door toward the cook house.

Mary Johnson glanced up at Adrianne but continued to press the flatiron back and forth over the shirt in front of her. "What's wrong?"

Adrianne did not answer but stood on the shaded porch, looking off down the creek.

Mary came to her side. "That smoke smells plumb pungent, don't it? Somebody must be burning off their old brush piles. Sounds like they are poppin' at the snakes comin' out, too."

Adrianne studied the thick, rising column of black smoke, her hands crossed over her fresh white shirt and short jacket. "They are not shooting snakes," she said as she turned. "Go to the house, Mary, and get the children into the gun room." Looking into Adrianne's face, Mary saw her lips form the words: "It's Indians." She ran toward the house with Adrianne following.

At the back door Adrianne paused, watching the sudden wind blowing dust across the yard, observing her home in the last peaceful moments before it, too, whirled away with the

45

dust. The doors on the horse barn swung and banged in the freshening wind. Farther away, penned cattle broke through the fence and charged out, pursued by warriors whirling ropes to drive them forth. She scanned the horizon, eyes hungry for the cowboys she knew were too far away to help.

"I shouldn't have sent Britt to get lumber." Adrianne sighed softly to herself, stepped inside, closed the heavy door, and dropped the bolt over it.

She crossed from the dining room into the hall just as Mary and Susan pushed the children down the stairs and into the gun room. This was where the family would make their stand. They had planned it. Mary placed the smallest children under the bed on the quilts spread there. Adrianne and Susan worked swiftly and without speaking. As Susan set the bolt over the door, her mother closed the thick shutters over the window and secured them. The women's eyes met and lingered.

"I love you, Mama," the girl whispered.

"I love you, my heart," her mother answered.

They went quickly to those children sitting beside Mary. Joe Carter was ashen, with his knees drawn up under his chin. Adrianne smoothed his hair. When he looked up, she smiled. Then, as Lottie caught her about the legs, Adrianne bent to lift the crying child. She walked with her to the rocker and sat down. "Susan, Jule, mind the guns like you were taught." Susan moved to a narrow slit cut in the door. Jule took a position in the corner, opening a slot in the adjoining wall. Racked in the wall near each were pistols and rifles and ammunition. The young mother and black boy began to check their loads.

Adrianne rocked gently with the child. "Lottie, don't be afraid," she whispered, brushing her lips against her oldest granddaughter. The only sound in the room was the empty,

46

metallic, ticking sound of the mantle clock. Outside, the rising wind carried the sound of many hoofs thundering toward the yard.

"Mama," shouted Susan. "Do you hear?" A bugle sang into the wind. "It's the cavalry! We are safe!"

As Adrianne looked up, Susan joyfully lifted the bar over the door and pushed it open.

Adrianne rose quickly. "Susan, don't . . . !" she began, but the door was open and the girl and Jule were on the porch. By the time Adrianne reached them, they had stopped, suspended in terror by the scene before them. Twenty Kiowa warriors, naked and painted, sat on their ponies in the yard.

Adrianne's eyes scanned the silent, painted faces. One of the horses switched its tail and kicked back at the heel fly annoying it. Her eyes came to rest on a tall erect man sitting at the center of the raiders. A bugle hung from a strap around his shoulders. His black eyes, hidden behind the black mask painted across them, watched her closely.

"Come back inside, Susan . . . Jule," Adrianne said calmly and quietly. "Back up slowly into the doorway."

"It's too late now, Mama." Adrianne reached for her, but Susan stepped boldly forward with the rifle. "You men clear on out of here."

One of the Kiowa men dropped from his pony and strolled indolently toward the house to the amusement of the others. The staunch little bulldog set himself and started to bark. A dozen arrows struck and silenced the dog. The man walked up the steps slowly. Susan thrust the rifle and fired. He staggered, but grabbed the barrel and threw the girl holding it into the yard. Now other men were on foot, approaching the porch from several directions. Jule tried to fight them. A tomahawk split his skull.

"Wait," shouted Adrianne. "Stop this!" She moved onto

47

the porch toward her stranded daughter. The men were touching Susan, causing her to turn about. One of the men caught the girl about the waist and threw her to the ground. She screamed as he straddled her. He brought his hatchet down on her head, spilling the brains onto her skin and hair. Adrianne caught a porch post to steady herself and the child she still held.

The tall man shouted words she did not understand to the others. Men went past her into the house. Behind her she heard Mary and the children screaming. She heard the sound of furniture falling. But she was still held by the man on Susan's body. He was unbuttoning her dress, stripping it away from her dead body. Adrianne's head jerked in short, involuntary movements. Setting Lottie on the stairs, she walked down into the seething yard full of men and horses. She took the pistol from the holster at her hip, cocked it, pressed it against the Indian's temple as he glanced around at her sudden appearance, and pulled the trigger.

Lottie screamed and ran from the porch toward her grandmother with a buck behind her. Adrianne turned and fanned the pistol twice, hitting him in the chest, sending him back against the steps. She caught up the running child with her left arm.

"*Heyyah!*" exclaimed Satanta as he watched the Kiowa and Comanche soldiers fall before the white woman's gun. He kicked his horse forward toward her. Hearing him, she turned, but he drove the animal into her, knocking her to the ground. He leaped from his horse, captured the gun from her hand, and jerked her up. His hand unbuckled the gun belt from her waist and threw it down. One of the young men quickly grabbed it up and placed the gun in it before handing it back to Satanta. Satanta stripped Lottie from Adrianne's arms and handed her, kicking, screaming, to the soldier. The big Kiowa

48

shoved the woman forcefully against the horse. "What are you doing?" he shouted at her in Spanish. "Why are you killing us?"

Now Adrianne swore her answer in Spanish. "You *pendejo estúpido,* you expect to come in here killing and not be killed!"

"Where are your men?" He continued to shout.

"None of your god-damn' business," she returned.

The back of Satanta's right hand caught her full force on the side of her face. Adrianne staggered, then straightened back to stare at his face with eyes blazing. His fist doubled, but he caught himself and suddenly looked away from her. He took several breaths, observing his men who were pouring in and out of the house with their struggling captives and booty. He caught Adrianne's arm roughly. "Look, you have saved nothing with your killing!"

The scene in all its horror unfolded before her eyes. The Kiowa soldiers were carrying whatever they wanted from the large house — cooking pots, cloth, clothes, guns, knives, ropes, food — good things, silly things, everything that a horse could carry. On the porch, in the midst of the screaming and tumult, two young men sat spooning her plum preserves appreciatively into their mouths. Others were ripping her pillow cases and bed tickings apart, emptying them of their feathers and filling them instead with the things they were taking. The feathers settled in a gentle snow over the dry ground.

Adrianne turned, trying now to locate her family. The young Indian still held Lottie, rocking her gently without thought. Mary and her children, Chuckie and Cherry, were already on horses in front of red men. Susan lay now fully stripped and scalped in the yard with chaos expanding around her dead body like ripples from a stone. Someone had split her torso, exposing, spilling the inner organs.

"Joe Carter," Adrianne whispered to herself, searching the

49

yard for him. Two Indians came around the side of the house carrying the boy like a log, one with his feet, the other with his shoulders. They dumped him unceremoniously in front of Satanta. The boy started to rise and run again. The two braves anticipated his move with their open, ready gestures.

"Sit down," commanded Satanta. The boy sat and caught his knees to his chest.

Adrianne twisted in Satanta's grip to see Mary as she was being taken away. "Where is the baby? Where is Millie?" she shouted.

"Inside. Way back under the bed the last I seen," Mary answered hoarsely as her captor tightened his rope around her neck. "Jule's dead." She added the last words as if Adrianne did not know, had not seen him fall.

"Burn the house," Satanta ordered his men as he saw that the looting was nearing its end.

The men trotted off to get fire as the horses from the lower pen surged through the yard. They shied at the bodies and veered toward Satanta. Without releasing Adrianne, he stepped back, speaking in Kiowa to the man with Lottie. The young soldier sat the little girl beside Joe Carter and quickly rode after the horses.

Then two Kiowas, carrying burning torches, walked through the front door of the house. They touched the curtain blowing in the now broken window. Inside, the flames ran up the material and leaped across with a flying fragment of cloth to the broken bed. The fire kindled and leaped within the room in an eerie dance. Adrianne broke from Satanta's grip, running with all her might toward the house and the children inside. Flames shot out of the window and doorway as the prairie wind circled through the house. Adrianne was nearly to the stairs, when Satanta tackled her from behind. She struggled in the dirt, trying to be free of

50

his grip, digging her way toward the house.

She kicked hard at the Kiowa. "My grandchildren are in there. Let me go!"

Slowly the man overpowered her, pulling her back through the dirt to him. He lifted her up and held her as the end of the porch collapsed under the fire. He started to carry her away, when they saw a man emerge from the flames with a small girl cradled in his bare, scar-filled arms. "There," he said. "The child is out."

"There is another," Adrianne struggled.

"That one is lost now," Satanta said, watching the timbers of the second floor fall through. "José, bring the horses." Satanta signaled the young Mexican captive who had helped him before. José brought up Satanta's horse and Adrianne's. "Bring the little girl," he instructed him. Then, turning to Adrianne, he said: "Get on." The woman hesitated. "It's your horse, isn't it?"

"It's my horse," she answered.

Impatient, the big Indian threw her onto the unsaddled gelding and began to tie her feet beneath its red belly. José handed Lottie into Adrianne's arms. Looking up, Satanta saw Joe Carter dart for the trees. He straightened, resting his hand on Adrianne's thigh. "Well, get him, José," he said in exasperation as the young man watched the fleeing child.

Chapter Six

France Peveler lowered the telescope for the last time. "I've seen all I can look at," he said to Perry Harmonson. The young Texan, already brown from the sun, had burned during the long October day. "There's Indians on three sides of us now. They've started a big fire up to the north. Guess they're dividing the loot. I never seen so many horses carrying things away. Shit, I even seen a bunch of dogs dragging travois."

When the Indians finally withdrew from Elm Creek, the settlers crept forth tentatively into the moonlight. Mart Bragg, George's youngest son, broke over the stile into his father's yard, yelling: "Don't shoot! Don't shoot!" His mother kissed him like the sinner once lost and now found.

Thornton Hamby lowered his gun. Since the last of the fighting, around sunset, the people in the cabin had regrouped. Both Thomas Hamby and George Bragg lay on the single bed. Gracella treated their wounds and fed them. The children sat wide-eyed around the table, staring at the cold supper their mothers had placed in front of them. Hamby walked to the bed, as Mart took a place beside the door.

"Pa" — Hamby sat in the chair beside the bed — "I'm going out and look around. Check on our folks and the rest of 'em. Gracella will be here and stay with you until Mother and the children come." He clasped his father's hand, shook it back and forth, then left the cabin.

Crossing the stile, Thornton caught the arm of the dead sniper and dragged him outside and away toward the trees. On his route that night, walking back along the creek, he found every cabin stripped of anything of value. It would be a poor winter along the Brazos that year. But the settlers Doc Wilson had warned had gotten to cover and had survived. Thornton found them all. He met Ruben Johnson, riding in from Weatherford. Guns ready, the two shepherded the women, who had hidden during the raid, to the little fort where Thornton and Gracella had stood off Little Buffalo and his Comanches. Mrs. William Bragg could not stop talking now that the danger was over. The loss of her Army son's new suit of clothes to the savages bothered her more than anything else. Thornton heard her walking briskly, never troubling to breathe as she talked.

"Yes, sir," Mrs. William Bragg observed. "It is proved out here today . . . God is good, movin' mysterious in His ways, but good all the same. We had some losses right enough, but still we got shelter aplenty, and the mens that's away is bringin' winter supplies. And consider this, them thievin' Indians left my cards and my wheel and my loom. And Clara, she found a big bag of wool left up in the rafters. Now, Thornton," her voice came through the darkness to the soldier, "I want you to stay just ten more days longer on your leave. In ten days, I can remake that suit, and you can take it with you for your cousin, Ed."

Thornton nodded, but his mind was not on a soldier's suit for his kinsman. After he had seen the women and children into the fort, he led Ruben Johnson away into the darkness.

"We have to check up at the Chastain place," he said grimly. The other youth nodded. The two walked away, listening to the night sounds, determined to find any survivors and to look at the carnage. They found Susan's mutilated body in the yard where it had fallen. Ruben lost his stomach there, for he had once thought to marry her. Thornton covered her nakedness and the gore with his coat. On the porch they found

53

Jule Johnson's body and, nearby, the bulldog's. Inside, the soft moonlight, slanting through the burned roof, revealed the charred remains of Susan's baby. The young men carried the bodies inside what was left of the house. Scavenging animals might not get at them there, until someone could come in the morning to bury them beside their people. They carefully closed the burned door when they left.

They cut across country from the Chastain place toward Fort Murrah on the other side of the river. Thornton thought someone, who still had a horse, should ride for help in case the war party came back the next day. On the way they came upon a sight neither would ever again forget. Laid out on a knoll behind Fort Bragg were the bodies of twenty Indians. The men saw them clearly in the moonlight, walked among them to count them and see the work of Thornton's guns. Some mules neighed, and the men went to investigate. There, in the rocks, they found a man wrapped in a blanket and tied with leather cords. They opened the shroud to find the chief, Little Buffalo, with a hole from a large bore gun in his black gabardine coat just above the second buttonhole. By the time the settlers would return, not a body would be left. The Indians would come back without their knowing it and take them all away. But these men had seen them in the moonlight. They were witnesses.

Thornton and Ruben made reins from their belts and rode one of the abandoned mules the rest of the way to Fort Murrah. Near the Brazos ford, they discovered something white shining in the moonlight. It was the body of Joel Meirs who had died so long ago that morning.

Satanta led his prisoners through the men around the leaping bonfire. Adrianne sat on the horse, holding Lottie tightly against her. She looked about for Mary and her children. But

54

their captors had already departed with them. She searched the men's faces, trying to identify the one who had taken Millie. Adrianne was struck now by the commonness of their savage faces — eyes and noses like everyone else. On many the paint had worn or run away in their sweat, and they looked little different from the men who worked her cattle or drove her wagons. Some played cards by the fire. A few were busy shaping the fresh scalps they had taken on willow hoops. Others were trading booty from the raid. The white woman thought she saw one of Carter Doe's good suitcoats change hands.

Satanta visited jovially with other men like himself. He turned occasionally and looked at her, but no expression crossed his bronze face or wrinkled it over his high cheekbones. José sat close beside her, holding her reins and those of Joe Carter's. The woman considered her son. He was more pale than usual, with a frantic energy in his eyes. "Joe Carter, are you all right?"

"Yes, Mama," he answered. "When are we going home?"

"As soon as I can get us there." Adrianne spoke softly, but there was resolve in her voice. "Just as soon as I can get us there."

A man beside the horse caught the calf of her leg, and she felt him pushing the skirt up over her boot top. "Get away!" said José, bringing his horse around, raising his quirt.

"Will you strike me, camp garbage? Are you a warrior?" snorted the fondler. "I will kill you and take this white woman for myself." His hand moved farther up her leg.

Adrianne saw that there were others watching him closely, willing to help him take the woman away from the young man and enjoy her before riding on.

Satanta caught the villain roughly. "Do you wish to fight me, Elk Call?"

The other man backed away slowly. Those watching with hungry eyes returned their attention to the fire. Satanta's eyes met and held Adrianne's. "Do you want to go with any of them?" She shook her head.

"She is Satanta's Woman," José said to the bystanders. "This is Satanta's Woman."

The chief mounted his horse. "I do not want to fight them, white woman. We will go home now." He trotted his pony through the firelight and out onto the dark plain.

"I'm hungry," Lottie whimpered as José led Adrianne's horse after the warrior.

"Shush, Lottie," said the woman, holding the child against her body. "We will eat when they do."

By the second day, Adrianne believed the Kiowas neither ate nor slept. They had barely allowed their captives to relieve themselves before they were back on the horses' bare backs, heading northwest. They watered their horses crossing the streams and scooped handfuls of water to their mouths without taking their eyes from the horizon. The two children were weak with hunger, exhausted by the unrelenting ride away from the Brazos and any pursuit. Adrianne felt little better. But the seven warriors with Satanta and José never tired. Leading their war ponies, now laden with goods, they walked and trotted and walked their regular horses over the open terrain with the wisdom of men who understood how to use and save their mounts. Adrianne knew, if the children cried or became a nuisance, they would be killed without thought. She turned to look at Joe Carter. He was slumped over the horse now, barely holding on. "Sit up, Son. Stay awake." She whispered: "Stay alive."

On the third evening, they crossed the Pease and rode deeply into one of the copper breaks. The metal had leached out of the red earth, leaving green and turquoise streaks. Two young boys ran toward Satanta as he drew up his horse and dropped to the ground. They took his horses and pointed to a fire where a dinner cooked. Behind her, Adrianne heard the other men already on the ground. They had been coming here all along, knowing this destination as surely as white men knew a town.

José untied her feet, and Adrianne drew up her right leg sorely over the gelding's withers. She sat facing his left side for a long moment before sliding to the ground and releasing Lottie. As she rubbed her neck and back, the woman turned to see Joe Carter collapse onto the ground. She went quickly to him. One of the men pushed her away, shoving her back toward the girl child. He jerked up his head, pointing with his chin toward the girl. "Go there," he said.

José quickly caught the woman and pulled her away from the man. "No," he said. "The boy must be a man. He is too old for women's ways. They already think he is a weakling. If you go to him . . . ," he hesitated. "You must not go to him or help him. It will be bad for him."

"He's my son. He's just a boy," protested Adrianne.

"These boys are his age. They do not hang to their mother's skirts," said Satanta from the fire. He was eating as he watched Adrianne.

Lottie ran toward the food and stopped. She turned to Adrianne. "They are eating, Marn."

Adrianne looked at the Indian. "Can she eat?"

He nodded and offered a rib to the starving child. Adrianne pushed her slightly, and Lottie quickly took the meat. Satanta lay back on his elbow, studying the woman. "Will you eat also, or is your pride enough to fill your belly, *mujer?*"

"Is my son allowed to eat?"

Satanta pointed to the boy, hovering over the food the other men had given him.

"I will eat," Adrianne said to him in Spanish, then added in English: "You stinking savage." So Adrianne Chastain ate Satanta's meat by Satanta's fire and fell asleep with Lottie in her arms.

"*Mujer,* wake up." The Mexican captive shook her. "You will not sleep here against the rock. There is a bed for you and the child."

"A bed?" The pleasing image rose in Adrianne's exhausted mind — clean, fresh-smelling linens, feather softness.

The boy motioned to a blanket stretched on the ground. "Satanta wants you there where he can see you. Come." He offered his hand.

Adrianne lifted the sleeping child and followed him. The captive talked as he smoothed the blanket over the sand. "*Mujer,* be careful of the boy. I was about his age, when I was taken. It is important how he acts. He must be a man. A woman must not touch a man and make him weak. Be very careful. I will talk to him and help him when I can."

Adrianne looked into the youth's eyes and nodded. "I will be careful, José."

Satanta stood above them as Adrianne lay Lottie on the blanket. José went away and returned with a buffalo robe. The Kiowa took it from him and walked to the edge of Adrianne's blanket and lay down. She moved away toward the child. He ignored her as he stretched himself onto the hard bed. Thinking of the raid's success, Satanta considered the stars.

"Where are my horses?" the woman asked with her back to him.

"Your horses?" Satanta puzzled over the question. "*My* horses have been driven ahead of us."

"The cattle?" Adrianne did not use the possessive.

"The cattle will be sold to the Comanchero, Tafoya. He

will get money for guns from the bluecoats in New Mexico." Satanta smiled.

"Fine. Just fine," the woman said to herself in English. She shivered in the cold, night air. Satanta drew the buffalo hide over her as he turned onto his side against her back. He lifted her arm and dropped his hand easily over her waist. The muscles in Adrianne Chastain's body tightened under his touch. The man took no notice, but drew her closer, getting comfortable for the night.

He touched the child's dress, smoothing it. "She is a very pretty child," the man whispered. "Very beautiful, very beautiful."

"If you touch her again," Adrianne seared the words into the man, "I will cut your heart out, if I have to crawl out of my grave."

Shocked at her words, Satanta drew back from the insult as if slapped by the woman. "I do not molest little girls. I am Satanta, Setainte, White Bear. She is a beautiful child . . . a child."

"Good," shot back Adrianne, settling herself firmly on the blanket, shielding the child more obviously from the man.

"*Humph,*" the Kiowa snorted to himself, studying her back. "You are very salty for a woman in such precarious circumstances."

"You mean I am not under your protection?" parried Adrianne.

"You are protected only because I claim you, because you are my woman. You are my woman to do with as I choose. I can keep you. I can give you to the ones who watch you like a dog watches meat on the fire and knows the old woman will split his skull if he tries to take it." Satanta moved his hand over her side, caressed the hip and buttock. "Giving you to them would please them, a gift for their part in the raid. They would fight over you, for turns with you." He spoke confidentially, softly, as he unbuckled her belt and drew it away. His hand found the opening in the skirt and eased inside. Satanta's fingers stroked the soft smoothness of her belly. "And each one would have you until his legs were feeble and it hurt him to sit his horse. But you would not care because your mind would be gone." His lips brushed her jaw, her neck. His tongue tasted the salty sweat. "I would leave you on the prairie, of course, or kill you then. You would be no further use to me. I would have to kill the child, too, because there would be no one who would want her, and she would be too much trouble. I could do that. Yes, I could do that. Turn toward me."

Adrianne lay still, thinking about Satanta's words. She turned slowly. "I will give you horses for my family and the others taken in the raid."

"I have your horses. You don't have any horses." Satanta opened the first button of the white shirt.

"I am a rich woman," Adrianne continued, concentrating on her words. "I can buy a hundred horses more for you . . . excellent horses, blood stock, the best stallions in Texas. And I will give you a hundred more to get the other white child."

As she talked, Satanta had worked his way down the front of the shirt and spread it slightly to reveal the curve of her breasts. "What is this child to you?" He touched the bare roundness gently.

"She is my daughter's daughter. You killed her mother," gambled Adrianne. "I want the child of my dead daughter."

"I killed no woman," protested Satanta, momentarily detained from his pursuit of her softness.

"You led the raid, and you sat on your high horse while your minion killed my daughter. That makes you responsible,

60

you red. . . ." Adrianne stopped to catch his hand.

"Have you no fear, woman?" demanded the chief.

"Certainly not," spluttered Adrianne. "You are the one who is in trouble here." She flipped onto her back and drew her shirt together.

Satanta laughed. "I am the one who is in trouble. Ha." He rolled onto his back, laughing. "I am the one who is in trouble here."

Before dawn Adrianne awoke under the weight of Satanta's body. He unceremoniously opened her clothing and satisfied himself. The woman did not resist him. She lay still, her eyes and her thoughts firmly fixed somewhere else. As he lay upon her, he ran his hand along her arm finding the fist clenched tightly on the blanket above her head. He rubbed her gently, nuzzling the cheek and earlobe as he opened her hand and covered it with his own. "Why do you not cry out with pleasure, little one?" he whispered against her ear.

Adrianne hit his chest with both fists, pushing him away. "What pleasure?" she spat out. Grabbing the kerchief from his neck, she wiped her legs and body. She threw the soiled rag at him. "Here, this is yours. You wear it all day. I don't want it."

Satanta lay back, observing her anger. "I am generally better received."

"You are generally better deceived," she shot back.

"Are you not afraid of me, at all?" the savage asked.

"Afraid of you? Why should I be afraid of you? You are only twice as big as I am, heavily armed, surrounded by men as despicable as yourself. You hold my children's lives in your hand. And you are a proven murderer and rapist. Am I afraid of you?" Adrianne stopped to breathe. "I am sure as hell afraid of you. But I, by God in heaven, do not like it."

Satanta watched her. "You are not pleasant in the morning," he concluded.

At first light, Satanta rousted the still sleeping camp boys from their blankets to prepare the men's breakfast. He was irritated and unsatisfied. "Is there no respect anywhere?" he mumbled as they scurried away to their work.

With the buffalo robe drawn high over his back, Satanta ate without looking at the woman. Adrianne watched him out of the corner of her eye and stayed well away from him. He threw his coffee on the fire and stood up. The others, sensing his mood, followed. One of the men tossed Joe Carter onto a horse. The boy slid limply off. The man jerked him up again.

"Get on the horse, Joe Carter," said Adrianne softly, watching the boy.

"You lay with that red nigger. You're a whore!" the boy screamed at her as the Kiowa warriors watched. Adrianne saw their contempt.

Quietly, the woman spoke. "I am your mother. Get on the horse."

"Slut! Whore!" the boy hissed.

"What did he call you?" Satanta caught her elbow.

"Nothing," insisted Adrianne. The Indian jerked her arm hard. She looked into his scowling face. *"Puta. Ramera."*

Satanta slapped the boy, knocking him to the ground. "I am Satanta, Setainte, White Bear. I do not bed with whores."

Adrianne forgot herself and went to Joe Carter, touched his bleeding lip gently. The Kiowa threw her back. She attacked him, slapping and punching at the hard muscles of his arms and stomach. Satanta backed away. Then, suddenly, his arm exploded forward, the back of his hand hitting her, knocking her to the ground. Unsheathing his knife, he knelt over her. "You will not treat me this way in front of my

62

men." Lifting her head by the hair, he hesitated, anger boiling in the black eyes. He drew the knife blade slowly down her cheek. A thin line of her blood followed the blade and flowed out onto her face and neck. He jerked her to her feet, held her upright, and kneed her hard between the legs. Adrianne buckled, but Satanta lifted her and slammed her down astride the horse. "You will hurt with every step. Every step, remember you and your little world exist only as you please me."

"The boy," the woman moaned.

Disgusted, Satanta grabbed the shivering child and put him up in front of the woman. He walked away. "José, carry the girl."

That day the band of warriors and captives crossed the Prairie Dog Town fork of the Red River and out of Texas. They rode steadily northwest, moving with each step farther into the depths and safety of their own country. Satanta watched the woman often during the day. He had hoped in the beginning to enjoy her suffering. But each time he saw her, she was fighting, struggling to hold the boy on the horse, struggling not to yield to her own pain, struggling to keep her integrity. Finally, the Indian could watch no more. Satanta rode far ahead, leaving the others behind. Late in the afternoon, as he sat watering his horse, the others began to catch up with him.

"Where is José?" he asked, even then turning his horse.

"With the woman," said One Arm. "That boy is killing that woman."

Satanta did not hear the words. He cantered slowly back. He drew up to watch their faltering approach. Before him on the rolling plain, José held the girl child and slowly led the horse carrying the woman and her son. The boy's leaning weight dragged her off the horse. They fell in a heap on the ground. José stopped the horses. The woman struggled to her feet, pulling the boy, positioning him against the animal, and lifting him astride. She nodded to José. He started again. She walked along beside Joe Carter, holding him as he tottered on the horse's back. José stopped again. Adrianne crawled atop the animal. They began again. A few more yards passed. The boy began to lean again, purposefully throwing his arms and head toward the side. The woman fought him back. But once again the pair hit the ground.

Satanta dug his heels into his pony's sides. Dropping beside her, he caught Adrianne by the shoulder of her jacket and forced her up and away from the boy. With one practiced movement of his knife, he slashed the boy's throat. Blood hesitated, then gushed forth. Joe Carter gasped and gurgled out his life. The child crumpled back, falling lifeless on the prairie. Adrianne tried to strike Satanta. He deflected the weak blows and drew her against him.

The woman pushed away and began rubbing her hands as if they were covered with spider webs. Satanta frowned at this new peculiar behavior. He looked up at José. The young man shrugged. Adrianne straightened abruptly and fell backward hard against the ground.

Lottie tugged at the Mexican slave. "Let me down. Marn is sick."

Satanta nodded. The captive set the child on the ground. Lottie came to the woman who was now absolutely still, rigid in the prone posture. Opening her grandmother's jacket, she removed a small wooden stick from a pocket sewn into the lapel. She squatted by the unconscious woman's head and tried to place the stick between her teeth, but failed. Satanta picked up the child and handed her back to José. He opened Adrianne's mouth, forced the small rod across her teeth as he had seen the child try. He watched the woman's frozen form.

64

The fingers of her left hand twitched slightly, and then the convulsions began, heaving her up and back against the earth.

"*Aagh,*" muttered José in alarm. His horse reared slightly and backed away from the woman. "She has power."

Hearing the words — "She has power." — Satanta looked at José and backed away from the woman. He watched the continuing convulsions. *Power.* Satanta and the Kiowas, like most native peoples, had an awe and respect for those they deemed touched by the supernatural. Gathering himself from his first fear, he moved forward again and bent to control the bucking woman.

"No," said Lottie. "Mama says don't hold her."

Satanta lifted his hands. Adrianne's body continued the involuntary movements for moments more, then settled quietly back against the winter grass.

"It's over, now," affirmed Lottie, although neither understood her. "She'll wake up pretty soon."

Even as the child spoke, Adrianne's eyelids fluttered and opened. Satanta stood above her. She raised herself to her elbows, trying to find the reason for her position, trying to remember why she lay at his feet. Finally, knowing, she sat up. Satanta watched her slowly, painfully rise again to her feet. As she saw Joe Carter's body, a low animal groan escaped her. She staggered. The Kiowa caught her, lifted, and carried her away toward his horse.

"Go on," he told José. He sat Adrianne sideways on his pony's back and flung himself up behind her. Holding her, cradling her against him, he cantered the horse lazily away from the dead boy. *Power. She has power.* The words echoed in his mind.

Chapter Seven

"Marn, you are hurting me!" Adrianne heard the child's voice through the mental fog that had protected her for the last three days as the Kiowa raiders rode north toward the deep sanctuary of their country.

"Marn," Lottie said again.

Adrianne looked down at the child she held so tightly in her arms. She kissed the nearly white hair on top of her head. The October sun was warm on her face as she rested her cheek against Lottie.

"What are they doing?" asked Lottie.

Adrianne's eyes wandered over the scene before her. Satanta and the others that rode with him had been joined by other men and boys. A horse herd grazed nearby under the watch of several young boys. She recognized the brands and markings of more than a dozen of her own horses. Adrianne sat up like a dreamer, wondering where she was. She turned on the mare's back, then moved the pony around with the pressure of her legs. The warriors were gathered in the trees beside the stream. Some bathed in the icy water. Others shook garments from rawhide cases. Still others sat here and there on the ground or fallen logs, painting their faces.

A cold wind shivered its way across Adrianne's body. Something was different. They were not running now. After so many days on a horse, she feared stopping. What ceremony was this? Were they preparing to attack some other unknowing family? Pulling her running thoughts together, trying to put what she saw into some understandable pattern, she continued to observe the men closely.

"Where did the horses come from?" she asked Lottie.

"They rode up on them yesterday afternoon. Then this morning, when we got here, all the men started dressing up," answered the child.

"Dressing up?" The term, used in her household for Sundays and special occasions, seemed incongruous to the woman.

"Like Satanta," the child pointed.

Adrianne followed the child's gesture. The Kiowa stood dressed now in white deerskin leggings, tufts of human hair running down the sides. The breechcloth was a long strip of fresh and vivid red flannel. He lifted his copper arms and carefully slipped the skin shirt over his freshly oiled hair, over the padded and fur-wrapped left braid. The shirt also bore scalp locks and a broad geometric design of red earth across the chest with yellow ochre below. Images of four-armed stars graced the sleeves that danced with long buckskin fringe. Taking a small mirror and paint from a beaded bag, he carefully drew the red and black and white mask over his face.

"Ain't he splendid?" whispered Lottie.

Automatically, Adrianne corrected: "*Isn't* he splendid, Lottie."

When Satanta finished, he turned, and José handed him the many-plumed war bonnet from the cylindrical case he held. Adrianne saw that the Mexican captive also wore a better shirt and clean breechcloth over his shabby leggings. A deer-tail roach dangling three feathers sprouted from the back of his head.

"Why are they dressing up?"

Adrianne shook her head. "I don't know."

José walked quickly toward them as Satanta mounted his war horse, also freshly washed and painted with hands and bugle. "Get down, *Mujer*," he said, offering his arms to take the child.

Lottie went to him as to a favorite uncle. Slowly Adrianne moved her stiff and bruised right leg over the withers and slipped down. She dusted her torn skirt and smoothed it down modestly. As she looked up, José jabbed a wet rag at her bloody cheek. She dodged the gesture and the pain. The boy stepped back and handed her the rag.

Staring at the soiled, wet cloth, she said quietly: "Thank you."

Making sure the horse shielded him from the other men, José drew a mirror from a bag at his waist. "Here." He handed it to Adrianne.

The woman stood silently in the middle of the horses and men, holding the looking-glass and wet cloth in her hands. "Clean up," José prodded.

Raising the sliver of glass, she touched the rag to her face and beheld what she had become since leaving the Brazos. Adrianne Chastain would have been hard pressed to identify the woman in the mirror. Physically, a raw and gaping cut ran down her cheek from her eye to her jaw. Dark circles bordered her blue eyes. A mottled bruise clung to a high cheekbone. Her sun-streaked hair hung in strings about her face. Only one earring remained dangling from her earlobe. Her shirt collar was brown with her own dried blood and begrimed from the journey. But more strangely a deep spiritual schism, between what she believed she was and what she now was, shown in her grief-filled eyes. Observing this phantom of herself, she dabbed at the dirt and dried blood until José nudged her.

"Hurry! I am supposed to put this on you." Adrianne saw a braided, rawhide rope in his hands. He quickly dropped the loop over her head and tightened it gently against her neck.

"Are you going to hang me?" Adrianne asked quietly, handing him the mirror.

"No. No." The boy shook his head impatiently. Gesturing at the sides of his face, mimicking Adrianne's disheveled hair, he gave her a broken wooden comb. She looked at it and at the boy. "No lice. Use it." Adrianne continued to stand. José pushed her shoulder impatiently. "Do it. You must not look beaten, *Mujer*. Walk straight and proud. If you seem weak and afraid, it will be bad for you and the child. You fight back. Don't kill anybody, but don't take anything, either." With the words he slapped the comb into Adrianne's hand, took the rag, and knelt to wipe quickly Lottie's face. The woman straightened, lifted her chin slightly, drew her hair back, and tied it loosely with a strip of braid torn from her jacket sleeve.

It is recorded that the triumphal procession of Cæsar as he entered Rome with his legions lasted for four days, one for each of his conquests in Gaul, Egypt, Pontus, and Africa. Royal captives marched before him — the princess Arsinoë of Egypt, the infant son of the King of Numidia, the noble, long-imprisoned Gaul, Vercingetorix, whose people Cæsar had so brutally and mercilessly pacified. These illustrious captives glorified the conqueror's procession, preparing the people for his presence. And when at last he appeared in a chariot drawn by white horses preceded by seventy-two lictors, he dazzled the citizens of Rome. They lined the streets, shouting Cæsar's name louder and louder, until it became a deafening roar as he passed by. Behind him marched his legions. Behind him came the loot and plunder of the nations he had conquered — furniture, silken fabrics, gold, jewelry, exotic beasts. Every cohort received five thousand *denarii* and every centurion ten thousand. Each spectator along the route received a hundred *denarii*. All were given also ten pounds of olive oil

69

and ten measures of wheat. And it is said that Cæsar's treasury was still full. In the following celebration the people were fed at twenty-two thousand tables and entertained with gladitorial shows, animal fights, plays, and miniature military fights. In the evening, the conqueror was escorted by twenty torchbearers on elephants to his home, and there the night was spent in revelry.

Satanta's return to the Kiowa village differed not at all in principle, but only in magnitude. Before the main party of warriors arrived, criers, accompanied by barking dogs and running children, rode through the large Kiowa encampment proclaiming their return. No faces were painted black, and the People knew from this that no raider from among them had been lost and that the raid had been a success. And their hearts leaped up as they left their lodges and work and went into the village street. When the People were assembled, young men and boys, captive and Kiowa born, pushed the herd of booty horses whose hoof beats carried the sound of thunder through the village. And the people drew back against their teepees because the herd was so large. The old men and many women, too, watched the herd closely and saw that these horses were good, sorted, and had been brought along the trail with care. A few mules and heavy horses needed for the women's work ran among the others, but the culls had already been sold along with the cattle. Behind the herd and young men rode the senior warriors, men of many battles and honors, and men who had distinguished themselves in the fight at Elm Creek. Before them all rode Satanta, leader, *toyapke*, of the raid. And behind him, tall and straight, walked Adrianne Chastain, holding her granddaughter's small hand.

Around the woman and child swirled a world of unknown sights and sounds. Women with long poles ran out and took from the returning men the fresh scalps of their enemies.

70

Carrying the grisly trophies stretched over small willow hoops hanging on the poles, the women paraded them through the village, shouting out the warriors' names. A few of the men rode double, their horses painted with hand prints, to show that in the midst of battle they had rushed in to rescue men who had fallen. Many of the men or their slaves led ponies laden with huge ticking sacks filled with the spoils of Elm Creek and the Brazos. And the hearts of the People leaped up for the giving-away time was coming soon. Women raised their voices in ululating waves as their warriors passed. Some young women caught their husbands' trailing moccasin fringes and walked beside them eager to be with their man again. But most remained to see the passing splendor of the procession.

Satanta's honored war pony danced with excitement among the pressing crowd. Adrianne gazed straight ahead, trying not to see the excited and unfamiliar faces of the captor people. As they walked, she drew Lottie closer to her side, resting her hand on the child's thin shoulder, still holding the small hand.

"Marn! Marn!" shouted Lottie as a woman from the crowd caught her arm and jerked her quickly away. The child dug in, pulling back against the woman's strong grip.

Adrianne shot out toward the woman, but the rope jerked her back with a searing pain at her neck. Her hands went to it, drawing the opening larger. She threw it away from her as she lunged into the throng after the woman, dragging away the child. The People backed aside from the women.

"Fall down, Lottie," Adrianne ordered the struggling child. The child fell, making the woman pull her full weight across the dry grass. The woman stopped and bent to pick up the child and carry her away. Adrianne dove into her, knocking her back on her behind. She lifted up Lottie against her. The child's arms grasped her neck. Her legs encircled Adrianne's waist. The Kiowa woman did not rise. Adrianne

71

waited, but she did not rise. The white woman turned slowly, observing the surrounding crowd. Her eyes defied them as she started back through them toward Satanta. She turned slightly to make sure the attacker did not follow. Yet she did not see the club that struck the back of her head and knocked her to her knees. Adrianne did not release the child, but held her tighter. She raised one knee weakly and attempted to stand. When she looked up, she saw Satanta sitting grimly on his horse above her.

"Take the child," he ordered José, who dropped down and moved toward the woman and child. As he took Lottie's arms, Adrianne stiffened and fell.

José looked up at Satanta. The black eyes of the chief flashed. "Move back!" The People moved farther away. "Put the stick in her mouth," he told José.

The boy's whole body shook. "I cannot," he said, backing away in fear. "She has power."

Satanta lifted his quirt, then popped it against his leg in silent fury at the boy's disobedience.

"Where is the stick?" asked Woven Blanket, coming through the crowd.

"Her coat front," gasped José, feeling relief.

The Kiowa woman patted the coat until she found the short rod. Placing one hand across Adrianne's nose and cheeks and the heel of the other against her chin, she pried the mouth open and laid the stick across her teeth. Adrianne convulsed against the ground. Woven Blanket sat back on her heels, watching. The crowd muttered, moving farther away.

Woven Blanket did not flee, but looked into Satanta's eyes. "What have you brought us, my husband?" she asked. The Kiowa shrugged, then rode slowly away.

When Adrianne awoke, she was in a small lodge. The coals

72

of a fire burned in a rock-lined pit, filling the room with deep shadows. Outside, the night throbbed with the steady rhythm of drums. Shouts and singing echoed through the night as the People celebrated their victory over the whites.

"Lottie," the woman called softly. There was no answer.

Adrianne found herself unbound, free, as she rose stiffly to her feet. She staggered, her head throbbing with fatigue and fear. Catching a pole to steady herself, she considered the unfamiliar space as it circled and narrowed above her. Somehow she knew it was a woman's place. Buffalo robes and parfleche boxes lay neatly arranged against the walls. A child's doll sat on one of the rawhide boxes. Food simmered in cooking pots, swinging from iron hooks over the fire. Tanned hides hung suspended in the rising smoke of the embers. A garment and sewing materials waited where they had been laid aside. Adrianne crossed the room to the door made of hide. Lifting it tentatively, she stooped beneath to half crawl from the lodge.

The night air was crisp and fresh against her face. Her eyes moved over the dim, lantern-like lodges, through the shadowed pathways between, to the great fire built in the center of the village. Two women passed her, carrying cook pots, oblivious to anything but their need to furnish more food for the feast. A young man proudly walked a fine pony between the teepees. Unheeded, unhindered, Adrianne ventured forth more boldly. For the moment she was invisible, it seemed. She watched unwatched. She moved into the shadows as a painted and feathered young man emerged from the door of a red teepee. She walked quietly, concentrating on seeing and not being seen. Dodging a group of young men coming toward her, she backtracked between lodges and found herself among the trees. Circling the distant fire, hungry to find Lottie, she eased through them.

"Unh. Unh." The moans came faintly through the cold air

faint above the drums. Adrianne stopped and stood very still, trying to locate the urgent sounds. At last her eyes found the shadowed shapes — a man and a woman against a tree. Adrianne had seen the young warrior before, but did not know his name. The woman groaned as he kissed her hungrily. She reached out for him, enveloping her embrace in a brightly striped Spanish blanket. Adrianne blinked, surprised by the open ardor. She quietly hurried away.

The noise of the drums and the singing grew louder as Adrianne returned again to the red teepee. Standing in its shadow, she scanned the faces around the fire, looking for Lottie.

"Well, White Woman, Taukoyma, what have you found in prowling about my village?" asked Satanta behind her.

Adrianne turned quickly. "Where is my granddaughter?"

"Are you going to take her, steal a horse, and run away?" queried the Kiowa.

"Where would I go?" answered the woman without emotion.

"You are a smart woman," smiled Satanta.

"Now, where is Lottie?"

The man put his hands on her shoulders and turned her toward the fire. "There." He pointed, leaving one hand on her shoulder. "She is dancing."

Adrianne gasped as she recognized the child dancing perfectly, foot down, trunk up, foot down, swaying the fringe of a small shawl. She carried a miniature scalp pole, dangling a scalp.

"Good God in heaven, have you no decency?" Adrianne turned on Satanta. "Is that her mother's or her uncle's scalp you've put in her baby hands?"

"Learn from the child," the Kiowa said. "She is already walking a new road."

"I do not want her walking *this* new road."

"Do you want her to live?" asked Satanta directly.

"Of course, I want her to live. She is mine."

Satanta caught Adrianne's face in his hand. "No, Taukoyma, White Woman. She is mine. You are mine. That is the truth. You must walk the road I say for you to walk."

Adrianne was shaking as she straightened and backed away from Satanta's hand. "I am not yours. Lottie is not yours. We are your prisoners, but we are not yours."

"It is the same thing," grunted Satanta.

"It is not the same thing," the woman said softly to herself as the Kiowa walked away. "We are here under duress, not by choice, that makes us prisoners. You cannot own us inside . . . where it counts."

"Do you talk to yourself, Taukoyma?" a woman's low voice asked. Adrianne turned to see Woven Blanket with a large stack of blankets. "Carry this," she said as she offered the stack to Adrianne. The white woman took them.

"When Satanta finishes dancing, he will begin the giving-away. He is a fine dancer," boasted Woven Blanket gently.

Adrianne followed the woman's eyes to the bright firelight and the dancer. With the steady throb of drums, the warrior bent and turned with shield and lance in a form of battle. His movements were graceful and strong. There was a difference from the dance of white society. Nothing frivolous or affected, the Kiowa danced with a male strength and power. His face seemed transformed in the firelight and shadows, far away, involved in something that Adrianne did not recognize.

"It is the *ohoma* . . . a warrior's thanksgiving dance," commented Woven Blanket. "Do you hear the music?"

Adrianne nodded absently.

"Do you hear the music?"

Adrianne turned to look at Woven Blanket. "I hear."

75

"No. I do not think you do." Woven Blanket studied her. "I think you hear only the sounds, but not the music. Only a Kiowa hears the music. When we dance, we become the music, the Sacred. We are in good relation with the sacred rhythm of life. See how Satanta manifests it in his movements."

As the man dipped and whirled and thrust with shield and spear, he began to sing to the drums. "Give us long life. Make us brave chiefs. Keep our enemies blind and deaf, so they cannot discover our cunning approach." Woven Blanket interpreted the words for Adrianne. "It is from the Scalp Dance. He remembers as he dances that he was not alone."

Satanta finished with the staccato-ending strikes of the drummers' sticks and walked toward the women. Beads of sweat stood on his forehead. Woven Blanket gave him his shirt, and he slipped it over his head and body. "I will give away the horses first," he said. While other dancers kept the eternal rhythms, Satanta moved away in the darkness and reappeared at the entry to the great circle of the People. José was behind him with a horse. Other herd boys held other horses.

"Come with me," said Woven Blanket. Following behind the splendidly dressed Kiowa woman, Adrianne was suddenly aware of her own tattered attire, the tear in her skirt that revealed a patch of bare, bruised, lacerated skin. Woven Blanket lifted her graceful hand to signal a stop, and the long, cone-wrapped fringes of her skin dress danced and murmured in the firelight.

Satanta now stood near the drummers who kept a soft, steady beat as he talked.

"I am giving away gifts to those who have helped me on this raid. These men are very brave. Cut Nose, I give this fine horse and rifle." The warrior came forward and took the

76

horse's reins and the weapon offered him by Satanta. As he went away, José brought another horse. Satanta gave it away to another warrior. Adrianne noted the brand was her own.

"Very generous, sir, with other people's property," she muttered to herself.

Woven Blanket turned slightly, silencing the white woman, then returned her attention to the giving-away ceremonies conducted by her husband. Slowly Satanta disposed of more horses to especially brave and honored men. Finally, he began to give brass tomahawks with ornate patterns of nail heads in the handles and steel knives in beaded cases with dancing feathers, and then bright trade blankets and shawls for the warriors' wives. As he spoke and each man or youth came forward, Woven Blanket took a blanket from Adrianne and carried the bright red or blue cloth to Satanta. Each was edged with decorative bands of fine beadwork. The men bowed slightly to her as they eagerly took the beautiful tokens of their chief's favor.

When Satanta's giving was done, Woven Blanket returned to the red teepee, beckoning Adrianne to follow. The white woman hesitated, trying to find Lottie again in the crowd. Satanta shoved her slightly and gestured with his head toward his lodge. "Do whatever Woven Blanket says. She is first wife. You are nothing, a slave, whatever she wants you to be."

Adrianne started after the elegant Kiowa woman. She heard the giggles of little girls running and felt Lottie take her hand. "Look, Marn," the child said. "Ain't I pretty?" Adrianne looked searchingly at the child, wearing an Indian child's dress, cheeks painted with bright red circles, blonde hair blowing in the prairie wind. "This is my friend, Speckled Light. She's Satanta's daughter . . . well, one of his daughters. He's got five."

Speckled Light was several years older than Lottie and

seemed to have adopted her, turning the white child into a kind of living doll that she could dress and ornament and take about with her. Adrianne nodded at the girl. The children ran away again, and Adrianne hurried to the red teepee.

Ducking inside, she found the lodge much more spacious than the one where she had awakened. Buffalo robes lined the walls and provided comfortable couches against woven backrests for Satanta and his guests. The men had not yet arrived, and Woven Blanket was making the final preparations for the revelry that would continue throughout the night.

Woven Blanket tended the meat, roasting over the coals. José knelt beside her, listening to her instructions. He slowly turned the skewered buffalo humps as she watched. At last, she gave her attention to the bedraggled woman standing in the shadows.

"Come out of the doorway," the Kiowa woman said in Spanish. Adrianne stepped toward her, pushing a strand of hair from her eyes. Woven Blanket rose and walked toward Adrianne. She circled her, talking almost to herself. "You smell and you are very dirty, too dirty to wait on Satanta's guests. Still, under the dirt, you are probably pretty. Satanta likes pretty women. Pretty is nothing to me. He has pretty wives and daughters, and as you can see none of them is here helping. What can you do?"

Adrianne started tentatively, then, realizing the importance of making a place for herself and Lottie among their captors, she became bolder. "I can . . . I can cook. I can sew. I can do laundry, make beds, and clean. I can mind children, or herd horses or cows. I ran a ranch, a store, and an inn and boarding house for a dozen muleskinners and cowhands besides guests. I doctored the sick, made garden enough to feed us all, raised my own chickens and pigs and milk cows. Sold eggs and hams

78

and butter and whatever wasn't eaten from the garden and made shirts and dresses to sell. I also pickle and make preserves. I can do whatever needs doing."

"Hmm." Woven Blanket cocked her head slightly. "Let me see your hands."

Adrianne self-consciously wiped her hands on her skirt before offering them to the Indian woman who observed the strong but gracefully tapered fingers. Adrianne turned them over, revealing light calluses that she was supposed to be ashamed of in front of refined, white women. In the past, when she had been busy or preoccupied, she often had forgotten her gloves or taken them off. It was a flaw that her grandmother had pointed out as unlady-like and would lead to just the calluses that she now possessed. Woven Blanket gripped her hand, testing the strength. Adrianne gripped back before letting go.

"Can you skin and butcher buffalo and tan hides?"

"Don't know," Adrianne answered with unfelt bravado. "Never tried."

"Ha," laughed Woven Blanket. "I will see you get to try, White Woman. Right now, you tend the fire and food. José, go and find the Sisters. If you cannot find them, Speckled Light will have to help me serve." Adrianne started toward the fire, circling behind it to face the door, stepping over an oblong stone on the floor. "No. No," corrected the Kiowa woman. "That is the altar in front of Satanta's place. Never touch it or get between him and the fire."

As Adrianne watched the meat spitted over the red coals, Woven Blanket placed a leather-wrapped bundle on the floor beside Satanta's place and untied it. Inside was dried cedar. Lighting the tip of one stem in the fire, she placed it on the stone altar. The pungent smell wafted up Adrianne's nose, mingling with the roasting meat. The tent flap opened. Both women looked up. Each smiled. Speckled Light towed Lottie into the warm room.

"Yes, Mother," the girl spoke softly.

"Dohasan is coming tonight. It is a great honor to have the principal chief in our lodge. Remember, he is your great-grandmother's brother. You will set the plates before the men on that side of the room, and I will serve Dohasan and your father. Later, when they have finished, you will collect the platters and bring water for washing the grease from their hands and towels for drying."

"Can't Flies Far do it?" asked the girl with a small pout. "I wish to keep playing with my friend."

"Do not think to do other than what is needed, Speckled Light," Woven Blanket said softly. "Tonight you must help me. You are my only chick, now that your sisters are married." The girl glanced at Adrianne. Her mother saw and cut off the thought that flickered over the young face. "This woman does not know our ways."

Adrianne pulled Lottie down beside her as the Kiowa mother and daughter spoke in words she did not understand. She bent and whispered so that only Lottie could hear. "Can you understand them, child?"

"Sometimes," said Lottie. "I think Speckled Light is to take food to one side of the room and her mother to the other."

The door cover lifted again, and a woman came in, wrapped securely in a striped Spanish blanket with a light-blue background. Adrianne looked hastily back at the fire. "Do you know who that is, Lottie?"

"Oh, that's one of Satanta's wives," affirmed the child.

The lovely creature removed the showy blanket and placed it behind a buffalo robe hanging from a cross pole laced between two teepee supports. Adrianne watched, focusing on the blanket and the fringed and painted skirt, confirming her suspicions of the woman.

"She is awake, I see," noted the woman as she came toward the fire. "Oh, she is loathsome and disgusting. How can you bear the sight or smell of this creature?" she asked Woven Blanket.

Adrianne did not understand the woman's words, but easily read the gestured pinching of the nose as a negative comment about herself. When the Kiowas spoke in Spanish, she felt some security. But in their tongue she could find no clues from inflection. She could not tell questions from statements.

"Is Head Of A Wolf coming?" asked Flies Far casually.

"He was very prominent in the raid," answered Woven Blanket. "Satanta must invite him."

Adrianne saw the small smile come quickly and disappear on the young Kiowa woman's face. "Do not look at me, white, stinking dog," the woman said and slapped Adrianne's head hard.

Woven Blanket glanced up at Satanta's youngest wife. "What has she done that you behave in this common way?"

"She was looking at me," Flies Far explained. "Maybe she is a witch. We all saw the fit she had. It may be that she is evil. Such colorless eyes are revolting. I hope Satanta can get a good ransom for this sorry thing and get her out of here quickly. I will worry about the children, until she is gone."

"Right now, we must worry about the guests." Woven Blanket rested her hands on her thighs. "Speckled Light, you will help us serve, but you do not have to wait for the washing. You may take the white child and play quietly behind the screen until you are ready to go to sleep. If you are needed, I can call you. Take the child and the woman there now. I can hear our guests coming."

Speckled Light took Lottie's hand and motioned that she

81

wished Adrianne to rise and follow her. The young girl led them to the place where Flies Far had thrown her Spanish blanket. Adrianne brushed against it as she sat down and pushed it aside as if it bore the corruption of the woman's adulterous act. She and Lottie lay in the nest of robes with the party in full progress beyond them. The sonorous tone was not unlike the political smokers her father hosted. Listening to the murmuring voices and laughter, Adrianne's eyes rested on the Spanish blanket. Perhaps a very keen and sharp weapon had been given to her this night. Feeling how far time had taken her from her father's house, she fell asleep, holding Lottie and the fragile thought that she was armed in some new way.

Chapter Eight

"We are moving north to the Sand Hill country," Satanta said as he ate his breakfast and talked with Woven Blanket. "I wish to visit my mother's people. And the grass here has pretty well played out while we were away in Texas. Last night we decided that moving would be good. Some will stay here, but we will go north with our horses. It may be that we will find some buffalo to hunt."

"Yes," agreed the woman. "That would be good for us. The buffalo will be prime now for winter robes. And before the *Kado,* the red teepee must be re-made. That will take many hides."

"How many hides?" queried the Kiowa.

"More than twenty," replied Woven Blanket.

"If we find buffalo, my son and I can kill many buffalo. But can you and the Sisters work up so many hides?"

"We have some already. And now with the white woman we have more help."

"I do not think this white woman will know how to help much," observed Satanta, looking at Adrianne. "I think she is used to having other people work for her."

"She is good help," defended Woven Blanket softly. "She is strong. She is experienced in managing a large household."

"*Humph.*" Satanta set his eating platter down. "Flies Far says she smells and has evil-looking eyes." He looked closely at Adrianne's eyes.

Woven Blanket watched her husband, scrutinizing the woman. "Does Flies Far speak for you, my husband?"

83

Satanta turned back to Woven Blanket. "She could be cleaner."

"Yes," agreed his wife. "We must see to that."

When Satanta left the lodge, Woven Blanket quickly began the preparations. "Get up, Taukoyma. We are moving today. Fold the bed robes and stack them outside, then take out the parfleches. José should be here by the time we have things ready, and we can take down the lodge and begin to pack everything onto the travois. Speckled Light, go and tell the others. Everyone should have everything packed and ready to go."

Speckled Light sprinted from the lodge past Adrianne, taking Lottie with her. Woven Blanket smiled. "The People like to travel. This is how to fold the robes."

Adrianne folded just as Woven Blanket taught. Occasionally the Kiowa woman checked her progress or brought a pillow or backrest to be folded into the bed robe. They undid the bed scaffolds and lashed the limbs together into bundles. The two women quickly had the red teepee stripped of its bedding and storage cases. They took down the inner lining and gathered the cooking utensils and the cord of dogwood arrow shafts drying above the fire.

"The men prefer bullets to arrows now," noted Woven Blanket. "But for buffalo hunting, bows and arrows or lances remain the best. Satanta keeps dogwood sticks to work into arrows in the winter."

The household of Satanta required several lodges — the main red teepee used for his purposes and entertaining, a small bachelor teepee for his eldest son, one for storage and the herd boys, and one for the women's separation and work. Each required Woven Blanket's supervision. By the time the stacks were shoulder high outside the lodge, José and the herd boys arrived with the horses. One of the boys stood on a horse's back and unfurled the lashing that held the teepee poles in place. Carefully and skillfully the boys and women unstacked the nested poles and lay them in place on either side of the patient ponies. The poles fit into padded straps laid over the animal's withers. The points were tied, and cross members were laid over the trailing ends to form platforms for the lodge and all its household furnishings. Woven Blanket hurried here and there, seeing that every bundle was packed and nothing left behind that was important. Adrianne followed closely, occasionally in the way, but willing to help.

In work, any work, she found purpose and forgetfulness, just as she always had. Adrianne realized how she had missed physical labor and its release. At last she stood up, easing her back, and looked about the disappearing village. Lodge after lodge slipped its skin, leaving a skeleton to be transformed into travois. Children ran in and out of the open frames. Many of the skins were brightly painted and bore designs. Long, colored streamers blew in the wind on the tops of the poles. The sun was bright and the sky clear. *It has a beauty,* Adrianne thought to herself.

"Now, you come," motioned Woven Blanket. "Everybody cleans up good for the journey." She led Adrianne down toward the stream. Along its edge women who had finished their packing were bathing and putting on clothing in the bright October sun. Traveling was an occasion in itself. The men and women wore their finest to ride in a dazzling procession with their herds and families. It was during traveling that the young men courted the young women, playing flutes, as they rode beside the chosen. Adrianne looked at Woven Blanket, at her own begrimed and disheveled self, and then back at the cold water and public bathing.

"Come on, stinking white woman," shouted Flies Far from the water.

Still Adrianne stood conflicted by necessity, modesty, and the chilly water. Flies Far and her sister, Looking Glass, ran naked from the water and dragged in the white woman. Pushing her under, they roughly scrubbed her head and stripped off the dirty clothing from her. Up-ending her to remove her skirt and high topped boots, they threw the garments on the bank.

"Look she is white all over," observed Flies Far to her sister and the women who had gathered around them in the water. "What can Satanta enjoy in this fish flesh?" Their hands were on Adrianne, pushing her, turning her. "Ah, feel here. She is woolly as a buffalo. White women are woolly as well as white."

The Kiowa women giggled, informed of this new, disgraceful fact. The Kiowas, women and men, plucked away all hair from their bodies, even that of their eyebrows. A few defiant ones, like old Satank or Big Bow, allowed wisps of mustaches to grow at the corners of their mouths. But for most, only the luxurious scalp hair was allowed to remain. Adrianne struck at the hands touching her. Someone shoved her deeply under the water just as she was starting to curse. She inhaled a mouthful of water as she fought her way to the surface. Coughing and spluttering, clawing the hair out of her face, she struggled for breath.

Flies Far caught Adrianne's hair and pulled back her head, scrubbing her face until the cut on her cheek bled again. She thrust the rag into the shivering woman's hand. "Finish yourself. No. There is José. José, come and scrub this white woman's private parts." A howl of laughter rose from the women as the Mexican captive handed a bundle to Woven Blanket and fled.

With the inspection and scrubbing over, the Kiowa women splashed out of the creek toward their blankets and clothes.

Adrianne stood, water to her chin, watching, dreading the moment she would have to rise from the cold water into the colder wind and vision of the few lingering captors.

By the time the women returned to their travel preparations and horses, Adrianne's teeth were chattering. Woven Blanket waited with the garments José had brought, folded over her crossed arms. Sometime during the battle in the creek, the Kiowa woman had changed clothes and was dressed for the travel procession. Adrianne's boots hung upside down on sticks driven into the loose bank.

"We are going away now," the chief's wife said. "If you wait too long, it will be difficult to catch up on foot." With the last words, she dropped the garments and went up the creek's edge back to the packed household and the departing Kiowas.

"Damnation," spluttered Adrianne, striking the top of the water with her arms as Woven Blanket cleared the rise, and she felt the cold wind on her wet flesh. "Damn, damn, damn!"

She dried hastily but not well on a fragment of blanket. Slipping a tattered skin shirt over her torso, she pulled up the skirt even before the shirt edge had fallen over her damp body. She looked for something to hold up the loose tube garment. She held it together as she ripped the belt from her riding skirt and secured it over the hide at her waist. She jammed bare feet into wet boots and listened to the *squish, squish* as she gathered her remaining old clothing and wrapped it in the piece of blanket. She was running and stumbling as she reached the top of the bank. The sight of the disappearing Kiowas made her run faster.

"What in the hell am I doing?" she panted to herself as she gasped for air. But she knew it was not the Indians or even her fear of being left in the empty land that drew her. It was Lottie and the thought of Millie, her younger grandchild, somewhere with other Indians in the vast unknown land.

87

Chapter Nine

The Kiowas' luck was good. They found a wide place near water with good grass for the horses. Even as the women unpacked and erected the teepees, one of the young warriors came in with a report of buffalo to the west.

The next day the main camp was fully set up along the bend of the river. All the family lodges were nestled together as before. The People would remain here until they had taken a sufficient supply of buffalo and prepared their meat and hides. As the herd moved away from them, some of the Indians would take small camping tents out toward the animals and return to the main camp only when they, too, had acquired an ample supply of meat and hides.

"We are not many warriors together now. We are well known to each other. Our young men are our sons and obedient," said Satanta to the men around him in the red teepee. "So I do not think we will have to hold the buffalo to prevent anyone from running into the herd before the rest of us are ready."

Cut Nose looked at the bright sun beyond the teepee door. "It is still warm weather. If anyone should break the hunt, the meat of running buffalo will spoil quickly. But it is as you have said. We have hunted together many times."

Other men in the circle nodded their agreement. The formalities of a large hunt would not be needed. Satanta summarized: "We will ride out together, with the warriors directing the circle. That will be enough. I am sure most of the women are already waiting for us." The men laughed.

"My wife was awake before the sun rose, sharpening her knives," added Hump.

As Lottie remained behind, playing with Speckled Light and the other Kiowa children under the supervision of Woven Blanket's grandmother, Geese Going Moon, Adrianne rode away beside Woven Blanket and the Sisters — Flies Far and Looking Glass. Along the way Woven Blanket gave the white woman instructions about her part in the anticipated hunt. They rode several miles into the wind, letting it wash their scent away behind them. Although the eyesight of the bison was not good, their noses were keen. One of the men directed the women into a wide arc at the base of a rise, as the other men fanned out, circling the bison that grazed in the winter sun beyond.

"When they yell out and ride down on the buffalo, we will go up to the top quickly and see where Satanta has made his kills," said Woven Blanket, as some of the women were already edging up the slope in anticipation. "He will kill only two or three animals for us today."

Adrianne considered the fact that a bison was larger than a cow, but still questioned. "That does not seem like many for such a large household needing winter provisions and many skins for re-making a lodge."

"That is enough to take from the buffalo today. We take only what we must have and no more from our kindred. And it is mainly just for me and you today. The Sisters will also help. Tomorrow he will kill some more and the next day some more. It is the same for every household in our village." Woven Blanket smiled. "We will see tonight if you still think that is so few. You will learn a lot today, Taukoyma."

A series of whoops broke the silence, and the women rode quickly to the brink of the hillock. Below, in the wide basin of the river, the Kiowa men sped down on the waiting buffalo.

Riding into the edge of the herd, the men took several animals before the others started to run. Adrianne raised her arm to shield her eyes from the bright sun.

"Which is Satanta?" she asked. All the men were stripped to moccasins and breechcloths.

"There," pointed Woven Blanket.

Adrianne searched in the direction she pointed. "Does he have a bow?"

"No, a lance. A lance is better, but more dangerous to use. It can be placed better and pushed down into the heart at once. The buffalo will not run far with a lance in it. The meat will not be tainted by long running." Woven Blanket spoke as she watched intently.

"How is it more dangerous?" asked the white woman.

"The shaft sticks up. A man or horse can be hit by it," explained the Kiowa woman. "Even now he is praying."

"About the lance, or does a skillful man pray for success?" asked the white woman.

"Neither." Woven Blanket continued to watch Satanta. "He asks the animal to give flesh to feed his children, hide to clothe and house them, to forgive him, and he thanks the buffalo. Watch his horse, White Woman. It is a famous buffalo horse."

Adrianne watched while many of the women along the hillside were shouting. They excitedly charged down after the men, going toward the places where their husbands' kills had fallen. "Are we not going?" asked Adrianne.

"Not yet," answered Woven Blanket. "I like to watch the hunt, and I do not like to get there before the animal is really dead. A wounded bison is very dangerous. Better to watch from here for a while." The hunt played across the plain before them as they sat on their ponies on the hill.

"He has picked his animal," said Flies Far excitedly.

90

Adrianne saw Satanta cut in behind a cow from the right. His pony ran unchecked as the man raised the shaft of the lance. His left hand held the sparkling point, aimed behind the last rib, and his right arm drove it down into the animal's vitals. Immediately the pony swerved to the right, taking him away from the danger of a wounded buffalo. A few running paces more and the cow skidded onto her knees and dropped. Adrianne's hand went to her mouth. The other women shouted. Excitement danced along the hilltop.

The herd and hunters went on down the valley, leaving the carcasses of the dead and dying behind. Slowly the careful women on the hill rode down with their travois onto the plain. Each rode in the direction of her husband's kills. The feathered shaft or lance marked the final owner. When more than one arrow had struck an animal, the men decided whose arrow had killed it and gave the meat and hide to that one. If either arrow could have made the kill, the meat was divided. Of course, sometimes, with the arrows driven with force at close range, the arrow went completely through the beast and into the ground or another animal. Deciding the owner then was a matter of a man's claim and a decision by the hunt leaders. But these instances were rare.

As the women rode, Adrianne saw that Satanta continued down the valley. "He has killed more than three animals."

"Yes," agreed Woven Blanket. "A very, very good woman can skin out and butcher three buffaloes in a day. That is going too hard except for show or dire need. Two is a good day's work for any woman, but we have several women. Satanta also kills some for those who are widows and in place of the men too old to hunt any more."

"Damned Christian of him," swore Adrianne under her breath in the muleskinners' best style.

Woven Blanket looked at her. "What?"

Adrianne did not look at her, but nodded toward the carcass. "Is that the one?"

The women circled the dead cow where José waited. From long experience, each knew their own and the others' parts. The young man had already straightened the young cow on her side. Woven Blanket bent and slashed across the neck at the brisket with her skinning knife. She peeled back the skin, exposing the animal's forelegs. As she continued the skinning, José disjointed the legs and removed them, handing them to Looking Glass who lay them on the winter grass. Woven Blanket worked along the animal, slicing the skin down the backbone. With Flies Far she pulled the skin away from the flesh. The carefully protected sinews along the spine were removed intact. She handed them to Adrianne and gestured toward the stack of legs. Adrianne placed the sinews there. José and Woven Blanket spoke in Kiowa as they considered the special problems of the situation. The young man again did the heavy work, disjointing the hind quarters, leaving the rump with the back. Woven Blanket, meanwhile, cut the flank toward the stomach. With Adrianne's help, she sectioned a thin chunk of meat along the body toward the brisket and removed it in one long, neatly rolled piece.

Adrianne like most frontier women had butchered before. She was not repulsed by the act or the blood and grease that soon covered her hands and clothes. As José sliced open the belly and removed the entrails, the smell of the fresh grass in the cow's belly floated into her nostrils, and for a moment she knew again the fragility of life, its vulnerability before man. Before her lay what had been a living thing, so recently feeding peacefully with its kind that a blade of grass still clung to the corner of its mouth. It had sought no confrontation with the men, had merely been in the herd pursuing its life. She sighed. Perhaps the Kiowas were right to thank and ask pardon of the

92

spirits of such giving creatures.

With the still warm liver in his bloody hands, the young captive offered it to the women. Each cut a section and ate it with relish. Woven Blanket noticed that Adrianne was not eating. She cut again and offered the flesh to the white woman.

Adrianne leaned away from the hand and flesh. Woven Blanket caught her arm with her free hand, holding the bloody knife. "Eat. Just try. You will be pleased. Try."

Adrianne considered the raw meat, the grisly hand holding it. Her face twisted slightly. Woven Blanket tugged on her arm again. The white woman took the piece of meat as the Kiowas watched.

Woven Blanket continued to nod at her. "Yes. Yes. Good."

Adrianne, by force of will, drew the purple pulp to her lips. She closed her eyes and placed the flesh in her mouth. In a quick bite, she cut into the porous organ. She chewed twice, gagged, and swallowed quickly.

José slapped her on the back. "Now you're a real Kiowa . . . a raw-liver eater." The Kiowa women laughed and continued to relish their portions of the uncooked prize.

By the time Satanta, his son, Eagle Child, and his father, Old Man Red Teepee, arrived, the ribs had been split from the sternum and the rib steaks secured with the other meat in the fresh hide. Only the animal's massive skull, bones, and sacred heart remained. The three men loaded the heaviest pieces onto the travois as the women wiped their hands on the long grass.

"There are four more carcasses," Satanta said to the women. "I will kill no more until you are caught up. Leave the next kill for White Crow's women."

"That means we will have to go far down the valley for our meat and carry it a long way back," murmured Flies Far. "It will take a long time."

Satanta looked at her, and then at Woven Blanket. "They are old. You are not yet," he said to Flies Far. "Leave the next animal, and, when we have finished with our buffaloes, you can help White Crow's women finish their work."

"You were not so mean to me last night in the warmth of our blankets," pouted Flies Far with a cunning smile at the chief.

Satanta looked away. "It will not hurt you to help the other women."

"It will make me tired, maybe too tired," simpered Flies Far.

"This is a woman's matter," said Satanta, going to his pony. "Woven Blanket will tell you what to do."

"I am going to take this hide and meat back to camp and show the white woman what to do," Woven Blanket spoke quietly to the Sisters and José. "As you finish each carcass, send in the hide and meat so that we can get to work. I do not want to have to wait on you or work after dark. Flies Far should stay and help the old women, when you finish here. It is expected. We will do without her help in camp so that she may help White Crow's women. White Woman, get on your horse and lead the travois horse." Adrianne did not hear what Flies Far said; she only saw Woven Blanket turn quickly on her. "Would you rather tan the hides and cut the meat for drying?" The junior wife shook her head.

Woven Blanket and Adrianne rode back to camp without speaking. The white woman had discovered another secret of the Kiowa household.

As the women arrived, the village already hummed with work. Adrianne soon realized that Woven Blanket was an efficient and generous woman. As soon as the meat was unloaded, she set the older women to slicing and seasoning the rolled flank steak in thin strips to hang over the drying racks.

94

"Looking Glass will come in soon and help us," she explained. "But we can begin. I will set the white woman to work and come and help you." Geese Going Moon, Woven Blanket's grandmother, and Satanta's mother, North Country Woman, elder women of the extended household, knew their work and went quickly about the meat preparation.

Taking large roasts, Woven Blanket called Satanta's youngest son, Feathered Lance. She placed the ten-year-old in charge of the little girls, and they began the delivery of the meat set aside for lodges without hunters.

"Take the hide and lay it there in the clear place," she said to the waiting white woman, and disappeared into the women's teepee. Adrianne carried the wet skin toward the spot and put it down, wiping her hands against her skirt. Woven Blanket dropped a number of wooden stakes onto the ground. "You will stretch out the skin flesh side up and drive the pins into it to hold it in place. Make it tight." She dropped a large, smooth stone for pounding beside the stakes.

"But come now, we will make the tanning mixture. It can cook while you drive the stakes into the hide," Woven Blanket said as Adrianne followed. "You will hate this, Taukoyma. This is a very smelly and revolting task, but you were not squeamish about the butchering. Maybe you can do this. It will be a great relief to Flies Far. This is often her task, when I am skinning and butchering and Looking Glass is cutting up the meat for drying."

Adrianne grimaced slightly at the thought of being useful to Flies Far who had yet to elicit any respect or sympathy from her. Woven Blanket handed her a battered bucket. "Do as I say now. Watch the proportions. They are important. Take about half the brain and put it into the bucket." Adrianne looked at the white mass that had become goo during the return to camp. She swallowed and scraped it into her hands

95

and dropped it into the bucket, dodging the smell. "Next, half the liver." Again Adrianne obeyed, plopping the liver on top of the brain. Woven Blanket scooped up a palmful of tallow, showed it to Adrianne, and dropped it into the bucket. Feathered Lance arrived with a buffalo paunch of water, and she poured a small amount into the mixture as Adrianne observed. "Now stir."

Adrianne looked up from the disgusting bucket. "I'll need a stick."

"Not yet," corrected Woven Blanket. "You can mash and mix it better with your hands."

Adrianne looked at the bucket. "Hands?" She lifted her hands from her lap and plunged them into the mess. She closed her eyes.

Woven Blanket and the other women laughed. "Work the mixture into a paste. You can add a little water, but, if you add too much, it will be runny. Let me look at it. Keep mixing. Geese Going Moon will tell you when it is ready and watch it cook while you stake the hide. I will look at it before you put it on."

As the tanning stew simmered, the white woman labored over the hide, pulling the skin taut against the driven stakes, and driving more. She did not look up, but worked steadily as Woven Blanket went away to check on Looking Glass and the others' progress and the children. Adrianne was just driving the last pin, when Woven Blanket silently returned to see the work.

"See if the tanning mixture is ready," she said to Adrianne who went to the fire where Geese Going Moon stirred the concoction.

"Take it. Take it," said the old one.

Adrianne returned to the staked hide and set the pot down for Woven Blanket's inspection. "Let it cool enough to put

96

your hands in, then work it some more."

Adrianne stirred the cooling liquid, then squeezed and mashed the organs into a mush of finer and finer pieces. She tried to work the consistency by feel, but occasionally had to look into the forming paste. After a time, Woven Blanket bent beside her and peered into the bucket. "Pour off some of the water and work it some more." Adrianne did as she was directed, too far immersed in the miserable mess to protest. Woven Blanket looked again. "Good. Now spread it evenly all over the skin and work it in."

"With my hands?" asked Adrianne.

"No." Woven Blanket handed her a rock. "Press or pound it in."

Adrianne soon discovered that pounding caused the tanning mush to splatter into her face and eyes. She smoothed and pressed.

"Harder," said Woven Blanket as she passed.

Adrianne pressed the liver-brain solution into the hide until the backs of her arms ached and her stomach muscles twitched. The foul smell saturated her nose.

Woven Blanket inspected. "The hair on this hide is not choice for a robe. You can turn it over and do the other side now," she said, and went away again.

By the time Adrianne had both sides coated and the tanning paste rubbed in thoroughly, Satanta arrived with meat wrapped in two more hides. He rode proudly with his father and son in front of the travois led by Looking Glass and one of the herd boys. Flies Far and José had remained in the field to help White Crow's women. As the others went on, the chief reined in before Adrianne. She saw the pony's fine front hoofs as she worked.

"So you have found your work, Taukoyma?" smiled Satanta, as Adrianne looked up. He chuckled as he rode away.

97

One of the boys came with the two other robes and dropped them in front of the white woman. She sat back on her heels with tears in her eyes. Lottie put a small sympathetic hand around her neck and kissed her. "Poor Marn."

"I'm just fine. You can go and play with the other children," whispered Adrianne. She searched the child's face. "How are you?"

"We took meat to some old people," the child said with pride.

"Yes," smiled Adrianne. "I saw you. That was gracious and generous."

"The children are nice," Lottie volunteered. She added confidentially: "Feathered Lance is very clever and in charge of the little children, except for Speckled Light, but I do what he says. He likes me." Adrianne smiled tiredly, stroking the child's arm until she hurried away after the others.

As Woven Blanket directed, Adrianne rolled up the first skin and lay it aside. She then began to spread the fresh skins. By sunset, she finished the last of the work and stood up to carry the hides back to the women's lodge.

"When you have taken that, you should go and bathe." Woven Blanket was again at her side. "There is food inside. Sky Living In Her Eyes has eaten and is playing with Speckled Light."

"Sky Living In Her Eyes, that's what you call Lottie?" asked Adrianne.

"Yes. It is a good name. Speckled Light chose it," answered Woven Blanket. "Now go and clean up. Wash your clothes and bring them back to the fire to dry." Adrianne looked at the Kiowa woman, too tired to protest, and stood up shakily. Woven Blanket laid a blanket over her shoulders. "Wrap up in this until your clothes dry. You have worked hard and well, Taukoyma. You hardly seem like a white woman."

Night was beginning to settle over the sunset as Adrianne knelt beside the stream. She washed her arms, scrubbing them with sand to remove the smelly tanning jelly. She had brought her white clothes and washed them in the moving water. Easing into the cold water, she stripped off the hide garments she wore and washed them and tossed them onto the shore before turning her attention to her body. Emerging from the water, she quickly reached for the blanket Woven Blanket had sent and wrapped it around her. It was thin, and the wool scratched. As she flapped out the leather garments, she noticed Satanta, standing on the bank above her.

"Well, how long have you been there?" She muttered to herself as she worked. "Got your eyes full, did you, you red buzzard?" She continued slapping the wetness out of the leather. "Go away. You do not need to watch me. You know I will come back," she shouted to the Kiowa.

"You are not safe here alone," the man said.

"Where are your weapons to protect me?" queried the white woman.

"You know that I myself am your protection, Taukoyma. Woven Blanket says you are too good a worker to be eaten by wolves. Come now. It is getting dark. I will walk you to the lodge."

Adrianne stood looking at the chief for a few minutes, then stooped and picked up her wet clothes, and climbed the bank toward him. "What are you going to do with us?"

Satanta looked down at the woman. "Keep you until someone comes for you."

"No one is coming," she said, as she drew even with him.

The Kiowa seemed a little surprised. "But you are a rich woman."

"And that, sir, is exactly why no one is coming. They are in control, when I am not there. No one is coming."

As she started past the chief, Satanta gestured toward the gently milling horse herd across the stream. The small fire of the herd boys burned brightly in the growing darkness.

"It is a good place for horses," he said.

Adrianne nodded. Her practiced eyes, too, had found the land good for horses. "On that we can agree." She shivered suddenly as the wind touched her. Satanta put his blanket around her shoulders. They walked back to the camp together in silence.

Chapter Ten

Geese Going Moon shook Adrianne's shoulder. The white woman groaned softly, feeling yesterday's lingering pain unhealed by the night's rest. "Up," said the Kiowa woman. "Get up. Get dressed. There is work to do." Her Spanish was as good as Satanta's and Woven Blanket's.

Adrianne sat up, noticing that Lottie and the other children still slept quietly beneath the winter robes. Drawing her blanket higher, the white woman went to her clothes, drying near the women's fire. She gathered the leather shirt and dropped the robe. Quickly thrusting her arms into the shirt, she stepped into the skirt and drew it up, belting it to hold it in place.

The ancient woman was already at the door as Adrianne struggled into her boots. "Take some food from the fire and come on. *¡Andale! ¡Andale! ¡Manosea la obra!*" Adrianne grabbed a rib and followed. She chewed as Geese Going Moon led her to yesterday's stack of coated buffalo robes. "Now," said the Kiowa grandmother, "you take these to the creek and wash them good, both sides. Woven Blanket says you will do right, but I will watch you, anyway."

Throwing the bone away, Adrianne lifted the heavy hide carefully to keep the mess away from her clothes and caught up with Geese Going Moon. The old woman sat down on a log and waited comfortably for the white woman to wash the tanning gel from the hide. Adrianne sighed as she slid the skin into the water and knelt to wash it. She scrubbed and rinsed until the skin was free of the jelly.

"Let me see," said the old woman. "Bring it for me to see."

Stripping off as much of the water as possible, Adrianne carried the hide to the seated woman. She held it up, dripping, for her to scrutinize. Geese Going Moon nodded.

"Take that one back and get another one," she said, and gestured casually over her shoulder.

As Adrianne worked on the second hide, she noticed that Geese Going Moon was dozing in the warm sun. She heard the restful sound of a little snore bubbling from the old one's lips. Despite herself, the white woman smiled. When she looked again, Geese Going Moon was not on the log.

"Ohhh. Ohhh." A low moan came from where she had been sitting.

Leaving the hide, Adrianne rushed to the log. Geese Going Moon lay on her back, trying to right herself. The white woman knelt quickly and lifted the old one's shoulders and back. Slowly they worked to get her on her feet.

"It is difficult to be old," apologized Geese Going Moon. "You do embarrassing things to yourself." Adrianne dusted grass and dirt from Geese Going Moon's back and legs. "And almost everyone you know is dead."

Adrianne said softly: "That happens not just to the old. Almost everyone I know is dead, too. I have only my grandchildren left."

"Then who will come for you?" asked the old woman.

"I will have to see to us," answered Adrianne.

"Can you do that?" asked Geese Going Moon, looking into Adrianne's eyes.

"I will find a way." Adrianne brushed a small leaf from Geese Going Moon's forehead.

"Maybe you are meant to stay," suggested the old one thoughtfully, taking Adrianne's hand and turning it. "Your hands are strong, yet gentle, even with an old one of your enemy." She looked up, returning to a previous thought.

102

"Woven Blanket is *my* granddaughter. My husband was killed. My sons are important men now, busy men with families. My sisters are all dead. My daughter died of the smallpox. There is only my brother. He is so old the bluecoats gave him a wagon to go about in. The younger chiefs, like Satanta, take their horses away from time to time so that his horses do not have to move about much to find grass.

"But Woven Blanket treats me very well. She spoils me. Satanta does not mind. He has great generosity. My daughter did not want Woven Blanket to marry him. She said he was ambitious, and Woven Blanket was only a way of adding to his standing. Woven Blanket is the daughter and granddaughter of Kiowa chiefs . . . an *onde* . . . high-ranking woman. Dohasan is my brother, you know. He has been principal chief a long, long time, since the Cut-throat Massacre, maybe thirty years. My daughter said Satanta called attention to himself. She thought that was a fault, but Woven Blanket did not. As it turned out, he has done well. He is a strong leader who speaks well in council. Woven Blanket has helped him. They have done well together." She thought a few moments. "I only do what I want to do." She smiled wickedly. "But I did not want to take my nap with my feet in the air."

Seeing the hide slipping away from the shore, Adrianne squeezed the old woman's arm and ran back to it as it drifted away on the current. "Damn," she said as she splashed into the water after it. Racing to retrieve it, she stepped into a hole and blubbered beneath the surface. She quickly emerged and started after the hide, but stopped, the water streaming from her ears and nose and hair. Satanta scooped up the skin with his lance and walked his horse through the water toward her.

"Why is it you are always a mess when I see you, Taukoyma?" he asked, and dropped the skin onto her.

Adrianne turned as he rode slowly away, spitting water

103

from her mouth and pushing the wet hair out of her eyes. "Damn," she said.

By the time the three hides were washed and staked again on the earth to dry, Woven Blanket returned with more hides and meat. The women of the household set to their work again. By now Adrianne knew the brain-tanning routine and went to it as the others tended the meat. By sundown, she had coated and worked three more hides and had them rolled beside the women's lodge to soak in the solution overnight. She and Lottie walked down to the creek together with a number of children and women. This time she washed and put on her ragged white clothes, unnoticed.

In the following days, Adrianne worked the cooked tanning solution into more hides, while the women of Satanta's household took up the task of fleshing and dehairing. After the hides had dried again on the second day, the younger women pulled the thickened and dried hides back and forth for hours through the scapula of a buffalo, softening it. Then Adrianne soaked them again in warm water and staked them once more to dry. The flesh and hair were next scraped from them. If the hair did not come off, the hides were soaked again overnight in a mixture of ashes, and then washed and staked again and scraped. When a robe was set aside without dehairing for a winter blanket, Adrianne expressed a small hallelujah. But she would not complain in front of the women, although her body ached and her hands were raw and bleeding from the abrasive mixtures she had used.

She saw that even as she worked hard, the Kiowa women also bent to their tasks. Geese Going Moon told the children stories as the women pounded the hides with buffalo bones and scraped with elk-bone tools. They worked steadily, knowing that winter was near. The dry meat must feed them throughout the cold weather, when game was scarce and hunting hard. The hides would provide them warmth as they turned them into garments and bags for themselves and for gifts. Some of the hides would be traded to the white men. Others would be stored for making new teepees in the spring. They worked with joy and conviviality, teasing each other by tossing things at each others' work or bumping one another or telling stories of foolish things they had done. Only Flies Far seemed to be thinking other thoughts. Woven Blanket watched her silently. And Adrianne watched them both.

At night in the red teepee, Adrianne heard the sound of the wind begin to change. Its breath grew colder during the day, and, even in the sunshine, the lee of the teepee provided little protection from it. The women's outside work continued with more urgency as the wind pushed dark clouds over the plains. Adrianne's task became carrying armloads of wood to lay beside the teepee doors. Her back ached as she broke limbs and bent to pick them up and carry them back. She wished for a chopping axe in place of the small hatchet she was given. But she needed no urging to push on. Even a white woman knows when winter is coming. Only once had Adrianne been struck by a member of Satanta's household, and that had not been for dallying in her work but because she was different from the others. It was a matter of pride to Adrianne to work hard, harder than the others, if she could.

When she set her last armful of wood down beside the woman's teepee, Woven Blanket opened the door flap. "Come inside, Taukoyma. We are waiting for you."

The white woman rubbed her frozen fingers as she bent to enter the lodge. The warmth of the enclosure drew her. All the women were seated around the fire.

"Come in. Come in," cried Geese Going Moon, and giggled with delight.

Lottie ran to Adrianne and caught her leg. "It's a surprise,

Marn." Adrianne unwrapped the ragged cloth that covered her head and shoulders above the thin wool blanket.

"Everyone," proclaimed Woven Blanket, "I am giving this fine buffalo robe to White Woman. She has worked hard and done well."

"And the grease. I am giving the grease for your hands, White Woman," shouted Geese Going Moon.

The women laughed with pleasure as Woven Blanket gave her grandmother's gift and the robe to Adrianne for her own. Tears swam in the white woman's eyes as she gathered the robe to her. She drew Lottie closer. They had not been found wanting among the Kiowa women.

106

Chapter Eleven

As the days passed, Adrianne became accustomed to the household routine. The Kiowas were an independent and self-sufficient people, preparing themselves well for the winter. With their larder full and many new hides, they relaxed and rested, telling stories long into the night, arising whenever they wished in the morning. There were no regular hours and no regular meals. Food always bubbled in an iron pot above the fire. Everyone ate as they became hungry, although the women fed the youngest children at the same time they ate. No guest ever entered the lodges without being offered food.

There was no privacy, except that given by the buffalo robes on the beds, or behind the robe screens in the red teepee where the women waited during formal gatherings of the men. When the children cried or when important guests appeared, Flies Far and Looking Glass took them away to the women's tent. Great care was taken not to disturb Satanta or his counsels.

Adrianne could not see that the children disturbed the Kiowa chief when he was alone with the family. They crawled over him, pulled his hair, stretched his mouth with tiny fingers, blew their breath teasingly in his face, and begged him for stories. Sometimes he slept with little bodies piled around him and on his stomach. Lottie, the white child, was undifferentiated. She leaned on him just as freely as the others, even as he patiently worked with Feathered Lance in the construction of arrows. The white woman saw that Satanta of the home fire was a different man from the raider who had ridden into the valley of the Brazos.

Correction of the small ones' behavior was gentle, repetitive, rather than strict. The children had much freedom, even the freedom to hurt themselves. When their fingers were burned by the fire, or they cut themselves on the many knives and needles used by the women, they were loved and rocked, not scolded. Then, the women explained again patiently the danger and its results. The children were cared for by whomever was available, so that the actual mother was often difficult to tell. Also, children from other households appeared and stayed as long as they wished, sometimes for days or weeks without their parents becoming concerned or their hosts seeking to be rid of them. There was no ownership of children. Adrianne's watchful concern for Lottie was seen as an unhealthy peculiarity. Among the Kiowas each child was just as free to be himself and choose for himself as an adult. There seemed to be no guilt or jealousy by parents whose children wandered away into other families, no sense of disloyalty on the children's part. There were no secrets hidden in the village, so no one restricted visitors from the intimate details of their lives. In the rich and strong household of Satanta, there was enough for all.

In time, the children of Satanta's household came to Adrianne as easily as to their own mothers. They followed her when she worked, ate from her plate. Soft Wind, Flies Far's daughter, sprang into her arms when a fierce dog dashed from behind a teepee. Adrianne's heart filled with sudden joy at the innocent and thoughtless gesture. She held the child tightly and drove the dog away. She loved the Kiowa children in return.

Among the Kiowas there was a hierarchy based on birth, but more importantly on achievement. A man or woman of high birth could fall through cowardice or low behavior. A

108

man or woman of low birth could rise through courage and nobility of character. Satanta and his family belonged among the *own-gope*, or *onde*, the highest class. These people were the leaders of the tribe, famed warriors and medicine men and their wives, women who were the daughters of such men. They were marked by their consideration for others and their generosity. They owned many horses and lodges, and slaves enough to maintain them. On their clothing and in their lodges, they displayed the trophies of many successful battles. Expectations of them were great. They could not be petty or small or run away from danger without losing their place. The *onde* were proud and did not tolerate disrespect. Among them, the *Koitsenko* were the most elite warriors. There were only ten of them, and each was so powerful in personal medicine and courage that he dared to stake himself to the field of battle and would not retreat unless released by another. Below them were the Black Legs, also very brave. They carried the bent, or curved, lance, a kind of shepherd's crook, but with a deadly blade attached. The vast majority of the People were *kah-on*, a respectable middle class who managed their households well and supported the efforts of the tribe in hunting and war. Unfortunately, even among the Kiowas, there were those who were either inept at the matters of life or do-nothings. These irresponsible, burdensome souls were called *daw-pha-gha*, or *dapone*. They were not in good relation with the People or nature.

No restrictions were placed on Adrianne's movements among the Kiowas. She came and went throughout the village and onto the prairie. They, as she, realized that to escape from them with a small child into the vast unknown country would not only be unsuccessful, but foolhardy. Still, when she was alone, taking garbage to the village dump or bathing the children or simply looking at the southern horizon, Satanta always seemed to appear. His eyes were often on her when she looked up unexpectedly from some task.

For her own part, Adrianne sought to make the most of what existed for herself and Lottie. If work and obedience could make any opportunity for them or reunite them with the lost grandchild, Millie, she could work and obey. Adrianne had not defied the People after the early incidents with Satanta. She had worked as she had been taught — not unto man, but unto God — meaning that, whatever she was asked to do, she did it as well as she could. And always there was the thought, greater than her hunger to get home, that she must find Millie. She believed that everything she had learned and did drew her closer to finding the child.

In time, Adrianne sorted out Satanta's wives and their children and the other members of the family. Flies Far had a four-year-old daughter and Looking Glass an infant girl of three and the boy, Feathered Lance. Woven Blanket had three daughters and the adolescent son of her dead sister. He was called Eagle Child and spent little time in the red teepee or around the women since he was coming into his manhood. He lived in his own lodge. And the women made him fine clothes and giggled at how handsome he was and how the girls watched him. Two of Woven Blanket's daughters were married to one of Satanta's warriors and had a household of their own. They were not traveling with the camp because one of the girls was pregnant. Woven Blanket missed them and was concerned that the girl might need her while she was away. But Satanta wanted his mother to visit her people, so Woven Blanket followed him north with the comfort that the grandchild would not be born until spring and the other daughter was with her.

Satanta's father, Old Man Red Teepee, and his mother, North Country Woman, maintained their own dwelling and life, but often shared the work and the evening fire. Geese Going Moon lived in the women's lodge, but visited the red teepee many times during the day. And, if she fell asleep before the fire, she was gently covered by Woven Blanket and slept there until morning. Satanta also had a brother, Appearing Wolf, who had two wives and several children. They shared tasks and came and went freely in the lodges.

Flies Far and Looking Glass spent much time with the children, especially when they were near Satanta. They eagerly sought their husband's attention. Flies Far was truly skillful, touching the man softly, leaning against him, rubbing his arm or thigh idly as she listened to his stories. Later, when he followed her to the women's teepee which the Sisters used as their own sleeping quarters, Adrianne thought again of what she had seen between Flies Far and Head Of A Wolf her first night in the camp. Sometimes Adrianne heard the Kiowa chief and Woven Blanket together beneath their buffalo robes. Watching the small fire from her own bed, she listened to the soft sounds of a man and a woman. Their coupling seemed remote and far from her own experience or desire.

Adrianne's night and day thoughts, when there was time and when she did not fall asleep in exhaustion, were on finding her grandchild and getting the two, Lottie and Millie, home. When she awoke during the night, sometimes she could not remember where she was. She fought off the dark hopelessness of knowing with thoughts of rebuilding the station and ranch. She laid her plans in detail, starting with the commercial barn and corrals where the wagons could be repaired and the oxen and horses shoed and tended. The horse barn itself must be bigger, nearer the house, and more secure. In her night-wandering thoughts, she considered and liked the lean-to barns built against the small workmen's cabins. No one could take a horse from them without being noticed, ex-

111

cept perhaps a white thief like Charlie Morehouse who had so cleverly given himself the red racehorse. In a moment of joy, she remembered that, perhaps, not all of the small cabins had been burned and might be waiting for her and the children to live in until the main house could be rebuilt. Later, these cabins might be filled again with people, strong men with young families wanting to get a start. The Brazos station must have a force of men.

This time she would build the house of stone with walls three feet thick and timbers made from whole trees. A frame house on the frontier was a vanity, disregarding the danger and ignoring the native building material. Carter Doe had thought it would attract travelers. It had, but not the right kind as it turned out. In the dark nights, when fear of never finding Millie, of ever getting away from the Indians, clutched at her, Adrianne laid out the house room by room, placing each door and window and hallway. She moved them about as she considered their convenience and inconvenience and now their security. She thought of the paper for the interior walls, the curtains and carpets, the pictures on the wall, and the furniture arrangements. She fancied a red glass lamp in the main sitting room. There were pecan trees in the bottom that could be cut and milled and made into wide plank floors and window frames and shutters and doors and beautiful bedsteads. If the cook house and laundry had been burned, she thought that perhaps the time had come to abandon cooking on the hearth and buy the biggest iron stove a span of oxen could haul. And the business must be rebuilt. With the railroads cutting across country in straight, hard lines, teams were needed to haul into the interior towns.

These were the thoughts that pushed back the fear and closed her ears to the night thoughts and sounds. She focused on them so completely that they created a vivid and living reality for her. She did not even notice at first when Satanta one night lifted the cover and lay down beside her. For moments his hands moved gently over her as his lips brushed her hair and cheeks before Adrianne realized the reality of him.

"Shit!" she exclaimed, jerking away in surprise.

The Kiowa pulled her back to him and continued his hungry, but tender, pursuit. "Taukoyma," he whispered, "my eyes hunt for you and follow you, when I should be seeing only the horses and what must be done with them. My thoughts wander to you, when I should be listening to the old men." The woman pushed away again. He drew her back, putting his leg across her and holding her with it. She quit fighting and lay back, folding her hands across her chest and looking at the ceiling. Satanta stopped. He had been spooked by the two seizures.

"Go ahead," Adrianne murmured. "Just go ahead and get it over with." She sighed in resignation.

Satanta sat up abruptly, brushing his hair out of his eyes. Anger boiling, he jerked the woman roughly to her feet and dragged her toward the teepee door. Opening the cover, he thrust her naked into the night. "If you will not be a woman, Taukoyma, you can be a slave. Go and watch my horses." He closed the flap.

Stunned, then suddenly angry herself, Adrianne shivered in the cold night. "Give me my clothes, Satanta. It is cold out here."

"How can you tell?" he asked as he lifted the door and tossed her clothing onto the ground. "Get dressed. Go and tend the horses. I do not want to see you." He closed the flap and secured it. "Go," he yelled so loudly the sound blew her away from the door.

Adrianne stood for a moment. Her breath coming in short,

fierce bursts, she pulled the buffalo robe around her and gathered her clothing. Everything was there. "Fine!" she shouted. "Just fine. I will not pay your filthy price. I can earn my way." She snatched a moccasin from the ground. "Always have. Have earned my way, and Lottie's, a hundred times over. Not to speak of the horses you stole from me, you red. . . ."

She walked away from the red teepee in her bare feet toward the stream. Dropping the robe, she shoved her arms into the Kiowa woman's shirt Woven Blanket had given her and pulled up the winter leggings and attached them with shaking fingers at her waist. Sliding a breechcloth into place over the hip thong, she stepped into the hide skirt. Tears streamed in salty rivers down her cheeks. She sat quickly on the ground, dusted her feet, and fought them into the tight moccasins.

"You would not leave my bed in tears, White Woman," a voice from the darkness said. Adrianne hastily brushed the tears away. Head Of A Wolf stepped from the trees. "Come away with me. My lodge is warm, and I am a tender lover. I will treat you well. You will be first wife to me, not the chore wife Satanta makes of you."

Adrianne hurled the leaves and rocks around her at the handsome young warrior. "Get away from me, you scoundrel. Every time I see you, you are dallying some woman. Where is Flies Far tonight?" Her anger grew as she thought of this savage, believing she was like Satanta's fickle wife. His audacity in daring to approach her made her furious. "Get!" she yelled, coming to her feet and continuing to hurl whatever she could find at the man. He backed away, laughing at her frantic stooping and throwing, at the impotence of her anger. She pursued him with rocks from the stream side until he turned and went away. Satisfied, she tossed the rock she was still holding. "*Sainpeet!* Snotnose! Squirt!" Finally, she recovered her robe and went toward the small fire where the herd boys

114

warmed themselves. By the time she reached the circle of light, her heart had slowed, and she had regained some of herself.

"What's to watching the horses?" she asked calmly of a young Mexican captive.

"*Nada, señora,*" the boy answered. "Sometimes you need to walk about and see that all is well. If the horses become restless, you go and see what is wrong. If they move off, then you must follow or circle them back. If there are thieves, you fight and yell until you get help. That boy and I will help you." He pointed toward the fire at a curled pile of rags that had toes.

"Well," the woman whispered, "I can do that. You go, lie down, and go to sleep."

The youngster nodded and eagerly crawled toward the other child.

"Wait," she asked, "where are your weapons?"

"There is a bow and some arrows. And we have clubs and sharpened sticks." The boy curled up.

Looking at the meager arsenal and the coiled lasso beside it, Adrianne did not feel secure. She laid a limb into the star-shaped fire and drew up inside her robe. Her thoughts raced back and forth over Satanta and the arrogant young dandy. She had been deeply absorbed in the mental scrimmages and battle for justice, when she became aware of nickering from the herd. Searching the darkness beyond the fire with her eyes, she listened closely to the stamping and snorts. A horse screamed, and the herd whirled away. Catching up one of the sharpened hardwood sticks and a heavy burning brand from the fire, she raced to the place where the frantic horse flopped and screamed. Running, she dodged the fleeing horses. She stumbled to the edge of a gully, barely avoiding falling into it. Below, in the light of the brand, she saw that a colt was down, and a bear was ripping at it.

"*Yah!*" she shouted, sliding down the side. "*Yah!*" She waved the brand as she ran. The bear glanced up with a snarl, but did not release the yearling. Adrianne flew at the bear. She slammed the brand down on its nose and began stabbing its face and throat with the sharp stick. "*Yah! Yah!*" She kicked and pounded the animal. He took a good swipe and ripped her leg, taking more skirt than skin. She dodged the other paw as he released the pony, and gouged the brand into his face. The bear backed up from her attack. "Go on! Go on! *Ha!*" The bear backed another step, then rose on its hind feet with both upper paws spread. "Oh, hell," gasped the woman, staring at the upright bear. She kicked at the stunned colt with her foot. It rose in a burst and shot away up the side of the gully. Adrianne backed up a step. The bear moved a step forward. Righteous anger burned through the woman at this final affront. Her eyes narrowed. "All right, bear. We'll just see who cuts and runs." She stepped up onto a rock and raised the bloody spear and burning club. She shook them defiantly. "*Aghhhhhh!* Now who's bigger," she shouted. The bear shook its head and growled, giving the woman a good view of the red interior of its mouth and the long white teeth. "Get the hell away from my horses!" she returned. Rocks were being pommeled from the top of the gully, striking the bear like hail. The herd boys had arrived in force. The puny reinforcements were too much for the bear. He dropped and turned. As Satanta and Eagle Child thundered off the rim and plunged into the gully, he ran into the darkness. The children rushed down to the woman. Her arms went around them as she sank weakly onto the rock.

More people from the village were on the rim now with torches held high. Men with bows and lances came down to look at the bear tracks. With the bear in flight, Satanta re-

116

turned and allowed others to follow the ursine bandit. He stopped his pony and looked down at the woman. He studied her closely. She looked back fiercely.

"Bears do not come out in winter," he said.

"Indians do not ride into the Brazos in the winter, either," she answered. "But they did."

"Something is not right," the man continued.

"*Heyah!*" shouted the medicine man, Lean Buffalo, from the hill. "This woman has fought the Spirit Bear. It is a Spirit Bear. She has done us good and driven him away." The People murmured. "Like Ah-tah-zone-mah, the bringer of Buffalo Medicine, she has fought with a bear. Her medicine is strong."

"You have done well, Taukoyma. You have saved a prized colt," agreed Satanta. "What will you desire of me?"

Adrianne looked down at the shivering children she was holding. "I want robes for these boys. They are too small and young to be in the cold without good clothes and robes."

Satanta nodded.

"And I want *both* my grandchildren and a lodge of my own until you return me to my people," she said, then added more quietly so that only the Kiowa heard, "and I want you to leave me alone. You will never again put me out in the cold where wolves and bears prowl around."

"You will get your lodge." Satanta spoke the words as a chief.

"And the rest?" she whispered.

"I have given you much already. Don't push it, Taukoyma." The man frowned. "It was only one bear."

"A Spirit Bear," the woman interjected.

Satanta leaned close to the woman's face. "You become increasingly desirable to me, Taukoyma. I cannot promise things that I cannot control. But I will not take you. And I will look for the other child."

117

"That is your word?" she finalized.

"That is my word." Satanta reached down and lifted the woman to the horse in front of him. He delivered her up to the People at the top of the wash. "Because this woman is brave, I give her the horse of her choosing. A Kiowa woman must have horses."

"I want the colt I saved, Satanta. It must be tended," the woman worried aloud.

"Bring the colt," Satanta spoke to José, and let Adrianne slide from the horse into the waiting embrace of Woven Blanket and Lottie.

"Taukoyma! Taukoyma!" The Indian woman was smiling as Adrianne lifted Lottie, but the smile faded suddenly as she saw the shining wetness of blood on the white woman. She caught a torch from one of the bystanders and lifted it above the wound the bear had made. The People murmured.

Lean Buffalo came toward the women. Adrianne stiffened at his fierce and commanding approach. He spread the neatly ripped claw marks in the garment. Adrianne looked at the wound.

"This requires Buffalo Medicine," opined the healer.

Woven Blanket squeezed her hand.

"Is this bad?" asked Adrianne cautiously.

"This is good. Buffalo Medicine is used only on open wounds of warriors," whispered Woven Blanket, as she continued to hold Adrianne's shaking hand. "Brave warriors."

"I'm just out of brave," admitted Adrianne very quietly.

Chapter Twelve

Adrianne lay in recumbent luxury on the soft buffalo robes before the fire. Woven Blanket heated water for the old medicine man and brought it to him. Dipping in a gourd, sprinkling unknown potions into it, he gave it to Adrianne to drink. She gagged. He waited, then tipped the gourd higher and higher, until the liquid ran from the corners of her mouth.

Woven Blanket peeled the skirt away and removed the blood-soaked legging beneath. Softly chanting, the healer added more medicine from his pouches to the remaining water and wet a rag. Carefully, delicately, with a healing touch, he washed the bloody wound. Finally, he sat back, studying the bare leg striped by the bear's claws. Adrianne looked at the marks with a sideways glance. They blurred before her eyes, and her head swam. She took a long deep breath. "Whew," she blew the word between her teeth. "What was in that?"

"It is just healing medicine," said Woven Blanket. "It will heal you, perhaps even of the falling sickness."

"Don't let Satanta get hold of it," muttered Adrianne.

"You are not making sense," Woven Blanket noted. "As you rest, I will tell you about Ah-tah-zone-mah, a Kiowa woman who brought the Buffalo Medicine. She was a beautiful young woman, Chief Yellow Wolf's daughter, captured by the Pawnees. Our people looked for her many, many days, but could not find her. The Pawnees guarded her closely and gave her to an old woman. She worked for the old one, but secretly put aside meat and made herself three pairs of moccasins for her long journey home. And one day, she ran away. She hid in the tall grass, while the Pawnees hunted her, all around her. Finally, she was free of these Indians, but it was still a long way home. She walked and walked until all the meat she had brought was gone and holes were worn in the three pairs of moccasins. A storm was coming, and she was very afraid alone on the open land. As the rain began to fall, she saw a buffalo carcass with hide still covering it. She crawled inside. There she was warm and dry. And there she had a vision for the People. She was given Buffalo Medicine to heal our wounds. When she awoke after the storm, her bag of meat was full and her moccasins were without holes. She began to walk again, but a bear came across her path. Bears are evil animals to the Kiowas. He would have kept her from bringing the Buffalo Medicine to us, but she drove him away with the sharpened hardwood spear she had brought with her. Just as you did. When she came home at last, the People were very happy to have her with them again and to have the gift she brought of healing."

"I thought all Indian women were drudges . . . nothing," murmured Adrianne sleepily.

"Don't be silly. The Kiowas are men. They are not so afraid of their women that they must make them nothing." Woven Blanket dipped the rag into the water and wrung it out.

Adrianne breathed deeply, contentedly, and added philosophically: "Well, that's about it, isn't it. It's the scared, pissy little bastards who are the greatest tyrants in a household or a society. That's the truth. It's a big man who can share control."

"It's a smart one." Woven Blanket smiled and wiped the sweat from Adrianne's face.

"Satanta's a smart man," confided Adrianne. "Hoppin' cats, what was in that junk I drank?"

120

The shaman went to the fire and scraped warm ashes into his hand. When he returned, he rubbed them into the slashes. "Because this was a Spirit Bear," Woven Blanket informed Adrianne, "he is putting ashes into the wound to mark it forever."

"What?" spluttered the white woman awake now. "He's tattooing me."

Woven Blanket pressed her down onto the robe. Suddenly Adrianne did not care that she would wear the scarified marks forever. She had fought the bear. She was brave. She deserved to remember. The thought flitted across her mind that she was turning into an Indian — brave fighter, trophy scars — going native. As she drifted away, she thought thankfully that no one would ever see the marks, no one. Through the fog, Satanta's face appeared and swam away, smiling. He touched the wound. "This is the only track we could find of the bear."

Lean Buffalo began to chant to the Buffalo Spirit Power. Woven Blanket spoke the words for Adrianne: "I am standing here on the buffalo trail, requesting of you, now alone somewhere, the Buffalo Power which I seek, so that I may relieve one needing help. Give me power and strength to overcome death, so this one's pain will be relieved . . . help me sustain this one with your strength, so that she may overcome death."

And then he sang the reply of the Buffalo Spirit Power:

On this trail I also stand.
I am the giver of strength, the reliever of suffering.
I am the giver of power to overcome death.

Chapter Thirteen

Sand Creek wound its way steadily south, turned with cutting force into the sand banks, and flowed east and west for a mile before again turning south. It was here that Black Kettle sat down for the winter, a hundred lodges or so, on the flat north bank of the nearly dry stream. Below was the camp of the Arapaho chief, Left Hand, with only a scattering of lodges. Among them was the family of North Country Woman, Satanta's mother.

With heavy loads of meat and many hides, the Kiowas moved north to meet the Arapaho people along Sand Creek. When Satanta's lodges were finally pitched among them, the men came together around the fire with Black Kettle's Cheyennes.

"I want to take the white man's hand," said Howling. "But I do not trust him."

"Why not?" asked Satanta with a smile. "Has he done something new?"

"He has ridden on us all summer," said Howling. "In the spring, soldiers killed Lean Bear. He went out to meet with them. He was confident because of the medal the Great Father in Washington had given him. We were at peace, but they shot him and then shot him again as they rode over his body toward the village. I saw this." He made the sign for seeing to emphasize his point. "The young men saw this. They began to fight the white men. It was fighting all summer. The Little White Man, Bent, told us that unless we came in and sat down near them, the soldiers would kill us as though we were fighting them. We had talked to the Great Father and seen the extent of the white men. We have women and children. We knew that we could not fight them."

"Who was fighting the white men?" asked Satanta.

"The young men and the Sioux. We do not know what bands of Sioux. We heard their people way to the north and east were killed by the soldiers. Many of them were hanged."

"What do the Sioux want?" pursued the Kiowa.

"They want to wash the white man away with blood. They plan to clean out all the white men who have taken this country from us just as the white men have taken the yellow metal. They are very angry. The Sioux will do all the damage they can to the whites," concluded Bull Bear.

"But it is ended," Black Kettle asserted. "We have come away from the warring bands. Our friend, Tall Chief, took us to Denver City, four hundred miles. We ourselves in good faith bought and gave them four white children taken by the hostiles during the summer. We visited with the white chiefs . . . Evans, Chivington. They told us to sit down near Tall Chief at Fort Lyon. Some of the Arapahoes even moved down to the fort. Tall Chief feeds them. We have done what they said. We are safe here."

Satanta shifted his legs. "Who is this Tall Chief?"

"He is a man," said Bull Bear respectfully. "The whites call him Wyn-koop. When Bent told us that the white men had put out a paper telling everyone to kill any Indians they saw, unless they were in certain places, we sent word to Tall Chief to come out and bring us in. We were afraid someone would kill us coming in. We offered him the four children as a token. He is but a young man, but he came. We were many. He had but a few soldiers, but he came. One Eye brought him to us. Tall Chief said he would kill One Eye, if he betrayed him. He was afraid of us, but he came. One Eye promised Tall Chief that, if the Cheyennes betrayed him, he would fight beside the whites."

"If the Cheyennes broke the trust I had gone out on, I would not want to live any longer," explained One Eye.

"Coming to us was like going through the fire for Tall Chief," continued Bull Bear. "For us, going to Denver was like going through the fire."

"We told them we wanted peace. We have made peace. We have done what they said," Black Kettle emphasized. "What comes from now on is on them. This is the road we have taken."

Bull Bear thought for a few moments. "I have never hurt a white man. I am pushing for something good. The whites can do us good. My brother, Lean Bear, died trying to keep peace with them. I am willing to die in the same way and expect to do so."

Satanta frowned. "You think more of the white man than I do. I would like to make peace, but I have not seen him treat those who make peace well. Once you sit down, he forgets you. Your women and children go hungry. Meanwhile, he gives gifts to those who fight him. The only thing I want from him are the breech-loading rifle and ammunition. *I* will feed my people as my fathers fed theirs."

Black Kettle took the pipe as it came around. He smoked thoughtfully. "This is the road *we* have taken."

Satanta returned to the red teepee near the Arapaho camp, irritable and with a heavy heart. Left Hand rode thoughtfully in silence beside him, chewing a stem of dried grass. Finally he spoke. "The white men are very many people, Satanta. We do not have guns to fight them. We do not have children to spare."

"The Cheyennes are honest men. Their word is strong." Satanta paused. "Stronger than the white man's."

"You know we cannot withstand the white man. Killing them does not discourage them or diminish them. There are always more. We let in a little stream. Now they are a river, a flood. It is getting so that there is no place to avoid them. They are everywhere. We must make peace for our own good," concluded Left Hand as the two rode through the Arapaho camp.

"I feel free when I roam, Left Hand, but, when I sit down, I grow pale and die. This country is mine as it was my fathers'. I am angry when I see the white man on my streams. I am angry when I see the white man killing my buffalo. The Cheyennes and Sioux are not alone in wanting to fight the white man. I took horses from the soldiers. While the Cheyennes were fighting here, the Kiowa men were also fighting this summer. Kicking Bird took many men against Cow Creek Station. Some of our people were starving, eating carrion cattle, while Long Beard Mathewson, who owns that place, *sold* the meat of our buffalo to other white men. But, like you, some of the Kiowas would still make peace. It may be necessary to make peace."

"The Kiowas tried to make peace this summer?" asked Left Hand.

"We lost many men at Cow Creek and got nothing. Even a few men with repeating rifles can do much harm to us. There were many men and many repeating guns at Cow Creek. I went with Dohasan's son to visit the Little White Man, Bent. Dohasan wanted him to make peace between us."

"Did Bent act for you as he did for us?"

"He has a Cheyenne wife, not a Kiowa. He just sent us to see other men at Fort Larned, but we did not make peace."

"That is too bad. As a man do you not want peace?" asked Left Hand.

"Perhaps it is becoming necessary to make peace. But, if

we do not make them afraid of us, they will forget us. The peaceful Indians are soon starving, while the fighting ones are given talks and gifts and food. If the white men are afraid of us, we can have a satisfactory peace," Satanta concluded.

"We have peace now. It is better. This is what I think," said Left Hand.

"The white man is taking what is sacred and pissing on it. That is a white man. He is in harmony with nothing." Satanta spoke angrily over his pony's back as he loosened the saddle. "This is what I think."

Left Hand did not reply to the fierce words. He was thoughtful about the Kiowa's observations. "The new soldier chief at Fort Lyon told us that there are many buffaloes east of here. He said we should go and kill them and feed ourselves, instead of getting rations."

"You see it is already beginning for you," Satanta spoke harshly.

"You are very angry. Perhaps in a few days you should go hunting for a while, away from the white men," suggested Left Hand.

The winter days passed pleasantly among the Cheyennes and Arapahoes along Sand Creek. There was much visiting. The family of Satanta and their guests ate and told stories. They played guessing games with pieces of bone and howled when the guesser guessed wrong. Adrianne thought that Satanta's black eyes were somehow darker. Sometimes during the games he seemed focused on something else. But he quickly returned and performed splendidly as host.

"Saynday was coming along," Satanta began with the traditional lines, and the children were already crawling over him and laughing as they got ready for the story of the Kiowa trickster with the little mustache. Lottie, understanding more and

126

more of the Kiowa words, joined in naturally with the extensive family of the warrior. During the horrifying journey away from the Brazos, the child had come to trust her captors, accepting them and the situation in ways Adrianne still could not.

With winter strong on the plains outside, blowing sleet and snow against the snug hide dwelling, the best time, the family time, had come. All gathered now in the red teepee — children and wives, brothers and their families. Adrianne could hear and see the joy as she followed Woven Blanket's instructions in twisting and pulling deerskin through a shoulder bone to soften it.

As a girl reading the popular captive stories of the day, Adrianne had formed a far different picture of the Indians. Like all white people she knew that Indians were beasts, bloody brutes who dashed out the brains of small children and ravished women. They smelled and were filthy. They never laughed, often grunted rather than spoke. There was occasional, transient goodness in an Indian woman, but there was no nobility in the noble savage. Every written word supported to the moral sentiment of the time that Indians could be exterminated justifiably and their land taken by civilized people who knew how to use it properly and live Christian lives. Adrianne's father had found and pointed out the fallacy of the captive stories and their purposes. He had known the Cherokees. He had seen the treachery of white men in high places. Yet her experiences during the raid on the Brazos and the journey north seemed to prove the Indians' savagery.

Adrianne glanced at the family circle with her own grandchild seated on the great man's knee, leaning comfortably against his chest. Confused, tears swimming in her eyes, she concentrated on working the hide.

"You can tear it, if you pull too hard," Woven Blanket observed casually.

127

Adrianne lessened the stress on the leather. Woven Blanket bent slightly to see her eyes, then sat back with a sigh. "You are quick and a good worker, Taukoyma, and you are brave. It may be that you will not be separated from your people too long."

Adrianne turned the skin, looking at it closely. "My people are all dead. Satanta killed them all, except for Lottie and Millie, my other granddaughter, who is lost among the Indians somewhere in this storm." She sawed the hide back and forth. "He cut my son's throat."

"You see how he is with the child. Are you afraid he will kill Lottie?" asked Woven Blanket, looking at the child in Satanta's arms.

"I'm afraid she is forgetting who she is, where she came from . . . her mother," said Adrianne.

"A child has wisdom above adults." The Kiowa woman spoke slowly, collecting her thoughts as she passed a sinew through a small pair of awl holes in the moccasin upper and drew it tight, laying down a column of beads. "We live and are alive in the present. When the past and the future cannot help us, we must put them aside."

"Can you forget your dead?"

"No." Woven Blanket pushed the awl back into the skin. "But the dead must not kill the living. They have their place. It is safe. They are warm and secure there with the People. Do you wish to leave this child and the other and go to your dead ones?"

"No," Adrianne smoothed the skin. "Of course not."

"I have seen it. There is much life in you. When my sister died, she left me her son to raise. He is a young man now with a lodge of his own, too old for mothers and sisters. But when he was small, I was carrying a big iron kettle full of water. It was very heavy and awkward. For some reason he became frightened and ran to me and grabbed my leg and held on. He would not turn loose. I could not put the kettle down or pick up the child. You are like that, Taukoyma. You have a burden to carry, but the past is holding onto you. What will you do?"

"What did you do?"

"Someone helped me."

Satanta stretched as he finished the story and unpiled the sleepy little ones. Slowly the guests said their good nights and vanished through the small doorway. Flies Far and Looking Glass took the little ones away to bed. Satanta stared into the fire.

"I grow restless and would like to move about some," he said to Woven Blanket. "Most of the men are going away to hunt tomorrow. Do you want to go along?"

"Yes," exclaimed Woven Blanket. "We will take only a small lodge. You and I and Taukoyma will go. The Sisters and grandmother and the children can stay here. It will be a holiday."

Adrianne thought of the butchering and hide work and could not think of hunting as a holiday.

Major Edward "Ned" Wynkoop — who had so bravely gone into the Cheyenne camp and who, convinced of the red men's integrity, had taken seven of their chiefs to Denver to sue for peace with Governor Evans and Colonel John Milton Chivington — was relieved of command of Fort Lyon, Colorado, on November 5, 1864. It was one month and one week after he had forced the peace meeting between the governor and the chiefs. He left his former command on November 26th, *en route* to Fort Riley, Kansas, to answer the accusation that the Indians were running things at his post. He carried two letters — one from his officers and one

129

signed by twenty-seven citizens, commending his efforts toward making peace.

Cheyenne warriors caught up with their trusted friend on the road in Kansas. They told him that Sioux raiders were again coming south and specified the route. He thanked them and drove on, jaw set and eyes forward, unable to see for the salty liquid that burned his eyes.

The Cheyenne men watched his stage roll out of sight and turned their ponies back toward the buffalo hunting grounds. The new commander at Fort Lyon had told them the hunting was good. They had found it so as they left their families in his protection, sleeping at Sand Creek.

Adrianne ground the tanning paste into the fresh hide. The air was cold, and the wind blew down the throat of her dress. Still, she sweated at the arduous work. Woven Blanket also worked on a hide as Satanta and José cut the meat into strips and hung it to dry. There was no formality in the small camp. The men killed and butchered the buffalo. The women worked the hides. All worked with haste, fearing the first drops of rain or snow as the clouds darkened over them.

Adrianne sat back on her heels and wiped the sweat from her face with her forearm. "What's that?" she asked.

Woven Blanket looked up. "Where?"

"There," pointed the white woman.

Woven Blanket studied the moving specks coming across the winter landscape. *"Aiiiy!"* The demi-scream came from deep in her throat as she rose to her feet and began to run. Satanta and José dropped their work and followed. Across the hunting camp men and women were running. Adrianne still struggled with the unfolding event. Then, she saw. Coming through the growing winter darkness were the Cheyenne women and children from Black Kettle's village. They were afoot — walking, staggering on blanket-wrapped or bare feet. Even warriors were on foot. There was no finery. There were no lodges. The scattering of horses among them dragged travois, carrying the severely wounded. Many of the women were bloody from the self-inflicted wounds of their grief. Adrianne dropped the rubbing stone from her hand and also ran to meet them, to find Lottie.

Looking for the Kiowas, Satanta and Woven Blanket and Adrianne pushed through the throng of weeping women surrounded by their frantic men.

"What has happened?" Satanta questioned as he caught the shoulders of a Cheyenne warrior.

The man shook his head. "The soldiers killed us."

"What of the Kiowas?" pursued the chief.

The Cheyenne said: "I do not know. It was Black Kettle's camp that was attacked. The Kiowas were farther away. But everyone who is alive is greatly scattered. Perhaps someone else will know. My wife . . . my children . . . I must go and look for them."

Satanta released the man.

The Kiowas ran along the long line, searching the faces for their own people. At last, far to the back, Woven Blanket saw Geese Going Moon. "There!" she said to Satanta and Adrianne. "It is Grandmother."

The old woman staggered, but walked on until Satanta picked her up and carried her back toward the small lodge and fire. Setting her down softly, he waited as Woven Blanket unwrapped the rags from her feet and began to rub the freezing toes before the fire.

"Tell me what has happened, Grandmother?" the Kiowa asked.

The old woman looked up with tears running from her eyes and nose, her cheeks red from the wind and cold. "The soldiers rode on the Cheyennes."

"Yes, but the Cheyennes are at peace with the soldiers," Satanta stated calmly.

"I do not know why, but the soldiers rode on the Cheyennes. Black Kettle waved his big flag on a lodgepole. He called to his people. The people ran to him to be safe there, but the soldiers rode on them just the same," the woman said.

"Was our camp hit?" asked the Kiowa chief.

"No," said Geese Going Moon.

Satanta sat back slightly.

The old woman gripped Woven Blanket's hand. "Some of the Cheyenne women buried their children in the sand to hide them from the soldiers, but the soldiers dug them up and killed them anyway."

"You were in the fighting?" asked Woven Blanket.

"No, no," muttered the old Kiowa woman. "These Cheyenne women got away from the soldiers. They came to our camp. I came to tell you."

"Where are Flies Far and Looking Glass and the children? My son?" asked Satanta.

"He is alive and taking hold," Geese Going Moon affirmed. "Eagle Child is coming along with Looking Glass and the children." Her eyes darted at Adrianne, then turned swiftly back to Satanta as she hurried into the next words. "He has the horses, also."

"Flies Far?" pursued Satanta.

"I do not know," moaned Geese Going Moon. "Flies Far took the child to visit and spend the night with the Cheyennes."

Adrianne's hand came over her mouth as tears burned her eyes. "Lottie," she whispered. "Where is Lottie?"

Geese Going Moon looked up. "She was with Flies Far."

132

Adrianne sank back against the robe with her hands in her lap.

Geese Going Moon continued her report that some of the people were going south to find safety with Little Raven and some north to the Sioux.

The white woman did not hear the questions Satanta and Woven Blanket put to the old woman. She stood up, finally, and walked to the door. Satanta's eyes followed her as she bent and picked up her saddle.

"Wait," he said to the white woman. "It is too late to travel. You cannot go very far."

"Wherever I go will be closer," Adrianne said, ducking under the door flap.

Satanta followed her and caught the saddle as she lifted it toward the pony's back.

"If you won't give me the horse" — Adrianne's voice broke — "I will walk."

"The horse is yours, Taukoyma. But go into the lodge now," Satanta said, holding her arm gently. "We must talk of what to do."

"I don't want to talk," said Adrianne. "I want to find Lottie."

"We must decide what to do."

"I have decided," Adrianne persisted, twisting her arm away from Satanta. "I am going to get Lottie."

"You have no plan," the warrior pointed out.

"I will make a plan as I go."

Chapter Fourteen

The bloodless Third Regiment of the Colorado Volunteer Cavalry along with men from the First, all under the command of Colonel John Milton Chivington, hit the Cheyenne village on Sand Creek on the morning of November 29, 1864. A Cheyenne woman ran into the teepee of the white trader, John Smith, and Army Private Louderback and proclaimed that many buffalo were coming. As the report spread, the few men left in the camp went out to see. Quickly realizing that the advancing force was cavalry, some went back into their lodges to get their weapons. Black Kettle raised his great American flag and told the Cheyennes to come to him, and that they would be safe. He had been told that no soldier would shoot the Cheyennes while they were under the American flag. He was wrong. Perhaps he recognized Chivington with whom he had so recently made peace. Certainly he did not understand the white man's shouted orders — "No prisoners!" — or comprehend the man's motive. White Antelope, who had also been in Denver, ran out into the middle of the dry streambed and shouted to the charging soldiers that they were at peace with the white men. He folded his arms signifying no resistance and stood there as the men rode past, until the soldiers killed him.

In the first moments of fighting, a group of white men cut off the pony herd from the village and pushed it to safety away from the Indians. Baldwin's battery of two twelve-pound mountain Howitzers near the creek ineffectively lobbed grape and canister into the village. Opposite them, two more cannons of the Third opened. Some of their shot landed among the Indians. Most landed among the opposite battery, accounting for some of the dead and wounded soldiers at Sand Creek. There were other such stupidities committed by the Third Colorado. They fired over, through, and across their own men in their drunkenness and slovenly discipline.

When the men and women and children around Black Kettle saw that the flag made no difference, they fled in every direction. The main group ran for protection down the creekbed. They dug holes in the sand to hide themselves and their children — holes that would give some of the men a chance to fight. Robert Bent, the trader who had been forced into Chivington's service, reported that a small Cheyenne girl was sent out from them with a white flag on a stick. She had not taken more than a few steps before she was shot dead by the soldiers. After that, trapped, betrayed, the Cheyennes fought furiously. But a hundred soldiers of the gutless Third sat on the high banks and shot them to pieces.

Captain Si Soule of Company D of the First Colorado refused to order his troops to fire. They rode about on the south rim of the creek during the fighting. Soule said later, during seven days of examination by a court of inquiry into the sanguinary incident at Sand Creek: "I saw soldiers with children's scalps during the day, but did not see them cut them off." He had moved on too soon.

By three in the afternoon of the 29th, the fighting was over and the looting and pillaging began. Every corpse — man, woman, or child — was scalped. Many had fingers cut off to remove rings. The women, as well as men, had their sexual parts cut out. Soldiers stretched them over their hats and saddle pommels. Bent reported seeing a pregnant woman split open with what looked like her unborn child lying beside her.

Many of the men's bodies were so badly treated that they

could be not identified or were misidentified by John Smith, the trader who knew the Cheyennes and lived among them. But in the final accounting, grossly mutilated with scalp, nose, ears, and testicles cut off, White Antelope was dead. Knock Knee was dead. One Eye was dead. These men had all traveled the four hundred miles to Denver with Black Kettle to ask for peace. They had believed they had it when they sat down under the Army's protection at Sand Creek.

The night of the 29th, Chivington wrote to his superior, General Samuel Curtis, that in a bloody battle with one thousand Cheyenne warriors his troops had killed all the principal chiefs and between four hundred and five hundred other Indians. He had had nine killed and thirty-eight wounded. All did nobly, he added. The soldiers, many drunker now on blood than whiskey, slept on their rifles on the battlefield under heavy guard. On the 30th, Chivington ordered the village burned. There was light skirmishing with some of the young Cheyennes who survived. Jack Smith, the half-breed son of trader John Smith, held in custody, was shot to death by soldiers. Horsemen dragged his body back and forth for some time over the field like Hector had been dragged around the walls of Illium. His father said later as he testified that he did not see it.

Most of the Cheyennes did not return to Sand Creek to find their dead. All the survivors knew what they had seen and would never stop seeing it. They cut their hair and slashed their bodies and grieved for the dead and for the living People. They joined with the hunting men, then split into two groups — the angry ones going north to find the Sioux, the broken-hearted ones going south with Black Kettle who had trusted the white men. Satanta and his women left their lodge and meat for the Cheyennes. Placing Geese Going Moon in a covered travois, they went to find the rest of their family.

Adrianne was far ahead when Satanta caught up with her. "And what is your plan?" he asked, riding beside her.

"I want to look for Lottie. I just want to see for myself." Adrianne rode with her eyes on the horizon, pushing her horse forward with her body.

"What if the soldiers are still there?"

"You think the white bastards are going to shoot a white woman?" she asked in reply to his question.

"Maybe they are drunk. Maybe the body of a dead white woman would justify this thing they have done," the Indian observed. "It has been done before."

Adrianne sighed. "There is nothing left of trust or honor, is there? They have whirled away in the wind of blind hatred and of self-interest. The Christian soldier is no better than the *Kiowa butcher*." Her pretty mouth twisted on the irony of the last words.

"The Cheyennes are honorable men," Satanta replied.

"And they were destroyed at Sand Creek," Adrianne said bitterly. "So much for that."

As the family rode toward the place where they would find their own, they met many Cheyennes and Arapahoes going away. The crime was detailed differently by each, for each had known it differently, each had beheld it with their own eyes and their own experiences. But one name was on everyone's lips — Chivington, Chivington.

Adrianne rode contemplatively after repeated encounters with the survivors. She addressed Satanta, speaking softly at last. "You know Sand Creek wasn't Chivington's first crime. In September, not long before you came into the valley of the Brazos, we heard Chivington had murdered some Texans. We knew them. Jim Reynolds and his boys had based at Fort Belknap. Said they were going to Colorado to recruit soldiers for the Confederates. They were more robbers and crooks

137

than cavaliers, but they didn't deserve to be shot still wearing hand and leg irons. Chivington got them out of Denver Prison and marched them away for an Army trial. They never got to Fort Lyon for that trial. He took them off the road and murdered them. No survivors. Damn, I hate that man and the men like him who condemn us all for tolerating them. Where do they all come from? From what garbage pile do they continually emerge, while the rest of us are just trying to get on with life? What's worse is that in minding our own business we give them the power to betray us, and pay them to do it."

Satanta's party of women and Kiowa men finally met their families coming away from Sand Creek. Eagle Child told his father what had happened and presented him his horses and household. The youth had been eager to join the other young warriors in harassing the soldiers. But he had been taught a man's first duty was to protect the women, the children, to deliver them to safety. Then he could turn and fight. Then he could fight for personal honor and glory. Eagle Child had even found Flies Far among the scattering Indians.

"Where's Lottie?" Adrianne confronted Flies Far.

The handsome woman looked at the ground and did not answer.

Adrianne caught her arm. "Where is my child?"

Flies Far twisted.

Adrianne jerked her. "Look at me. Where is Lottie?"

Flies Far looked at the white woman briefly, then once more turned her eyes away. She shrugged, indicating her lack of responsibility for what had happened to the girl. Adrianne drew back her fist.

Satanta caught her before she struck the Kiowa woman. "That won't do any good," he said.

"It will make me feel a whole lot better," muttered Adrianne.

"Settle down," the Kiowa ordered, tired of the confrontations between the women of his household.

Irritated by his interference, Adrianne blurted incautiously: "Do you know what you are married to?"

Woven Blanket rose quickly behind Satanta and placed her finger over her lips.

Seeing her, Adrianne dropped her belligerence. She took a step away from Satanta. More softly, but firmly, she said: "I want to know where Lottie is. And I want to know now."

Woven Blanket intervened with Flies Far. "Do you know where the child is?"

Flies Far shook her head. "We were running away. Then I did not see her any more."

Adrianne chewed her lip and watched the Kiowa woman intently as she spoke. "Did you look? Or were you too busy saving your own pretty ass? You . . . you . . . !" Adrianne rubbed her face with her hands and walked away toward her horse. "I will just look till I find her," she murmured to herself.

"She should not look alone, Satanta," whispered Woven Blanket. "She is your wife. Our household. We will all come and help."

"No," spoke the Kiowa. "We do not know who may be there or what may happen. I must see this thing with my own eyes, with my men. She will not be alone. You keep going away. We will find you."

The Cheyennes fleeing Sand Creek had walked more than forty miles to reach the hunting camps. They were women and children, the old and the injured. Their march had taken several days. By the time Adrianne and Satanta returned to Sand Creek, all danger from Chivington had passed. There was no sound of bugles and sabers, no sound of clinking cups and canteens, no sound of creaking leather, no sound of horses' hoofs striking the soft sandy earth, no sound of their labored

139

breathing as the cruel men used them as accomplices to crime. The cold, shivering land was still, silent.

Long before they arrived, the man and woman saw the circling sentinels in the sky. Vultures and other carrion eaters were not unfamiliar or unexpected around Indian camps. Every big village drew them as they scavenged the waste that was thrown away. Sometimes trappers and traders even used the big birds as guides to find the Indians. Neither Adrianne nor Satanta spoke into the silence as they rode.

Stopping on the high south bank, they could see the whole valley. The once busy village was black, burned out, dotted thickly with the bodies of dead human beings and horses, lying where they had fallen. But in the great emptiness, they were not alone. The land teemed with birds, screeching as they competed for the People's flesh, flapping great wings, giving way as the larger animals, various canines, drove them off with bared white teeth in bloody muzzles. Dogs, once members of the camp, now feasted with their brother wolves on their masters. Here and there across the flat land, a few living People hunted for their dead and sought to understand the meaning of their deaths.

Satanta had seen the carnage of many battles. He read it with experienced eyes. "There was Black Kettle's lodge." He pointed to a scorched circle on the earth. Adrianne looked as Satanta continued to talk with the other Kiowa warriors. "There are many bodies there."

"It is as the Cheyenne women said," agreed Touches The Enemy.

Satanta turned his head and rose slightly in his stirrups. "There is a trail of bodies going away. They ran off that way toward the bluffs, down the creek. Come." He turned his pony, following slowly the direction in which the People had fled, studying the tracks of shod horses where he rode. He

140

pulled up with Adrianne and the other Kiowa men at his side. There were no words now. Around them the ground was torn up from boots and hoofs, littered with the refuse of men and animals and guns. Below them in the creekbed were the holes. Below them were the bodies of sixty women and children, slashed and torn open, scattered, piled in and out of the pits in the blood-soaked sand. Tears gushed down Adrianne's cheeks. Her chest was tight, and she opened her mouth just to breathe. She suddenly wanted to see the strength of Satanta's face. When she looked up, he, too, was weeping, silently weeping. All of the brave and seasoned warriors were weeping.

Adrianne choked and pushed her pony toward a defile leading toward the creekbed. Among the dead, she dropped to her feet and began to walk between the bodies, looking for the child, Lottie. For a little while Satanta was with her, then a warrior called him away. Adrianne thought, perhaps, one of them had found the child and come for the man who would break it to her. She watched them closely, but it was a man's body they stood over. Filling the cup of wisdom pungent with bitterness, Satanta and his men searched the camp for any scrap of information and understanding. Adrianne wandered alone among the dead. She could not look away for fear of missing the child. Her eyes grew old seeing the bloody, desecrated meat that had been human beings. Sometimes she stooped and turned a body. Sometimes she recognized a woman who had come to visit Woven Blanket in the Kiowa camp. She did not find Lottie in the sand of the creekbed. Leading the horse, she walked through the village and beyond, wherever a body had fallen. She found them under brush and against trees. Sometimes the soldiers had piled them indecently in naked, necrophilious acts of copulation. It was night when Satanta found her, crying silently, holding the body of a child.

She looked up when he touched her. "This is not Lottie," he said softly.

"No," whispered Adrianne as if the child slept. She spread the tiny fingers in her hand. "But is she not perfect? Each finger, each eyelash is perfect, fresh and perfect for a life. But she is dead." She looked up into Satanta's eyes. "Why is she dead?"

"Because she is other, nothing more to the men who killed her," answered the Kiowa. "In these white men there is no harmony with us, no harmony with the earth, no harmony with the beautiful, no harmony with the Sacred. Such men are not alive. All that is good has been forgotten, forsaken by them."

On December 1, 1864, Chivington withdrew his crew from Sand Creek. He sent a dispatch to the *Rocky Mountain News*, reporting his intention of going north to tie into the Sioux on the Smoky Hill. Fifteen miles down Sand Creek, he made camp. There he met the supply train from Fort Lyon. The wounded and dead cavalrymen from Sand Creek were sent from there back to the fort. The following morning, Chivington turned south, not north, seeking the small, weak Arapaho band of Little Raven who had not trusted the soldiers. He had taken his people away from Fort Lyon and Sand Creek. During the next several days the Third Colorado vigorously sought the Indians, but each time they found a camp, it was deserted. The warning from Sand Creek had preceded Chivington's soldiers.

Satanta and his handful of Indians with Adrianne in their midst followed Chivington's trail south, observing his course, waiting to see what he would do. Of course, the soldiers never knew. Their report noted they had searched the countryside and found no Indians. Captain Soule, the traitor who had been sympathetic to the Indians, was sent out with twenty men to scout for hostiles. The Indians knew Soule. He had gone with them and Wynkoop to Denver. His men had not fired on the Cheyennes at Sand Creek. Later, the deposition of Lipman Meyer, a freighter who accompanied Soule, would be offered in Chivington's defense. Chivington wanted to destroy the honor, the credibility of the man who had defied him and testified against him. Meyer stated that Soule was so drunk during the scout he did not know one direction from another, that he refused to check a reported Indian camp because he was afraid of Indians, and that he was a thief who had stolen Meyer's blankets.

Soule was certainly drunk, so drunk that he did not believe the apparition that appeared in the doorway of his tent. Gazing with blurred vision, his reactions slow, his comprehension tainted, he finally backed up toward the head of the cot and drew his knees toward him. With tangled tongue he asked: "Did you come out of a bottle?"

"I came from Sand Creek," the voice said.

A shiver ran over Si Soule.

"I walked among the dead, but I did not find my child. Have you seen Lottie Doogan. She is a white child, five years old. I am her grandmother, Adrianne Chastain."

"Jesus. God in Heaven," shuddered the soldier. "This can't be real."

Adrianne walked toward the bed where the man cowered. She hit him as hard as she could across the face. "I *am* real, sir."

Soule shook his head and turned to put his feet on the tent's dirt floor. He held his head in his hands.

Standing so close, Adrianne smelled the Dead Shot whiskey that sweated out of his pores. "Are you sober enough to

143

make sense?" she asked above him.

Soule held his head moments longer, then looked up. "I am."

"I asked you if you had seen a white child. Was a white child taken at Sand Creek?" Adrianne persisted.

The haze was still thick on Soule's mind. "A white child? There were Jack Smith and Charlie Bent. I got Charlie away before they could kill him. Charlie's safe. The Third killed Jack. And there were some other 'breed kids . . . little ones, a papoose or two, John Smith's kids, I think."

"Lottie is white."

"What's a white kid doing with Indians?" the soldier queried, then blurted as the realization of Adrianne's words struck: "My God, was Chivington right? Were there white captives in Black Kettle's village?"

"Black Kettle had nothing to do with us," Adrianne said firmly. "All the guilt at Sand Creek is on Chivington and you."

Soule wiped his parched lips. "That's the God's truth . . . the God's truth." He spoke the repeated words softly and slowly, savoring their fullness.

"You are sure there was no white child?"

"No white child, Missus Chastain." The disheveled man stood up and straightened himself to reassume his trust as guardian of the Republic and its citizens. "I offer you my full protection, ma'am. I will guarantee your safe return home from the savages." He cleared his throat as the word soured in his mouth.

Adrianne lifted the door curtain. "You don't have my child, and the Indians do. I have no reason to go with you."

"Wait," Si Soule said, taking a step toward the door, but the woman was already gone. "Wait." The officer ran across the small camp, pulled an armful of blankets from the wagon,

144

and hurried to the edge of the darkness where the woman had disappeared. He staggered awkwardly across an opening between the trees, slipped and fell down the incline, but managed to keep the blankets out of the dirt and water. When he sat up, he saw them — five warriors and a white woman. They made no move toward him, but watched him closely. After a few moments, he stood up and walked toward the woman. He handed her the blankets. "I thought all that night how cold the children must be, freezing to death maybe, dying just the same as from the guns. Take the blankets for the children." Soule stepped away.

Satanta raised the tip of his lance and set the keen blade in the dimple of the white man's throat.

"Go ahead," said the soldier, looking straight into Satanta's black eyes. "Be a relief."

Satanta lifted the point and rode away into the darkness with the others behind him.

In the morning, after consuming half a pot of strong coffee, Soule wandered casually to the edge of the trees as if about his morning routine. When he was out of sight of the camp, he scampered down to the spot where he had met the Indians the night before. He comforted himself that there were no blankets on the ground. He knelt and touched the track of an unshod pony. Even a drunken soldier could tell there were six horses. It had not been a dark dream.

Chapter Fifteen

Adrianne Chastain had made a decision as she dropped the flap on Soule's field tent. She was going back to the Kiowas. She was going to find the children. The children were with the Indians. She would find them. It was that simple. It was settled, she thought. But the battle was not won.

The voice of fear whispered in the long hours riding across the winter prairie. *You will never see either of them again. They are forever lost.*

Adrianne pushed it back. "No," she said to herself. "They are not lost. They are with the Indians. I will find them. I will." She said the words over and over to herself, and sometimes spoke them aloud to drown out the sentient, knowing voice of doubt. The Kiowa men occasionally looked up, but, not understanding, seeing that she rode in a world of her own, they turned calmly back to the road ahead.

Yet, when the whispered voice failed to dissuade her, dark imaginations arose. She saw the children dead and mutilated as the Cheyenne children had been at Sand Creek. She heard their screams. Her tortured heart ached at their fear, their aloneness. She saw her daughter, dead — her son, dead — Lottie, dead — Millie, dead. She condemned herself, alive. She saw herself mad, another woman of the plains, wandering, searching, asking strangers: "Help me, please. Help me. I cannot find my children." Adrianne considered madness a frail security. Whether it was a haven of rest from reality or a hell of never-ending hunger for what could not be found, it would not solve her problem. She fought it away, making herself feel the warmth of the sun on her skin, inhale the crisp, clean air.

Looking about, she saw the Kiowa men riding far ahead of her. One of the warriors passed jerky to another. They laughed. The woman saw then the great emptiness of her own life. Where before there had been hope and future, there was now only a void, darkness. Rising out of her body, she saw herself alone in the great empty sea of grass. The higher she rose, the more emptiness there was and the smaller Adrianne Chastain became, until she was a mere speck lost in the endless land, caressed by the ever-blowing wind.

"God," the prayer escaped her lips softly, "I can't stand this. I can't do this alone." Adrianne jumped from the horse.

José pulled up suddenly to keep from riding over her. "What is wrong, *Mujer?*"

"Nothing," Adrianne said, shocked at the human voice and the bright world around her. "I just want to walk a while. Go on, I'll catch up." So Adrianne walked and rode and fought the inner battle that the Kiowas could not see or know. "Dammit to hell, Adrianne," she said to herself. "You've got to find something bigger than yourself. Take hold, dammit. Where is your faith?"

But I cannot bear this, she heard the whine of her inner weakness, her self-pity. *You do not have to,* another voice said. The words of her faith sang through her mind: *Through many troubles, toils, and snares, I have already come. 'Twas grace that brought me safe thus far. And grace will see me home.*

"So there it is," the woman said aloud. "Hold onto it. It's all you've got. You can't grieve and feel sorry for yourself and find the children. Use what brains you've still got for better things. Get on with it, Adrianne."

The men were beyond her sight by the time the white woman ceased her meditation. She caught up with them as they stopped to water their horses. Easing the pony in beside

147

Satanta, she dropped down beside him, caught a handful of water, and brought it to her mouth.

Satanta looked at her, so pleasing to his eyes. "I thought, perhaps, I had lost you, perhaps you would go back to the soldiers."

"The Indians have my grandchildren, not the whites. I want my children, Satanta. Once you gave me your word that you would look for them." Adrianne pushed the horse's head away from her as water spilled from its moist lips.

"There is great confusion now," Satanta spoke calmly, thoughtfully — as a chief — but he could not keep his eyes from drinking in the woman. "The peoples are scattered. Everyone is trying to get right again. Many necessary things were lost. Food is scarce. People are going about looking for help. Lottie could have been taken to other bands of Kiowas or Comanches or even to the Sioux when the Cheyennes fled."

"Millie?" asked Adrianne.

"We will be traveling to understand what is going on among the tribes and bands," the Kiowa said. "We will ask and look for her as we go. Will that satisfy you?" He looked at Adrianne.

She raised her arm to shield her eyes against the sun and nodded. "It is a beginning."

In many days' riding, the small group, who had gone out to see what had happened at Sand Creek, reunited with the larger band. The several Kiowa households that had gone north with Satanta slowly stripped themselves of any extra food, clothing, blankets, and lodges as they shared with the Cheyennes and others they met. Eagle Child gave away his lodge and moved in with the herd boys and two other young warriors. Although no parent demanded the sharing, it was expected that even children of the household show generosity.

148

They understood. The little girls parted with leather dolls and their cradleboards. Their small teepees for playing house went, one by one. Under Woven Blanket's supervision much of the meat gathered in the fall disappeared into the mouths of the hungry.

One late night in the red teepee, when Flies Far and Looking Glass had taken the small children to the women's lodge and Satanta had not yet returned, Adrianne watched Woven Blanket, the sewing resting in her hands, her thoughts far away, her eyes fixed blindly on the fire. "What are you thinking, Woven Blanket?"

The woman looked up. "I am wondering if there will be enough food. I have given so much away."

"Is it different from other times you have come through? Don't the Kiowas call this The Moon when the Children Cry from Hunger?" asked Adrianne.

Woven Blanket looked into the white woman's eyes. "*My* children have never cried from hunger. Now, it is possible. Help me understand, Taukoyma. In the past we often have had trouble with enemies, the Osages and Utes and Navajos, even the Cheyennes. Now it is the white man, but he does not just come and take horses or fight warriors. The white man kills us all, even the babies. He does not go away and let us rest from killing. He chases us about, looking for more killing. Why is this, Taukoyma?"

Now the white woman looked into the fire. "I do not know. Perhaps it just comes down to thinking you are the center of everything . . . like a child, a child in a vast unsupervised candy store. I remember once, when I was a little girl, there was a cloud of the most beautiful birds, thousands of bright, beautiful birds. Their bodies made a shadow that ran over the green fields. They settled in living waves on the trees, anointing them like sugar icing spilling over a cake, ornamenting

149

them with brightness. Their wings and calls filled the air with their soft sounds. I loved those birds, their gentleness, the colors, the wonderful noises. But pretty soon I heard other noises. The men were killing them. In their innocence, the birds did not fly, but fell before the guns by the thousands. When the shooting finally stopped, the ground under the trees was thick with their bodies, ugly now, bloody and blown apart. The trees and sky were empty, and the world was silent. I asked my father why they had killed so many birds, since they could not eat all that they had killed. He said it was a sickness men have, a blood frenzy, an uncontrollable greed sparked by bounty and the fear they won't get enough. The men who gathered up the birds and burned them said it was because the birds would eat the grain. But there was no grain. I saw my father was right."

Woven Blanket spoke softly as she saw the picture Adrianne painted with her words. "I have seen this among our people, too. Will the white man wipe us off the earth?" she asked.

"Some like Chivington would," answered Adrianne truthfully. "Others will fight for you. But as long as some men serve their own self-interest in getting rid of you, you are in danger."

"Many children will die this winter," the Indian woman said. "I have given away to everyone I could. Now we must be very close, until we can find the buffalo again."

"You will always find the buffalo, Woven Blanket," Adrianne said without thinking. "The Book I believe in says that those who give to others receive again full measure, pressed down, and running over."

"Then why do the white men take everything?" puzzled Woven Blanket.

"Because they want less of God than they do of the Indian. God threatens their self-interest more deeply. They might

150

have to admit there is something greater than themselves."

"There is no harmony in such men," the Kiowa woman concluded. "They are out of harmony with all that is good and worthwhile."

"What do the Kiowas think is good?" Adrianne asked suddenly.

"To live in harmony is good. To live in harmony, we must have a good relationship with the earth who is our mother, with the Sacred who created us and brought us out onto the earth and is all around us, with the beautiful which makes our lives pleasant and graceful, and with one another, for we are human beings."

Adrianne thought often of Woven Blanket's words as she carried water or worked a hide back and forth across a pole, as they traveled from starving camp to starving camp. It occurred to her that, even as she smelled the stinking tanning paste and worked it into the raw hide, she had risen in the world. She had come into a distinguished household. She was no longer the wife of a successful man or a business woman or rancher in her own right, she was a witness to the workings of a great household which carried the weight of a people.

With frugality, Woven Blanket managed her family through the cold winter. Always in the snow time, even when the buffalo hunts had been successful, the Indians dispersed over the land. They could not stay together. They had to hunt to live. And wherever there were people, the animals fled away. Satanta's Kiowa band traveled restlessly about, not only in search of game, but in search of the thoughts of their People. As a chief, Satanta needed information. And as they traveled, they also pursued the children, Lottie and Millie.

Everywhere they became a little thinner as they shared with the ones who had less or nothing. The story spread that a young Sioux chief called Crazy Horse had turned the fleeing

151

Cheyennes away to save his own. The People shook their heads. It was not the way of the People. A great man was greatly generous. He had power and trusted it to provide. The Cheyennes stored Crazy Horse's actions in their hearts. They said the time for remembering would come.

The United States government estimated that more than sixty children, weakened by hunger, vulnerable to diseases, died that winter on the plains. It was a statistic to them, black words on white paper. But Adrianne saw in every new camp that women had cut their hair and gashed their arms and chests to grieve for the children. Beside meager fires, men sat with heads down, wondering what to do in a world that was changing, wondering what weapons would stop this relentless enemy that brought death and famine beyond the natural. Seeing the grief and pain, its commonness across the land, the fear grew in Adrianne that some high scaffolds built to hold the tiny bodies of the dead would hold her Lottie or Millie. In her heart, she asked if any child, white or red, could be safe in a world that allowed such things? In her heart she asked God to spare her motherless children, all the children. In her heart, she asked God to bring fair weather and buffalo to her enemies, the Kiowas, for they were sorely pressed. In the camps they found, they did not find the children among the dead or the living. Finally, with their clothes becoming rags and their bellies gnawing in emptiness, Satanta changed their course. The band hunted their way south, following the scarce game toward the Cañon del Rescate.

Chapter Sixteen

Like many whites who came onto the plains, Adrianne assumed the Indians roamed about at random in the manner of hogs searching for acorns, finding something here, something there, chancing on water and game, idling through their lives in disgusting laziness or pastoral bliss. That was before Adrianne realized the Kiowas were men like other men. Although their patterns were not discernible to the unseeing eye and their time was not registered on the face of a clock or seed-company calendar, they moved with deliberation, design, and purpose. Water and grass largely determined the rate and direction of travel. Rarely were the Kiowas more than a day from water in a land the white man often found dry and barren. Sometimes the white woman saw the principal men stopped on a high place, pointing to a landmark, checking their directions as the families and herds moved confidently below them. Moving south from the Smoky Hill River over the limitless plain, Adrianne was shocked to observe wagon ruts and a wide, clearly visible trail, meandering before the Kiowas. Texans and Americans, men in business like her father-in-law and husband, said there was no way across the Llano Estacado, certainly no way for wagons or herds.

If the Kiowas had turned their horses up the trails, instead of down, they would have found themselves in New Mexican towns like Las Vegas, Puerto de Luna, Santa Fé. For a hundred and fifty years, Comanchero traders had met the Indians with their contraband in the deep cañons of West Texas. Poor men at first, the traders brought a few trinkets, never more than twenty dollars' worth. They found a market and returned home with robes and pelts. As the years and seasons passed, the prosperity of the traders grew. When next they came, it was in *carretas*, two-wheeled carts and wagons. They could offer more and carry away more. And the Indians, too, had more to trade. They learned that stolen horses bought many desirable things, delicacies like a sweetened, sprouted-wheat pone called *panocha* or its cousin *cemita*, *manta* or calico for their women, blankets, paint, ammunition, and guns the government agents would not give them. And there was also whiskey carried in gourds and barrels. Some Indians would trade an entire herd for a barrel of whiskey. Knowing their customers, some traders buried the barrels, made their trades, directed the Indians to the buried barrels, and got the hell out of there before the crazed victims became violent. During the American Civil War vast Texas cattle herds, thousands of head, disappeared into the cañons driven before the Kiowas and Comanches. They reëmerged and followed the wide roads over the plains back to New Mexico, driven by *peones* who walked along peacefully beside them. Army officers at Fort Bascom, indeed, knowledgeable people throughout the territory, knew where the cattle came from. But they had little or no desire to fight the Indians or end the economic benefits brought by the Comancheros. Nor had they a corresponding desire to help their Confederate enemies in Texas. Seeing their unrecoverable cattle in the corrals of the United States Army, men like Charlie Goodnight and Oliver Loving and Jesse Chisholm and John Hittson swore and blustered and later took matters into their own hands. But the trade flourished. An officer's wife reported that for a copper pot and small Navajo blanket she received twelve head of cattle. Everyone, she noted, did it. No one cared about the bloody raids along the Brazos that secured the cheap cattle for the New Mexicans.

No one cared when the Comanches and Kiowas brought more than cattle from Texas, when they brought women and children taken in the raids. In the Valley of the Tongues where many languages were spoken, in Valle de las Lagrimas where many tears were shed, the women and children were parted, traded to other Indians, or bought by the Comancheros.

As Satanta's people traveled south, the weather grew better. They let their heavy robes slide from their shoulders onto the horses' backs and wrapped them about their hips and legs. The land became more empty still, uninvaded by the white man. The People began to relax. At Palo Duro the band divided, some of the men taking their women and children into the deep, hidden cañon to stay with the Comanches and other Kiowas. Slowly the travelers were becoming a leaner, more combat-capable unit. Still Satanta kept his women and children, unwilling to leave them again to anyone else's protection. Finally, when the moon had become full, the Kiowas reached the head waters of the Casas Amarillas and rode into the Cañon del Rescate, the Cañon of Redemption.

Once the teepees were set up and the household gear unpacked, the women began the cooking and settling in. Adrianne accompanied the children down to the wide streambed.

Speckled Light had stayed very close to Adrianne since Lottie had been taken away. She seemed to sense the woman's need for a child's company. Now the woman watched the child carefully set a leather cradleboard and doll against the base of a tree. She unlaced the cradle and removed the doll. "I thought you gave your doll away," observed Adrianne, lowering a buffalo paunch into the water to fill.

"I did, but this is Sky Living In Her Eye's doll. The one Geese Going Moon made for her," said the Kiowa child. "When she comes back, she will want it."

Adrianne knelt beside the child, then sat beside her, wait-

155

ing for the paunches to fill. She took the doll the child offered. Turning it in her hands, she studied the soft leather dress with its neat rows of green, yellow, black, and white bead work through teary eyes.

"Those are Kiowa colors," Speckled Light informed her.

Adrianne could not speak then, but nodded. "Geese Going Moon makes beautiful dolls," finally came from her constricted throat.

"She has made each of us one. They are very special. Now, I guess, she will have to make us some more. Grandmothers are good at that," the child confided. "She made the cradleboard, too."

Adrianne held the small work of art. The pointed wooden back braces were lashed with rawhide just as a human baby's cradle would be. Small brass tacks decorated the wood. The beaded cover or sack was lined with calico. Its top formed a diminutive sun shade over the interior. Adrianne lay the doll in the cradle and pulled the soft flaps over her without tying them. She was taken by the care and detail of the cradle and the love the maker had put into it. It was a perfect replica of the infant carriers the young mothers carried. "How extraordinary."

"How do white mothers carry their babies about?" asked Speckled Light.

"Oh, in the wagons, they sometimes have a wooden cradle, but usually they just put their babies on blankets or rags in a wooden box." The image rose in her mind of the coarse boxes of the frontier women.

"But how do they carry them about on a horse or when they work?" persisted the child.

"They sometimes ride with the baby in their arms," the woman said, seeing the frown wrinkle the small Kiowa girl's forehead. "You think that is not safe?"

Speckled Light nodded.

"Well, I think you are right. The Kiowas have a much better way . . . soft and pretty and safe. Some white women make a kind of sling from a blanket for the baby and tie it to their bodies." She removed the long scarf from her neck and put the doll in it and tied it about Speckled Light's waist. "I have worked that way." She studied the makeshift baby bag. "But it is not pretty like your cradle."

"I think I have enough soft scraps to make you a new teepee for the dolls," Woven Blanket spoke above them. Then she, too, sat by the child. "Of course, you girls will have to get lodge poles. Speckled Light, why don't you and the little ones see if you can find some. I think there will be many good sticks along the creek." The child handed Adrianne back the ragged shawl, but kept the doll. She started away, then hesitated.

"Can I leave the doll with you while I look for poles?" she stopped to ask.

Adrianne nodded, gently taking the child's toy, Lottie's doll.

"You will find her, Taukoyma." Woven Blanket touched her hand.

"Yes, I will find her," Adrianne nodded, looking up from the doll at Flies Far and Looking Glass with the little girls near the shallow water. "I still get very angry when I think Flies Far left Lottie. You must see how she behaves around men." Adrianne considered her next words, but proceeded. "You must know about her trifling. Why did you stop me from telling Satanta?"

"If Satanta knows, he would have to do something. So far it is only trifling. Flies Far is not pleased with her place below me and her sister. But she knows that she might be in more trouble if she goes to another man. She is very young. I talk to her."

157

"What if he just let her go, good riddance?" asked Adrianne, remembering Flies Far in the embrace of the young warrior, remembering Head Of A Wolf hanging about the night Satanta sent her from the teepee to the pony herd and the bear.

"If he let her go, he would be humiliated before the other man. That man would rise up in power, and he would crow about beating Satanta out of his woman. If things got too bad, Satanta would have to fight him, maybe kill them both. If he took her back, he might cut off the tip of her nose to show what she had done. Wouldn't those be terrible things to happen to our household?"

"They would be terrible," agreed Adrianne, looking at Flies Far, walking slowly with the little ones before the young men watering their horses. "But I don't think your words will stop what's coming. I think she just hasn't found a man that she thinks can take Satanta."

"Do not think such things," Woven Blanket whispered softly.

"*Yah. Yah,*" the man's voice shouted above the sharp crack of a whip. The women turned toward the noise.

"*Los Comancheros,*" said Woven Blanket, rising to her feet.

A huge wagon lumbered along the streambed with colorful outriders around it. Another wagon appeared, and another. Beside Woven Blanket now, Adrianne saw the Kiowas running toward the Comancheros as toward lost friends.

"They are traders," Woven Blanket informed her. "They bring us many good things . . . and bad. But they always take more than they give us. They are white men."

The Kiowa woman looked quickly at Adrianne. The white woman smiled back, knowing the truth of Woven Blanket's exasperated words as well as the woman's concern for her feelings. The women gathered the filled water paunches and chil-

158

dren and walked back toward the center of the camp where the first wagon came to a stop before the red teepee.

"Tafoya," Satanta greeted the swarthy Comanchero who swung down from his horse. "You are welcome." He shook his hand, then added: "If you have brought what I paid you for."

The Mexican removed his wide sombrero, revealing a bright kerchief tied around his forehead and fastened at the nape of his neck. A gold earring sparkled in his ear. "You know I would not come here if I had cheated you, Satanta." He smiled.

The men walked to the first wagon. Tafoya threw back the tarp as the Kiowa men crowded around. Inside were long boxes clearly marked for the United States Army, Fort Union, New Mexico. Satanta smiled. Leaping into the wagon, he broke open one of the cases. He tossed a new Sharps rifle to Eagle Child. The youth whooped and lifted the weapon with one hand high into the air for the other men to see. "Come," motioned Satanta. "They are paid for." The men pressed closer. José began to hand out the new guns as Satanta and Tafoya disappeared into the red teepee. One of the other Comancheros ducked inside with a heavy bottle.

When Woven Blanket and Adrianne passed the wagons, the Mexicans were opening them for the Kiowas to see. The few women and children in camp huddled close as the treasures were revealed. Inside were many bright and wonderful things — blankets, calico, copper pots. Flies Far and Looking Glass and the children joined the others. Woven Blanket walked on with barely a sideways glance. Adrianne looked at the rough, hungry-eyed men and followed her.

Satanta, Tafoya, and his lieutenant, Gomez, were seated before the cooking fire, toasting the success of the joint venture with a jug of fairly decent whiskey the Mexican kept for his best customers. Woven Blanket glanced disapprovingly at the jubilant Kiowa chief, dampening his good spirits slightly. "Feed our guests, woman," the man countered. "We are celebrating."

Woven Blanket and Adrianne began preparing the food that was always offered to guests.

Tafoya watched them. "Gomez, bring some bread as our gift," he said.

The lieutenant finished his cup of whiskey and went toward the door. Adrianne looked up into his blue eyes as he purposely brushed against her. "You ain't half bad," he grinned through dirty teeth. Adrianne looked back at the meat she was slicing.

Satanta watched the Comanchero over the rim of his tin cup and leaned back against the woven willow rest behind him.

In a short time the Comanchero returned with an armful of the sweet bread the Kiowas craved. Standing above the working women with outspread legs, he dropped the bread around them. Neither woman looked up.

Satanta observed the man, but spoke to his leader. "And how much is this generous gift going to cost me, Tafoya?"

Adrianne easily followed the conversation in Spanish as she worked.

"We made good on the cattle you sent us. Your men brought them in good condition. Some of the horses were pretty good, too, but you always keep the best," the Comanchero asserted. "We will not worry about small things."

"It will be the first time, then," joked Satanta.

"Then you are satisfied with the weapons you have received," continued Tafoya.

"I am never satisfied, when you cheat me," the Kiowa said mildly. "But, Tafoya, you are a good man. You cheat me less

160

than the other Comancheros."

"And I make special deliveries, out of season," boasted the trader. "On time and in good condition."

"If you had not, I would have cut your heart out," smiled Satanta. "You are smart not to cheat me too badly for so many cows and horses."

"We've known each other a long time," the Comanchero stated. "We know what can be done."

Satanta nodded and took a deep drink.

"Will you have more cattle soon?"

"Soon," agreed the Indian. "When the ponies fatten up some on the new grass. I will want more guns, so bring them, instead of making me wait and trust you." The Kiowa's black eyes looked directly into the Mexican's.

"It is hard sometimes to get guns, and it is dangerous to travel about with them," noted Tafoya.

"If you are afraid, I will send men to protect you," offered Satanta.

"And who will protect me from your Kiowas, when they have guns and ammunition?" joked the trader.

"It is not in our interest to kill you, Tafoya," stated the chief. He smiled. "Not yet."

The Mexican rolled back merrily, but his eyes were not laughing. "Have you nothing to trade me now? No robes or pelts?"

"It was a hard winter," said the chief. "We gave away much and did not hunt successfully."

"Pity," observed the trader. "There are many things in the wagons that the women will want."

Woven Blanket spoke in Kiowa to Satanta. "His prices are too dear."

"Nothing of significance to trade," the chief told the Comanchero.

161

"You have the white woman," Gomez said casually.

"She is not for sale," Satanta said quietly.

"She is worth more guns and ammunition than fifty horses," Gomez pursued. "I thought your people needed guns."

Satanta looked coldly at Tafoya's *segundo*. "She is not for sale."

"Too good to let go, eh?" Tafoya asked slyly, shooting a glance at Gomez. Adrianne blushed at the insinuation. "She ain't bad-looking, but I can see her skin through the tears in her clothes. Must have been a real hard winter. I have never seen your women in rags before, Satanta."

"These are our old work clothes," Woven Blanket spoke in Kiowa to Satanta.

The Kiowa looked where the trader's eyes were directed at the women working on the meal. He wiped the moisture from the corners of his mouth. Tafoya was right. In the winter travels among the starving, desperate northern peoples they had lost much of their pride.

Without looking up, the Kiowa woman continued. "We are wearing our old clothes to work in. We do not need clothes from the white man. We are just now sitting down to make new clothes for the *Kado*." Woven Blanket did not want any obligation to the trader nor did she wish to make a demand on her husband that would force him into close dealing.

"What's your name, woman?" Tafoya asked Adrianne in English as the Kiowas conferred.

She did not answer him, but continued with her task.

"Too ashamed of lying with these red bucks to tell it?"

Adrianne straightened and looked straight into the Comanchero's eyes. "I am not ashamed of my behavior. My name is Adrianne Chastain."

162

The trader's eyes played over her, trying to place the name. "Where from?"

"Elm Creek on the Brazos," she said, and went quickly back to her work as the shrewd trader stroked his well-kept goatee.

"Do not talk to my women, Tafoya," Satanta concluded the exchange.

Tafoya turned his attention back to Satanta. "I guess you were not the only ones with a hard winter. Another Comanchero told me some *indios* were hard hit at Adobe Walls. Kit Carson burned three hundred lodges and their winter supplies."

"This is not news," said Satanta. "I have heard this."

"Could have been worse, I heard." Tafoya chewed the corner of his mustache philosophically. "Comancheros warned them and sold them enough ammunition to turn old Rope Thrower back. By the time it was over, he was fighting for his ass. The Comancheros and the Kiowas have been friends a long time."

After the hospitality meal was served, Tafoya and Gomez left the lodge. The *jefe* paused near one of the wagons to light a *cigarillo*. "Bring me that Kansas *cibolero*. I want to ask him about the woman."

Gomez brought Tafoya's *cibolero,* buffalo hunter, through the trees to the Comanchero's tent.

"I have been good to you, Bill?" the *jefe* asked.

The unshaven *gringo* nodded affirmation. "Real fair, Mister Tafoya."

"I need some information that you perhaps have," Tafoya continued. Again the hunter nodded. "You ever hear of a woman named Adrianne Chastain?"

"Sure, I heard of her. I drove a wagon for her father-in-law for a while. Hard old man he was, too. No drinking on the job

163

and no women around his place that weren't wives or daughters. But paid honest and prompt. Many's the time I ate at that woman's table, but she wasn't called Chastain. She was Adrianne Doe, then. She's a right fair cook and a good-looking woman, though that was all wasted as fer as I could tell. She was straight as the old man."

Tafoya studied the table top in front of him, ran his finger along a crack. He was pleased with Bill's fountain of information, but wanted to be sure the man was not blowing hot air. "And where was this, Bill?"

"Elm Creek on the Brazos, not far from Fort Belknap. Had me some good times in Belknap," grinned the man. Seeing the Comanchero's face, he quickly added: "But that bunch was hit hard by Indians back last October, I heard. Killed a lot of settlers. I think they burned out Missus Doe, killed her daughter, and carried her and some kids off."

Satisfied that the buffalo hunter knew whereof he spoke, Tafoya leaned forward. "Someone would want this woman back?"

"Well, old Carter Doe and his son, Alexander, that was her husband, was murdered about four or five years back," Bill said, trying to think. "She remarried pretty quick to a sweet talker, but he got kilt or lit out. Maybe she run him off. I don't know anyone else would want her, 'cept maybe the government, if she was took in. Have to be in Kansas, though, the Rebs ain't got no money or organization to speak of in Texas."

"The government is not generous." Tafoya considered the table top again.

Bill rubbed the stubble on his face as he thought about Tafoya's words. "Well, she's rich as a foot up a bull's ass. I reckon she'd pay her own ransom."

Tafoya smiled broadly, revealing dazzling teeth. "*Señor*

Bill, after we finish our little talk, I want you to go shave and comb your hair, maybe take a bath," he added, wrinkling his nose. "Gomez will see you get a new shirt off the wagons. Then, you see if you maybe recognize Satanta's white woman."

"Missus Doe," the hushed voice came from among the trees as Adrianne reached for a piece of firewood. "Missus Doe, it's Bill Cox." He stepped into her sight as she straightened. "Remember me? I used to drive for your father-in-law, old man Carter Doe."

Adrianne frowned at the freshly shaven face, trying to place it. "You had a brother, didn't you? Both of you were drivers."

"That's right," Cox nodded. "Me and him left to hunt buffalo, *cibola*, that's what these Mesicans call 'em. I took a bunch of hides to Santa Fé, trying fer a better price, and now I'm ridin' back toward Kansas with these fellers. I'm a-cuttin' loose from 'em, goin' on from here alone. But if you're a mind to leave these red niggers, I'd be pleased to see you home. All we got to do is follow the Brazos east from here."

"I'm not ready to go home, Mister Cox," Adrianne said, and walked away from the freshly scraped buffalo hunter with her armload of wood.

"Shit . . . !" swore the man, rubbing his head, tangling the recently combed hair.

Chapter Seventeen

"She what?" exploded Tafoya, rising from his chair. He had already counted his ransom money and suddenly felt himself robbed.

"That's what she said, Mister Tafoya. Ain't ready to go home yet," restated Bill Cox.

"By God, she *is* ready," the old Comanchero said. "She just don't know it."

"Why ain't she ready, Bill?" Gomez calmly asked.

"Well, I don't know that. Maybe she's sweet on that big Kiowa. She was gettin' a pretty bad reputation for gettin' married so quick after her husband got kilt, then got married two or three more times to boot."

"Find out, Gomez," ordered Tafoya. "Somebody in this camp knows why she ain't eager to get out of here, when she gets a chance."

Bill Cox lifted the teepee cover and crawled under. "What in the name of heaven are you doing in here?" blurted Adrianne at the intrusion into the privacy of the lodge.

"Missus Doe," the man mumbled apologetically, trying to reset his battered hat, "I got to talk to you."

Adrianne scrambled to her feet, headed toward the door. "Talking to you'll get us both killed. Kiowas don't like uninvited men in their homes or around their women."

"I know where the little girl is," the *cibolero* cried out desperately, as she raised the door cover. "I been trying to get you alone to tell you for two days."

Adrianne studied the man lying on his stomach under the teepee bottom. "Go down to one of the trade wagons. I'll come down there. Go now." The man placed his gnarled hand over his hat and backed out from under the lodge cover. Adrianne stepped into the light and walked briskly to the place where the women were looking at pots in the wagon bed.

Flies Far lifted a mirror and considered her face with pleasure as Adrianne began to rummage among the trinkets displayed by a Comanchero. "Pretty things," the man said, offering a mirror to Adrianne. She ignored it, and reached instead for a silver bracelet. "If you was to treat me right, I'd see you got away from these savages."

"Shut up, Nate." Bill Cox shouldered him aside. "I'm leavin' pretty soon, Missus Doe, and I just wanted you to know about the little girl. I didn't mean nothin' else."

Adrianne turned her back to the wagon as she fingered the bracelet in her hand. "Where is she?"

"Back on the Brazos," the buffalo hunter answered.

"My place was burned out," Adrianne noted.

"Sure, that's right, Missus Doe. She's with Missus Hamby. She's safe with the Hambys. They always was good people," the man elaborated.

The white woman had not looked up at the man, but continued to touch idly pieces of the heavy, silver jewelry. She nodded. "Yes."

"There's just one problem," the hunter ventured.

Adrianne looked up. "What problem?"

"Well, the Hambys got hurt pretty bad in the raid. And the last I heard, they was thinkin' to travel, maybe when the weather got better, but before the Indians was about. Maybe they'd better pull out, go back east to Weatherford, or maybe just chuck it all and go on back where they come from. The girl ain't real well since her ordeal. Don't know as she could

167

make it. I mean, she could end up in some little unmarked grave somewhere along the way, and you'd never know. If she did make it, maybe you'd never find them or her again back there." The Comanchero added: "The Hambys won't wait much longer. The weather's gettin' better ever'day, Missus Doe."

With her blue eyes and attention fixed on Bill Cox, Adrianne had not noticed that Flies Far and the other women had disappeared. She only saw the red muscular arm shoot past her and catch Bill Cox by the throat. Satanta threw him over her head to the ground. As the *cibolero* coughed and strangled in the dirt, Satanta caught her roughly and pulled her away from the wagon toward the red teepee. Adrianne stumbled blindly beside him, trying to comprehend what had happened. Then, at the door of the teepee, she saw Flies Far smiling. Adrianne stopped and jerked her arm out of Satanta's powerful grip.

"You are hurting me," she protested.

"Good," muttered Satanta, pushing her with a stiff arm.

Adrianne turned abruptly. "What's the matter with you?" she shouted at the Kiowa.

"You will not shame me," he shouted back.

"Shame you? How did I shame you?" she asked fiercely.

"You are acting wantonly with the white man."

"Wantonly! Wantonly!" Adrianne could barely see, the anger was so full within her.

"It is immodest, brazen for a Kiowa woman to look at a man like that." The chief's chest was heaving with his own anger.

"Like what?"

"In the eyes," the savage shouted.

Adrianne continued to seethe. "I don't understand your damned heathen ways. I wasn't immodest with that man, or

168

any other." She pointed to Cox who still sat in the dust. "I've never been a loose woman, and I'm not now. I won't have my character questioned by you or anybody else." Looking at the tall, handsome Kiowa, she suddenly took the offensive, driving a finger into the man's chest. "How in the hell can you question me? You can burn my house, steal my cattle and horses to buy those damned guns to kill more people. That's what you are going to do, isn't it, kill more people? I don't understand how you can tell little children stories part of the time and cut my son's throat without a blink. I don't understand how you can do all you've done to me and then jump on me for looking a man in the eyes. In fact, I haven't understood a thing in so long, I'm beginning to wonder if there is any sense to anything. But there's damn' sure something wrong here. You can kiss my foot."

For a long moment she stood with her hands on her hips, glaring at the Kiowa. Finally, she stooped to pick up the tie from her hair that had come off during the altercation and fallen into the sand. Satanta planted his foot on her behind and pushed, sending her sprawling onto her stomach. He looked down at her as he walked proudly past. Adrianne rolled over and moaned when he took Flies Far's arm and went to the women's lodge. Catching Bill Cox's eyes on her, she nodded.

That night Adrianne lay on her elbow, listening to Geese Going Moon singing softly a Wind Song become lullaby to the sleepy child beside her. Her voice was low and soft, soothing to the child and usually to the white woman's soul.

That wind, that wind
Shakes my teepee, shakes my teepee
And sings a song for me,
And sings a song for me.

169

But tonight the wind sang in Bill Cox's voice: *"The girl ain't real well since her ordeal. Don't know as she could make it. I mean, she could end up in some little unmarked grave somewhere along the way, and you'd never know. If she did make it, maybe you'd never find them or her again back there. The Hambys won't wait much longer. The weather's gettin' better ever'day, Missus Doe."*

When the fire had burned low and the family slept, Adrianne gathered her robe and left the lodge. She took her saddle and went to the pony herd. Taking her horse without waking the sleeping herder, she rode off to find the *cibolero* who had departed in haste down the Brazos after his run-in with Satanta, to find the child, Lottie.

Chapter Eighteen

Bill Cox and Adrianne rode in silence throughout the night along the river's twists and turns. By daylight, they had covered many miles and come out on higher ground.

"Yes, sir, ma'am," the man ventured. "You hardly need me at all. Just follow the river."

"I'm grateful for your help, Mister Cox. And I will be happy to pay you for the service you are doing me on this trip." Adrianne noticed the man looked back frequently. "I don't think Satanta will follow. He let me go once before."

"Well, that'd make travelin' a whole lot more pleasant. But I got this itch at the base of my skull. All them little hairs is standin' straight up." The hunter rubbed the back of his sunburned neck.

"You don't think the Hambys have left already?" Adrianne focused on the urgency of their mission.

"Not them Hambys, no ma'am. You'd have to blast them Hambys out," Cox said, forgetting the lie that had propelled Adrianne on the ride.

"I thought you said they'd be pulling out, when the weather was good for traveling," Adrianne pursued the thought.

"Oh, sure, Missus Doe." Cox had caught his mistake. "They ain't likely quitters. Usually the Hambys would rather do anything than pull out, but they're licked, plum licked. Goin' back to Ohio."

"The Hambys are from Kentucky," Adrianne noted.

"Well, I got that wrong, didn't I, ma'am. You knows yer neighbors better than me, that's a fact," admitted the buffalo hunter. The man slid from his saddle and adjusted the girt, but his eyes searched the back trail.

Adrianne turned to look over the miles they had ridden. "Satanta won't come, Mister Cox. He let me go before."

"Well, that was before. I reckon he'll come this time. Him and a bunch of wild Indians with him." Cox threw himself back atop the horse. "But we'll get to the others 'fore then. Then, we'll see what happens to that *big* chief."

"Others, Mister Cox?" queried the woman.

"Best move on now, ma'am." Cox handed Adrianne a piece of jerky, then turned his horse downstream.

Adrianne held the jerky, but did not move.

The man looked back.

"You said *others*. What others?"

"Well, Missus Doe, I figured I couldn't handle that Kiowa by myself, so I got me some help," explained the hide hunter, eager to push on.

"Who are they, Mister Cox?" Adrianne asked still not moving.

"Why," the man scratched his chin, "just some ol' boys."

Adrianne sat looking at his face, waiting for the answer.

"Well, there's Nate and Gomez and a couple or three others, maybe four."

"Tafoya's men," she clarified.

Cox nodded. "That's about it."

"Maybe seven men?"

"Maybe seven, maybe eight or ten. Come on, lady. We're losin' precious time," Cox urged.

"I thought this was between us, Mister Cox." Adrianne sat firmly.

"You didn't think I'd go up ag'in' that Kiowa by myself, did you?" smirked the hide hunter.

"I guess I didn't think about that," answered the woman.

"I was just thinking about Lottie."

"Well, it's a good thing I did." Cox reached over and caught the reins of her horse and pulled her.

Adrianne, taking back her reins, rode several more miles, following the *cibolero* across the empty land. "Where are your friends meeting us?" she asked, pulling alongside the man.

"Ain't far now." He spat a stream of tobacco. "Boy, will that damned Kiowa get a surprise! Ha!"

"You're going to ambush him?"

Cox did not see the frown knit itself between the woman's blue eyes.

"Maybe so," grinned the man. He pointed his finger and cocked his thumb, suggesting a pistol. "Pop. Pop. Dead Injun!"

"Even ten men may not be a match for the Kiowas," speculated Adrianne.

"Ten men with brand new Sharpses are," Cox assured her.

"You just delivered guns to the Kiowas. They have rifles, too," protested the woman.

"Yeah, that's a fact, they do. But we got ammunition, and they don't," boasted the hider.

"They let you sell them guns without ammunition?" asked Adrianne incredulously.

"Hell no, they wouldn't go fer that. And Tafoya knowed that, if they had bullets *and* guns, we might not make it out. So we buried it. That's the way business is done with whiskey and guns and Injuns. They have to go twenty-five miles in the other direction to find the whiskey barrels and ammo. And Tafoya's guide won't show 'em the right place this time."

"They'll kill him," Adrianne said flatly.

"Oh, he'll show 'em the whiskey first. And then tell 'em where the ammunition is, and they'll trust him 'cause of the whiskey. Then he'll light out, hell's a-poppin'. But, if he don't

173

make it, one dead greaser ain't no big loss," laughed Bill Cox. "Jus' think of all them damned Injuns, diggin' and kickin' for something that ain't there. How they goin' to whup us, then?"

"I see you have this all well thought out, Mister Cox." Adrianne rode, studying the horizon, thinking.

"That's right, ma'am. All thought out real careful." The man beamed, dropping his rough hand on Adrianne's knee and winking. "Hot time in the old town tonight!"

"Why are you winking at me, Mister Cox?" she asked crisply.

Cox leaned over slyly, cunningly. "Oh, you know, Missus Doe. You been around the bush a few times yourself."

Adrianne drew her horse to a halt. "I'm paying you to deliver me home to my granddaughter. I don't want anything else from you, and I don't want Satanta harmed in any way."

"See here," the man grinned. "You been around the bush with that there red nigger and his friends. What's wrong with us goin' around a couple of times, too? 'Specially if we got to fight fer you. Little bit on account, so to speak. Fightin' kind of stirs up ol' Shorty."

Adrianne remained unshocked by the man's lascivious insinuations as a realization appeared with great clarity. "You don't know one damned thing about my granddaughter, do you?"

"No, ma'am," said Cox. "For a fact, I do not." As the man answered, the pair rode up over a roll revealing a wide expanse of the flat, almost dry, Brazos River. "Ayeh, lookey, there's the camp." He spoke to himself, for Adrianne had turned her pony and was lying over its neck as it sped away across the rolling land.

"Well, shit!" exclaimed Bill Cox. He pulled out his heavy pistol and fired twice. The men in the camp below looked up. Cox signaled with his hat. "Come on. Come on. I ain't

174

goin' to do ever'thing myself."

Adrianne put distance between herself and the Comancheros as the *cibolero* waited for reinforcements. She slid into a seam in the land and sped down it, heading back toward the distant Kiowa camp. She slowed and began to lighten the horse's load, dropping her robe, the bundle of her tattered white clothes and boots, then the small bag of food and gourd of water. Lifting herself over the high cantle onto the horse's hips, she placed her knife beneath the girt and cut it, flinging the saddle away. Any large man riding an American horse with a heavy saddle would never catch her in the open. Adrianne followed the wash to a cutback, then turned into it, and trotted down it. Seeing the defile growing shallow as it spilled gently into the wide Brazos bed, she squeezed the pony into a canter and prepared for the full-speed burst that would carry her into the open. Unaware that her enemy had anticipated the direction of her flight, she did not expect Nate Thorn when he flew off the bank above her, knocking her against the far side. She fought, biting and kicking, until Gomez, who had joined Thorn, hit her with the rifle butt. They threw her limp body across the Indian pony and led her back to the camp by the riverbed.

By the time the Comancheros returned to their comrades, Adrianne was groggy, but awake. Gomez pulled her roughly from the horse onto the ground. Standing above her, he unbuckled his gun belt and began to strip off his bandoleros and short jacket. "Time to pay the piper, you Injun-lovin' bitch," he growled. While both arms were still on the jacket, a bullet ripped into Gomez's chest.

Fascinated, the Comancheros watched as the man's body kicked backward for a long, slow moment with the bullet's impact. In sudden realization they scattered for their guns. Adrianne looked back in the direction of the shot. Satanta

175

sat calmly on the roll of land.

"Aye!" Satanta raised his rifle high over his head and yelled his defiant war cry into the vast sky. Bursting off the knoll, he thundered the seasoned pony toward his confused enemies.

A ragged line of Comancheros formed with rifles raised. They fired excitedly, kicking up dirt fifty feet in front of the Kiowa. "God dammit," shouted Bill Cox. "Aim yer cussed shots, yuh stupid greasers."

The men worked to settle shaking arms and hold their sights on the advancing menace. They fired spasmodically, randomly, the dirt kicking up around Satanta. Still he came.

"Dios mío!" one of the men exclaimed. "He is dead, but he rides."

"He isn't dead. Stop shooting!" Adrianne shouted above the guns.

Nate Thorn raised his Sharps and cocked it. With narrowed eyes he sighted thoughtfully down the barrel. His index finger curled gently over the brass trigger. "We'll just see about you, Mister Indian," he whispered.

Adrianne plunged into Thorn's legs, throwing him to the ground. She crawled frantically over him, fighting toward the Bowie knife in his belt. Thorn backed away like a man suddenly covered by insects, attempting to brush her away. But Adrianne had the knife and drove it into his heart.

Looking up from Thorn's body, she saw that the magnificent Kiowa still pounded across the open land. He rode erect, long legs relaxed and natural over the pony's belly. He lifted his repeating rifle and aimed, firing two quick rounds into the line of men.

"Aggh!" A Comanchero fell near Adrianne, gripping his thigh. "I'm hit. I'm hit."

Adrianne grabbed his rifle.

One of the other men dropped beside him to check the

wound. "Let's get the hell out of here while we still can."

"The rest are coming over there," shouted another Comanchero.

Only Bill Cox looked in the direction the man pointed. "Ain't nothin' over there 'cept trees."

"*Sí*, they are coming from the trees, *muchos indios*," the man said. "*Madre de Dios*, they will overrun us. They will kill us all over a woman that is nothing to us." With the last words, he turned and fled. Seeing him bolt, the other Mexicans ran toward their horses.

One man besides Cox remained, rifle trained on Satanta. "That's it!" encouraged Cox, trying to reload. "Nail that red bastard."

The concussion of the Comanchero's gun exploded in Adrianne's ears. She turned without thought to see if Satanta were hit. The shot cut two feathers from his shield. He did not notice, but rode harder, throwing down his rifle, drawing forth the gleaming tomahawk.

"Fire again. Keep firin'," commanded the hider, struggling with his weapon.

But Satanta was already on the Comanchero. Pushing the horse's body into the fight, he slapped the Comanchero with his hand, then split his skull with the 'hawk. He rode over the body into two other Comancheros, trying to catch and mount their frantic horses. Twice more he swung the battle axe in the jostling hand-to-hand turmoil.

"Shit . . . !" The *cibolero* spat a stream of tobacco juice onto the ground and scampered to his horse, undiscovered in the chaos of battle between Satanta and the remaining Comancheros. He was halfway to the knoll, when the Kiowa noticed his flight. Satanta turned from the wounded and vanquished, allowing them to escape.

"*Yih, yih, yih,*" he yipped as he pursued the buffalo hunter.

177

He caught him going up the hill and, with one vicious stroke, severed his head. Adrianne shivered as the man's head bounced along the ground.

The white woman sat down with both bloody hands crossed over the top of her head. She looked about the devastated camp with the bodies of the slain. The last of the Comancheros disappeared down the river as Satanta gathered their abandoned weapons. At last he gently loped the bloody war pony toward her. As Adrianne rose, she looked up into the angular bronze face, transfixed by the fiery black eyes. The man smiled slowly and offered her his hand. A small smile lifted the corners of her mouth. She reached out, and he swung her up behind him. They rode away with her arms tightly around his waist to retrieve her horse, the discarded gear, and the spooked horses left by the Comancheros in their flight.

Satanta and the woman made camp along the Brazos. Adrianne built a small fire as she had become accustomed to among the Kiowas. Satanta washed his pony and bathed in the red water of the river that glowed in the fading orange light of the evening sun. He hobbled his war horse with Adrianne's and the others taken from the Comancheros and came back to the meager meal beside the fire. Adrianne held her food, but did not eat as she watched the man chew his vigorously.

"I'm as bloody a savage as you are," the woman said at last, staring blindly at the fresh scalps Satanta had drying over the fire.

"I am not a bloody savage," countered the Kiowa in good spirits. "I have bathed. You have not."

"You know what I mean."

"I know we are good together. You are making a fine

Kiowa woman." He smiled, then became more serious. "I did nothing for which I am ashamed. I killed my enemies in open battle. I even counted coup on them, took horses and guns. This was an excellent fight. Do you think your prospects were good with such men?"

"No, of course not," Adrianne admitted.

"You did enjoy yourself," laughed the Kiowa.

"I did not," she protested. "How can anyone enjoy killing?"

"It is not the killing you enjoy. It is the risk, the testing of yourself against other men. I enjoyed this very much, and so did you. It is very exhilarating. You did well."

"Thank you," Adrianne said forlornly. "I am as bloody a savage as you. How come you haven't cut my nose off for running off with that man?"

"Because I have killed him and am well satisfied." The man struck his chest manfully, then he grinned. "Because José heard him tell you about the little girl. You went with him for the child."

"You let me go to Soule, when I wanted to know about Lottie. What was the difference?"

"Soule was a man, a warrior. These men were pigs. They lied to you and meant to use you badly. You are still under my protection." Satanta lay back comfortably on his blanket. Adrianne shivered with the thought and the cold wind. "Come, Taukoyma. I will share my blanket."

The woman looked at him across the fire. "We tried that before. It didn't work out too well."

"I thought it did," the man said. "Except you were not very pleasant." He studied the oval face with light hair spilling around it, then the well-shaped body as she added a stick to the fire. "Why are you so squeamish? You had a husband."

"Nope," the woman poked the fire. "I had three husbands."

179

The Kiowa turned his head, suddenly alert. "Three men?"

"Yup. Three. *Uno, dos, tres.* Number three was nothing. Actually it was probably my most successful outing. I needed a cow boss to run my ranch. He was a good one, nice man, very polite, too. Never got past ma'am, never came to my bed . . . strictly business. Then I caught him rustling my cows for Charlie Morehouse. We parted company. He joined the local rangers, got killed.

"Number two was a sweet-talkin', darlin' man. He told me everything I wanted and needed to hear. Chastain was his name. He drank and gambled and spent my money. But he *was* sweet. He didn't even mind that I. . . . He just drank more, gambled more, spent more money. Pretty soon we both knew it was a mistake. When his company was transferred, he went gracefully away. Killed fighting in Virginia, leading a gallant charge up a nameless hill. Pity, though." Adrianne looked down at the ground, sighed deeply.

Satanta's horse whickered from the grassy bank of the river. The woman raised her head. "Oh, look, the wild horses are coming to drink." Adrianne breathed in deeply the scene before her. A faint, remembered music — the *Laudate Dominum* from Mozart's *Vesperae* — seemed to float on the wind of the prairie twilight. The horses moved cautiously behind the lead mare into the sandy riverbed. The fire in the long sunset reflected orange and yellow off their sleek coats while the shadows on the land absorbed the soft lavenders and deep blues of the coming night.

The colts beside their mothers nuzzled the water and pawed it with their tiny hoofs. High on the riverbank, the stallion kept his watchful guard.

"*¿Y uno?* What about number one?" Satanta interrupted Adrianne's reverie with the horses.

"Oh. That's too unpleasant to speak of when the world is

so beautiful," the woman whispered against the lovely silence.

Satanta observed her closely, sensing that here lay a deep hurt. "Speak of it. Perhaps the harmony of this place will drown it and wash it away."

Adrianne thought about his words, hoping, believing suddenly that, perhaps, this place and time and beauty could cleanse her spirit of its sorrow, its humiliation. "I've never talked to anyone about it." As she looked at him, Satanta nodded quietly, encouraging her recitation of grief. "When I was fourteen, my father's debts became too large for him to carry. He was a soldier and scholar, not a careful manager of the land he inherited or its finances. He had a good friend, Carter Doe. Carter Doe had a son, Alexander. A marriage was arranged between us. Alexander was thirty-four. The debts were paid, the land saved, but I was lost. I knew nothing, except to do what my husband, my master, said. We didn't start off very well. When I caught his arm as he lay me down, he rebuked me as a common whore. He folded my arms across my gown and performed his conjugal duty, then he left. As long as we were married, he never saw my body, never kissed me, or held me. I never touched him again."

Satanta was alert to her words. "What kind of marriage is this?"

"A proper marriage," Adrianne answered.

"He did not caress or kiss you? You did not touch him?"

"He would have been offended if I had, or if I had cried out with pleasure as you say." Satanta's black eyes were on her as she explained. "I was a wife, a proper woman. A proper, decent woman does not take pleasure in copulation. She endures. He expected this. A proper husband does his duty properly by making children with her, finding his own release quickly, and leaving her."

"This is primitive," muttered Satanta in shocked amazement. "There is great pleasure between a man and a woman."

"Not between a proper husband and wife," Adrianne assured him. "A woman who enjoys sensuous pleasure is wanton, a harlot."

"*Pfft,*" Satanta blew in disgust between his lips. "You call me savage, but I would not do this to a woman I loved."

"Ah, but he did not love me. Once, when I was in the city on some trivial errand, I saw Alexander in the street with a beautiful dusky woman and her small child. He put his arm around her waist as they crossed the street and gently led the child. He was kind and loving with her, with them. It was a revelation to me of a side of him I did not know, had never seen. When I had his child the year after we were married, I thought that things would change. I thought, then, he would care for me. But he did not. In my foolishness, I blurted what I had seen between him and the octoroon. 'Why can't you love me?' I asked him. He answered very simply, very directly. 'Because you are not lovable.'"

The woman's eyes swam with unshed tears as she found herself again unacceptable, but she continued. "I was pretty much finished as a woman after that. But I did my duty. I was diligent and hardworking, filling my days with work and my leisure with more work and my evenings alone with books. I kept his house and desperately endured his efforts to beget a male heir, knowing that he found me, my very flesh, abhorrent." Adrianne stood up suddenly, unable to endure the pain and memory more. "How I dreaded those transient hells. How I wanted to give him an heir and be done with him. It took eight years and two miscarriages before Joe Carter was born."

Seeing her anguish, Satanta rose and came to her. "Come with me," he said, taking her hand. "Let these once spoken thoughts blow away forever on the wind. I will show you the wild horses as the Kiowa sees them."

Adrianne turned to him innocently, following him carefully as they stalked the ever vigilant horses. "Neighing they come. Prancing they come," Satanta sang and translated the song. "A great horse nation they come." Drawing her before him, they watched from a rocky outcropping. He placed his hand on her shoulder as he pointed to the herd. "See over there. That is the boss."

Adrianne looked where he pointed and then toward the reigning stallion. "But the stallion is over there."

"The stallion is not the boss," confided Satanta. "He is the progenitor in season and the protector always. He guards the mares and colts from predators, but also from other stallions. He is never in the herd, always on the edge. That full-bellied bay mare is wise and wonderful. She knows things. She finds good grass and clean water. She disciplines the colts and the foolish by driving them away from the safety of the herd. She holds them away with her undaunted eye. They are very afraid, because, without the herd she holds, they will be prey to the wolves. They watch her eye for any wavering. They paw and toss their heads and walk with their chins on the ground. And finally, when they are humble, she takes away her hard gaze. She releases them and lets them return. She welcomes them and grooms them affectionately. They are grateful. It is the way of the wild horses. A man cannot forget the wisdom of Earth-maker when he sees the free ones as He made them."

Satanta turned the woman to him and kissed her gently, her forehead, her cheeks, her soft lips. Adrianne yielded, kissing him warmly with her lost need to love. Satanta's embrace and kisses grew stronger. Suddenly, she stopped and pulled away. "I can't do this," she whispered.

Satanta reached out, catching her. "I can make you forget the others."

183

"You cannot make me forget my children." Adrianne caressed his hand on her arm, then lifted it away. "This beautiful hand killed my son." She looked into Satanta's eyes. "Loving you, I would betray him." She walked away back toward the small camp.

Satanta captured her arm. "I have won you. I can take you."

"You already have. Was it satisfying?" Adrianne asked softly, sadly.

Satanta drew her to him, kissing her passionately, trying to kindle the fire he had felt and knew was within her. Adrianne offered no resistance. Finally, the Kiowa released her. "It is like rubbing life into a stone."

Crying, Adrianne moved away down to the stream. Satanta followed. She stepped into the shallows and began to wash her face. Looking up at the disconcerted man, she spoke very softly: "If my body cried out for you, Satanta, my mind and heart would still remember my dead children. I could not give myself to you." Then, walking into the depths, stripping off her clothes, she floated into the glowing red embrace of the Brazos, or, as it was written on the Spanish maps, Los Brazos de Dios, The Arms of God.

Chapter Nineteen

Time passed in a soft and seemingly eternal rhythm as the Kiowas moved over the primordial sea of the plains with their ponies' manes blowing in the incessant wind. The teepees shook before it, but endured in their perfected design. Slowly Adrianne discovered a harmony between the Kiowas and the world they inhabited. In their natural habitat, far away from the white men and their bustling, clattering, tempting settlements, the People lived with a pattern and purpose just as the wild horses had without corrals and men. It was this harmony that the white man would never see or, if seeing, never understand.

"Behold, look at this," sang the Kiowa voices. "I stand in good relation to the earth and its creatures. Behold, I stand in good relation to the Sacred. Behold, I stand in good relation to the beautiful. Behold, I stand in good relation with you. Behold. Look. See. I am alive. I am alive . . . truly living, whole, complete as Earth-maker made me to be."

But even on the far plains, the seeds of disharmony blew from the white fields and took root. There were not so many buffalo that spring as there had been the spring before. The women knit their brows and thought of hunger and clothing and shelter from the ceaseless winds. The men went to see what was happening to the animals.

Everywhere, among all the tribes and bands, the Indians saw more white men settling along the free-flowing rivers and streams, polluting them with the soil that came from their plowed fields and the filth that came from their excrement.

They saw the hunters with guns that fired from great distances into the grazing herds. They saw the woolly beasts fall unheeded by their comrades who, in turn, were picked off. They saw the traders' wagons haul away the meat to feed soldiers and citizens in Kansas City, to make extraordinary profits at twenty-five cents a pound for men who invested little and cared nothing. They offered their own beautiful robes, taken for their thick fur in the winter, worked diligently by the women, and saw their trade value drop as men hunted year around to fill carts with stiff hides to be sent over iron rails to be commercially tanned into shoes and bags for soldiers and citizens in the East and in Europe. A thousand men, never more than two thousand, hunted the great herds to death to fill the warehouses of two traders, E. H. Durfee in Leavenworth and Charlie Bates in St. Louis, men who controlled the hide market and supplied the world with leather. They bought the hides for six dollars, sold them wholesale for sixteen dollars. Business was good. It was their inalienable right to make a living, their destiny to shape the world in their own image. Nobody noticed, or gave a damn, that the harmony was broken, that living things could not, were not created to, feed continually machines and industries without rest.

They also saw the little everyday men, the frivolous sport hunters with their full bellies and insatiable bloodlust. They saw the stupid, the ignorant, shooters who fired indiscriminately out of the windows of train cars, killing the buffalo, speeding on across the prairie without time to take the meat, wounding the buffaloes to let them die in agony.

When the hides and tallow and humps and tongues were gone, the Indians saw their children hungry. They saw these human things, and they were bad. But worse, they saw the mindless, arrogant breaking of the harmony, and they hated the white man.

186

Neither did the Indians forget the slaughter at Sand Creek. This, too, was disharmony, treachery. Men killed for honor and glory, a warrior's life for a warrior's life, but not to annihilate a people.

Eagle Child, a cherished son, took the manhood road that year. It was time. He was proud, stepping forward to join his father and grandfather among the Kiowa men. Satanta and Woven Blanket had done all they could for him — horses, weapons, skills, guidance, love. They watched him, released him from his childhood bonds, and let him go. As Adrianne saw the Kiowa mother hand a small bag of food to José to give to the boy, she knew the parting joy and grief. She had watched her daughter, Susan, leave with her young husband. It was not the same, she told herself — a young man taking the warrior's road could be killed. But then, she thought, a young girl, taking the woman's road, also takes her life in her hands as she bears her husband's toil and children and the risks he takes. And even the children, Lottie and Millie, somewhere on the windswept plains were on a perilous road.

Woven Blanket made herself and the household busy to fill Eagle Child's absence. She threw a party. After she and Adrianne gathered and sorted the accumulated hides, she invited all the village women for a meal and amiable conversation. She gave each woman a hide as they parted. Adrianne considered this as the laboriously tanned skins departed.

"Why are you frowning, Taukoyma?" asked the Kiowa woman in good spirits.

"I guess I am too much a white woman to take pleasure in giving away what took so much work to make."

Woven Blanket laughed, jostling her friend's shoulders. "It is the custom in building a new lodge. There is so much work that all the women share in it. Look around you. Each lodge you see, I helped that woman build. Now she is helping me.

187

With only one skin to soften, it is not a burden, and it does not interfere with her own work. It is just one skin to soften. As each woman twists and turns it through bone or around a post, she silently prays for, and blesses, a new lodge of the People. When a young woman marries, all the women give a skin to help her start well. We invest our work in her home. Because she knows that we work hard to tan and soften a hide, she knows that we want her success. Every new lodge is a blessing to the People."

When all the hides were made soft by the women's strong hands, Woven Blanket held a second party. This time the women brought and laid the buffalo skins down on the ground. An honored woman, the most skillful designer and cutter of lodges, arranged and rearranged and placed and trimmed them for the others to sew together. The women laughed and talked, their hands never stopping. They punched their awls through the hides and stitched the edges together until the new cover was completed. With the work ready for painting by the men, Woven Blanket, Adrianne, and the others of Satanta's family laid out a splendid feast. The women ate and laughed and watched appreciatively as Woven Blanket made the gift of a beautifully beaded belt set, including an awl case and awl with deer-horn handle, to the most honored woman, the teepee builder.

The old red teepee was eventually cut apart and reused to make the small lodge Satanta had promised Adrianne. The women of his household helped her cut new lodge poles and strip off the bark. Woven Blanket showed her how to make the raised racks for beds. Together the women wove a willow backrest and headboards. They furnished the teepee with several robes and other things for housekeeping. They came and sat by her small fire to sew the fine garments they would wear at the summer *Kado*, the Kiowa thanksgiving gathering.

Adrianne, skilled in sewing herself, learned their patterns and the expertise required for the fine lanes of bead work that scalloped the fringed hems and ran across the bodices and skirts of leather. When Woven Blanket and Geese Going Moon had gone back to the new red teepee and the Sisters and their children returned to the women's lodge, the white woman felt how empty and lonely her dwelling was without them, without Lottie.

Even as the women found their comfort in activity, Satanta could not sit in camp thinking of the boy. He was himself a warrior with a warrior's business. He and several men rode away. For Adrianne the camp became lonelier still. But she found the children were comfortable with her and came to her as to their own mothers. Geese Going Moon taught her to make the small, treasured cradleboards and dolls for the little girls. As the girls grew, their dolls and cradleboards, as their clothing, were replaced.

The arrival of Woven Blanket's daughters and their husband provided new purpose and joy for the household. There were many things to prepare for the arrival of the grandchild. Woven Blanket became occupied with a full-scale, beaded cradleboard. Geese Going Moon made the two small umbilical pouches. One would contain and preserve a tiny portion of the child's navel. It would be hidden. The other, hanging openly on the cradle, would serve as a decoy so that any evil spirit that came looking for the child's life would find it by mistake. The heavily beaded bags were made of soft deerskin in the shape of a turtle and a lizard. The totems were both small animals, vulnerable as the new-born Kiowa. One was noted for long life and the other for quick escapes without serious harm.

When the door opened in Adrianne's lodge, the women looked up from their work. Satanta stepped happily through.

The children ran to him. He touched them gently and knelt to receive their hugs and kisses.

"What? What, Father?" squealed the littlest one, finding that the Kiowa had a sack gathered from a blanket in his hand.

"Just see," he said, arranging the children and dropping the sack for all to see. He slowly opened it, watching their faces. Inside were gifts for each child. The gifts for the women were all silver — earrings, bracelets, rings studded with turquoise, bridle fittings, heavy conchos for their belts and drags. Woven Blanket chose first as senior wife and then bestowed the remaining items according to the women's professed desires.

"Taukoyma," the Kiowa woman said. "This is for you." Adrianne came into the circle slowly. "Here. Here. Take it." She offered the white woman a handful of conchos. "I will show you how to make a belt for the new dress." Adrianne smiled, for she had seen the beautiful belt Woven Blanket wore around her waist with three-inch conchos and a drag of the graduated circles hanging down past her knees ending in a silver tip.

She thought of the belt later when she waited for the buffalo paunch to fill beside the stream. The sound of a flute drifted over the twilight. Down the stream, she saw the shy courting of a young warrior.

"I could never play the flute," complained Satanta above her. "So much courting is done as the water is carried."

Adrianne stood up beside Satanta, looking at the young lovers. "They are so young. So much is ahead for them."

"So much is ahead for all of us," the Kiowa said. "I have a gift for you."

"I already have a gift."

"This one is mine for you," the man answered. From his

190

belt he removed a small pouch and handed it to the woman.

"This isn't a finger or something, is it?" asked Adrianne, seeing the size of the bag and knowing the Cheyennes' custom of cutting off the index finger of their slain enemies.

"I am not a Cheyenne." Satanta bent over the gift. "Well, open it," he said, looking into her face.

Adrianne's fingers pulled apart the leather strings. She dumped the contents into her hand. Bold silver earrings in the shape of broad crosses winked up at her.

"Well?" Satanta searched her face.

She smiled and touched him lightly. "They are beautiful."

"Put them on," ordered the Kiowa. "I want to see you in them."

Shyly the woman fitted the dangling silver crosses into the holes in her ears. She brushed back her hair for the Kiowa to see. He smiled and gently placed his arm around her shoulder as they moved back toward the lighted teepees. She did not shrink away, but accepted the bond that was between them.

"Are you courting me?" Adrianne asked.

"I am," responded Satanta.

The screams of a child startled them both. Adrianne froze, trying to see what was happening. Just at the edge of the camp, two Kiowa men were holding a small boy who kicked and thrashed in their grips as a third man bent over him and attempted to strip away his pants. The woman dropped the water paunches and started toward the men. Satanta caught her.

"No," the chief said. "You are going to make trouble again. They are *dapon*. The child will live."

She turned. "What are they doing to him?"

"They are going to castrate him," the chief said, looking into her questioning face. "They think he will be a better slave, if he never thinks of women."

"No!" Adrianne shouted, and started to run toward the

191

men. The Kiowas looked up, but did not release the child.

Satanta's mouth twisted as he shook his head. "This woman," he muttered, and walked calmly toward the group of ragged men. Adrianne was already in their midst and had a hand on the small boy when he arrived. He removed her hand from the boy. Seeing her mouth starting to form a protest, he instructed her in Spanish: "Do not say anything, not one word, nothing at all." Then he spoke quietly, casually, to the men in Kiowa. "You must have had a good raid, Elk's Ear. When did you come in with this captive?"

"We are just coming in. This captive child is for our mother," the man answered proudly.

Satanta looked at the white child. "He is scrawny."

The other Kiowas looked critically at the child. "He will do to work for an old woman."

"If you cut him," Satanta offered, "he will stay small."

One of the men smirked. "But he will keep his mind off our women."

Elk's Ear said: "It is our mother's wish. She does not want him to become a problem."

Satanta reached out and roughly turned the boy to examine him, but also broke him from the men's grips.

Adrianne quickly pulled him to her and covered his small chest with her arms.

Satanta frowned. "This white woman is a lot of trouble." He sighed. "You see how it is. She does not understand our ways. She has lost her child. I will give your mother a horse for this one."

The Kiowa brothers looked at each other. "A horse, Satanta?"

The warrior nodded.

The brothers considered the offer. "She would rather have a mule," said Elk's Ear.

192

"A mule and a horse," put in the other brother.

Satanta looked at the scrawny boy, and then at the white woman, shaking his head. "A mule and a horse," he agreed.

"Take him," Elk's Ear answered quickly.

"Take him away from here, Taukoyma," Satanta told her. To the men he said: "I will bring your mother's horse and mule tomorrow." The chief moved away from the men, walking far behind the woman and child. He bent slightly with his hands crossed behind his back, studying the ground over which he walked. "A lot of trouble," he murmured to himself.

Adrianne waited for him outside her small lodge. "Is a human being nothing to you?"

"I bought him for you, did I not? A word of gratitude would be pleasant to my ears, since I have now exchanged a mule and a horse for this." Satanta considered the scruffy waif. "A horse and a mule for this bit of hair and hide and bone."

"I do thank you," Adrianne said.

"Good," the Kiowa acknowledged her words. "It was for you I bought him."

"You cannot buy people like horses and cows or sacks of potatoes, Satanta."

"You are too intense for me, Taukoyma. Just take the child. And do not weary me. A child is a child, important only as it is important to me and those I love."

"Those you love?" The Kiowa's words had startled Adrianne.

"Yes," Satanta said gruffly. "The rest, like this one, are as they are, leaves on the current."

"You see no farther than that?" she asked.

"No."

Adrianne lifted the hide door and gently pushed the child through. "Then your own children will never be safe or live in peace."

Chapter Twenty

"My name is Adrianne. What's yours?" Adrianne asked the little boy.

"Hermann."

"Hermann what?"

"Hermann Kaltwasser," the child answered.

"Well, Hermann Kaltwasser," Adrianne continued, "how old are you, and how did you get here? Where did you come from?"

"Sank'n Tone," lisped Hermann. The unusual contraction meant San Antonio to the Texas Germans from which he had come. "At least dat's the closest *vhere* ve got. I have ten years. I vas gettin' in the cattle, but the Injuns got me, instead."

"*Habst du hunger?*" Adrianne asked.

"*Ja, ja,*" nodded Hermann. "Dem damn' Injuns don't eat." Adrianne smiled and filled a gourd eating bowl. She watched him as he shoveled down the meal, and then filled the bowl again.

"You're a good eater, Hermann."

"Dat's vot dey say." The boy continued eating.

"Were your folks harmed?" Adrianne asked as the boy slowed his eating and began to look around.

"*Nein.* But I expect dey miss me. I vas gettin' good size to help with de verk."

"Well, I suspect they will miss you for more than that," the woman assured the child.

"You like dese gott-damn' Injuns?" queried the boy, poking food in his mouth.

Adrianne nodded. "They are not all bad, Hermann." Satanta's words — *those I love* — ran through her mind.

"Vell, dat bunch dat had me, dey like to fix me up pretty goot."

"You'll be safe now, I think," Adrianne said. "Satanta has bought you from Elk's Ear." *For those I love* — the words had been clear and sharp in her ears.

"He the big damn' Injun?" asked Hermann.

Adrianne nodded.

"How *kommst du hier?*"

"My ranch on the Brazos was hit by a big raiding party last fall," Adrianne answered.

"You are beautiful voman," burped Hermann. "Vhere'd you get dat scar?"

"It's a long story." Adrianne filled his bowl again.

"How ve goin' to get the hell out of *hier?*"

"You in a hurry, Hermann?" The woman smiled.

"Sure, got the plowin' and plantin' to do. And my cow's goin' to throw a calf pretty soon."

"Well, Hermann, I have to get something before I can go or take you home," Adrianne told the boy.

"Vot you got to get?"

"My granddaughters. I have to find Lottie and Millie."

Adrianne fell asleep with thoughts of Millie and Lottie, with the sound of Hermann's gentle snoring in her ears, and the words of Satanta — *those I love.* It seemed that all her life she had wanted to hear those words that had escaped him. Now she could not receive them.

Hermann Kaltwasser proved a good and quick companion. He took up with Feathered Lance, Satanta's younger son, and began to learn the Kiowa ways and language. At first, Adrianne thought he would adopt the Indian life completely because it was so rewarding for a boy. All the work, hunting, riding horses, making bows and arrows, were play to a white boy. But as much as Hermann liked the riding and freedom, he usually fell asleep telling Adrianne of the spotted cow he had been given and the heifer calf he was anticipating her to have. "It's got to be heifer," Hermann assured her sleepily. "I'm goin' to have a dairy and sell milk in Sank'n Tone. Texas is full of cattle, but none for milk and cheese, yust steers." When the woman thought he was finally asleep, he mumbled. " 'Course, I could use a good bull, if I could buy some more milch cows. Papa's got a good bull, Friedrich. *Ja,* dat Friedrich's a bull."

Hermann also proved to be a creature of habits. As good as he was at sizing up and adapting to situations, in the evening he wanted his dinner and his bed. No matter where he was or who he was with, at dusk Hermann concluded his day and came home. The routine was, Adrianne decided, as much a matter of blood as training. The Kiowas did not understand the little boy, but they allowed him to be as he was.

Hermann often helped Adrianne gather wood or chips for the fires of the household and carry water from the streams where the People camped. He naturally went to the tasks because they had been his jobs in the well-organized German family from which he had come.

The day was fast failing when Hermann showed up beside Adrianne. Together they walked toward the light timber along the creek. "Let's go over that way today," the woman directed. The pair walked across the area behind the village where the People dumped the waste and garbage from their households. *Gehenna* — the ancient Hebrew word rose in Adrianne's mind. Surely, she thought, the nomadic children of Israel had such a place, a place of vile separation, a symbolic demi-hell, but no fires burned here. The approach of human

196

beings caused the carrion birds to lift before them. They flew up, or skipped away, then resettled behind the pair.

"You must not come here at night, Hermann," Adrianne instructed the small German as he studied the refuse for possibly useful things. "Wolves, sometimes mountain lions and bears, go through the meat scraps and bones at night." Hermann picked up a piece of discarded rope. He tested it in his sturdy hands until it broke, then dropped it as he walked on.

"Hey, look," the boy said. He trotted a short way, recovered something, and returned with it to the woman. "Vot you tink, dese damn' Injuns read the Bible?" He handed her a stitched signature of pages.

Adrianne took the fragment and looked at the frayed and torn pages. She put it against her body, wiping it clean of dirt and trying to flatten the wrinkled pages. "No, Hermann. Indians put books inside their shields." She saw the boy's unasked question in the earnest blue eyes. "To stop bullets. Makes them thick and solid between the rawhide, but not too heavy. I guess this piece didn't fit or wasn't needed. How'd you know it was a part of the Bible?"

"I know dat word. It's my brother's name in English." He pointed at the bold black type — **John**. "And it's laid out like de Bible at home. *Meine mutter's* hot on dat book," the boy answered.

"Can you read any more words?"

Hermann said. "We ain't had time for much school. But I can read pretty goot in German."

Adrianne thrust the fragment into her dress as they walked toward the woods. "We'll read some at night before bed. That way, when you get home, you'll know how to read English." Adrianne contemplated the pleasure of again reading words on a page, watching them magically turn into ideas and expe-

197

riences. She did not see the face Hermann made, but it soon returned to normal as he decided to make the most of another bad situation.

Adrianne and the boy worked slowly through the words on the soiled and stained pages. " 'In the beginning was the word,' " the woman read before him in the firelight.

"Ain't dat interesting," the boy said.

Adrianne looked at him curiously to see if he meant what he said or was merely delaying the task of taking the book in his own hands. " 'In . . . the . . . ,' " Hermann struggled through the text as the woman listened and corrected. Later, when each had retired to his own bed, Hermann asked a question. "What did you say 'word' was?"

"On one level it is meaning . . . in the beginning was meaning, and meaning was with God. Traditionally, it means Jesus, the promise, the kept word of God. The names or references to the Father, Son, and Holy Ghost are always capitalized in the Bible," the woman answered sleepily.

"You believe in ghosts?" asked Hermann warily.

"Just that one," Adrianne said. "Go to sleep, Hermann."

"What is the Holy Ghost?"

"It's the Spirit of God inside you, to guide you and teach you all things." She spoke without thought as she herself had been taught.

"How can that be?" pushed the boy.

"It's a mystery," muttered the woman. "Go to sleep, Hermann. We'll talk theology another time."

In the beginning was meaning. . . . Adrianne heard the thought at the edge of her consciousness. *And what was the meaning?* She slid away into the formless void as the answer moved over the face of the deep. *Love . . . incomprehensible, defining love.*

Over the next nights, the two traversed several pages of the book only to discover that a whole chunk of pages had been torn out, jumping them from the lovely words of John to an abrupt end with a few snippets from Corinthians. Hermann was becoming a good reader, but Adrianne still read first to give him the vocabulary and some of the meaning. She lay on her stomach beside the boy with the firelight warm on their faces and the pages of the tattered book. "All right." She cleared her throat. "This is the last of it." She flipped the page back and forth. "We'll have to start over tomorrow night. Can you see those words?"

"No," the boy said, looking at the begrimed text. "The mud and blood ruined it."

Adrianne grimaced slightly, thinking of whose blood might be on the page. She skipped down to the legible words below. " 'Therefore, if any man be in Christ, he is a new creature; old things are passed away; behold, all things are become new. And all things are of God, who hath reconciled us to himself by Jesus Christ, and hath given to us the ministry of reconciliation; to wit. . . .' "

"What is to wit?" interrupted Hermann.

Adrianne thought a moment. "It means . . . this is it, or here it is." The boy nodded. She continued reading. " 'That God was in Christ, reconciling the world unto himself, not imputing their trespasses unto them. . . .' "

Hermann touched her arm. "Imputing?"

"Holding against. Because of Jesus Christ, God does not hold our sins against us."

"Is Christ Jesus's last name?" the boy asked, rolling away from the book onto his arm to look at her.

Adrianne closed her eyes. "We are not making much progress here, Hermann." She looked into the boy's calm face. "No,

Christ is not Jesus's last name. It's a kind of title, I guess. In Greek it means anointed." She saw the next question forming. "Here it means chosen, appointed, empowered for a special purpose . . . reconciling the world unto God, making peace between God and man." She looked to see if he understood and went on over the stained text looking for legible words. "Shoot, this is ruined." She picked up the thread of thought again farther down the page. " 'Be ye reconciled to God.' Well, that's pretty much all that can be read on this page."

When she turned to Hermann, he was asleep. She lay aside the book and moved Hermann to his bed. Then lay down in her own. As consciousness slipped away, she considered the strange words often passed over — *be ye reconciled to God* — suggesting so clearly that it was not God who delayed, but man who cherished his separation.

"How come you know Greek?" Hermann suddenly interrupted her dissolution into sleep.

"When I was a little girl, my father taught me. He was a scholar of languages. Then, when I got older, I read a lot. It was a great comfort. There are lots of good stories in Greek, stories about gods and men, beautiful women and fierce warriors, long and perilous journeys." Adrianne nestled in, trying to regain the pre-sleep state.

"We don't believe in gods, right?" confirmed Hermann.

"Right." Adrianne spoke through a yawn, as she rolled onto her side, looking at the teepee hide. "Isn't it curious we didn't find a piece of the ILIAD or ODYSSEY? Those would have been good reading for a boy."

"I can't read Greek for sure, Adrianne," muttered young Hermann Kaltwasser. "And I don't want to . . . ever."

Adrianne smiled.

"Huddletay! Huddletay!" Flies Far sang out as the two

workers came in sight. "Hurry! Hurry!"

Adrianne looked up, but did not hurry for Flies Far who had no authority and for whom she had never been able to gain respect. Generally the white woman avoided her, ignored her, if forced into her company. Whenever Adrianne saw the Kiowa woman, she thought of her moonlight tryst with Head Of A Wolf, her tattling and her pleasure in seeing Adrianne humiliated as a low woman in Satanta's eyes because of Bill Cox. But most of all she remembered that Flies Far had lost Lottie.

Adrianne and young Hermann Kaltwasser leisurely made their way to the water to fill the buffalo paunches.

Ignored, Flies Far continued dressing her hair and gossiping with her sister and another Kiowa woman. They giggled as the boy followed Adrianne, carrying the buckets. "Little husband! Little husband! Satanta will be jealous," said Flies Far, and laughed.

Adrianne stopped and turned, putting Hermann behind her. Her Kiowa was not perfect, but she understood the words and felt the sting of their implication. Little boys in Indian households generally had two mothers, their natural mother and a near kinswoman who took many responsibilities for them. Dividing the boy child kept the real mother from favoritism. Thus, she would not make him into a weakling from overprotection, nor would the child displace her husband in her affection. That Satanta's jealousy would be provoked by her attention to the child meant that she had truly become his woman on the return from the Comanchero fight. Giving her the earrings, meeting her in the evening as she drew water, even buying the child proved it.

Adrianne bent over Flies Far and lifted her to her feet. The Kiowa woman did not resist, but stood quickly, anticipating the confrontation both knew was coming. The white woman's eyes danced with her anger, but she suddenly turned away. "I will not contend with you or defend myself from your dirty thoughts. I am not a savage." She took a step and started away. Flies Far extended a moccasined foot and tripped her, sending her onto her hands and knees.

"Can you not walk so good, Taukoyma? Has Satanta made you too sore between your legs to walk?" Flies Far bent tauntingly above her.

Adrianne rose with a roar — "Aaah!" — striking the contemptuous woman across the face with the back of her hand, knocking her upside-down over the other women. Adrianne pursued, stumbling over the others, grabbing Flies Far, and throwing her against a tree.

"Get her!" yelled Hermann to his mentor, whacking his clinched fist into his other palm. "Yihah!" The little German danced with excitement.

Against the tree, the Kiowa woman drew the knife from her belt. Adrianne grabbed her arm, twisting and throwing herself against the Indian woman's body as she caught the knife hand. Wresting it from her, she shoved her hard against the tree and brought the knife to her throat. Even as she continued to hold Flies Far, pressing the dagger against the soft flesh, a sharp light burst off the blade, blinding the white woman.

Adrianne, the voice from the light said, *why do you war against me? All things are of God. Be ye reconciled.* Realization flooded through the white woman. Flies Far in her sensuous sin was no worse than she was in her coldness and unforgiveness. God loved this despicable, sinful creature, just as He loved Adrianne and wished to heal her brokenness. His love was encompassing, forgiving, renewing, freely offered to anyone. It was even given to the self-righteous, tortured by their own bonds of rules and duty and justified unforgiveness.

It was not misery and punishment He sought, not condemnation, but wholeness, acceptance of His love. *Be ye reconciled* — the phrase echoed through her soul as a graceful, gentle, joy filled her. Adrianne took the knife from Flies Far's throat and released her.

"*Haw. Haw.* Yes. Yes," the two Kiowa women who watched approved, getting to their feet. "Taukoyma is a true Kiowa. She knows when to fight and when to forgive. She has true power."

Adrianne touched the tiny puncture on Flies Far's throat where the tip of the blade had cut her. Wiping the small run of blood with her fingers, she looked into the other woman's eyes. "Forgive me."

Flies Far saw the peace where fury had been moments before.

Adrianne walked away from the women.

Watching her go, Flies Far caught Hermann and took him to fill the water paunches. They saw the white woman cross the creek as they carried the filled bags back to camp. Adrianne sat for many hours, watching the grazing horses.

Chapter Twenty-One

Adrianne slept peacefully. "Get up!" Hermann shook her. "Someting's goin' on with the gott-damn' Injuns."

"What?" the woman asked, brushing the hair and sleep from her eyes.

"Don't know," the kid said. "But it's bad. Dere's a dead guy laid over a horse."

Adrianne struggled up and went to the lodge door. The People were coming out of the teepees behind a rider, leading a horse. The rider's face was painted black, making him difficult to identify at first. Her hand came to her mouth. "Oh, no. It's José," she whispered to herself. "He's bringing home Eagle Child." Tears flowed from her blue eyes.

"Vot?" demanded Hermann.

"Satanta's son, Woven Blanket's son, has been killed," Adrianne explained. She looked down at the German boy. "Feathered Lance's brother is dead."

"Shit," whispered Hermann sympathetically.

José stopped his pony in front of the red teepee as Adrianne and Hermann watched. He slipped from its back and reached for the door, but it burst open before him as Satanta emerged. The mature warrior knew what the black paint on the young man's face meant. He did not speak, but went past the messenger of death to his oldest son's body, lying across his war pony's back. Adrianne heard the wail escape him as he saw the boy. He lifted Eagle Child into his arms. Satanta carried the body past the women to the boy's bachelor teepee. Even as he passed and the women saw the boy's dead

204

face, they began the lamenting death song. José lifted the door, and Satanta took the body inside. Woven Blanket followed her husband and dead son closely. Flies Far, Looking Glass, and Geese Going Moon cried the plaintive death song outside. Drawing their knives, the family women cut their heavy hair by chunks and dropped it on the ground. They cut the hair of the little girls who cried in fear at the women's horrifying behavior. The women slashed their arms, open wounds bleeding. Their song and grief were taken up by the women in the camp.

José emerged from the teepee and motioned to Adrianne. "Come," he said. "Woven Blanket wants you."

"Hermann" — Adrianne took the boy's thin shoulders in her hands — "find Feathered Lance and be his good friend." The woman followed José into the lodge.

After she ducked into Eagle Child's teepee, she stopped. Satanta lay over the boy's body, weeping in agonized sobs. Woven Blanket's arms touched both child and husband. With tears running down her copper cheeks, she looked up at the white woman.

"José," Adrianne spoke softly, "help me with Satanta."

The two knelt beside Woven Blanket and gently lifted the man from the mutilated body. Adrianne suppressed a gasp. The corpse was swollen and black — odiferous. The boy's chest was filled with closely-spaced bullet holes, a pattern of careful shots. He had been scalped.

Desperate, Satanta caught José by the neck. Black eyes filled with tears and anger, he demanded: "Who did this?"

"Buffalo hunters. Near Los Escarpados," answered the Mexican captive. "He went to take a horse by himself. They caught him, tied him to a tree, used him for a target."

"Where were you and the others?"

José wiped his mouth in his own agony over the boy he had

205

brought home to his father. "His riding horse became lame, and he did not want his war horse to suffer from lack of water. He sent us ahead to the water. It was not far, just a few miles. He must have seen the hunters and tried to slip up on them and take a horse. When it got dark and he had not come in, I went back, but I could not find him. We looked for him for two days."

"The Comanches helped you look?" asked Satanta.

"Yes, they helped. When we did not find him, they said he had turned back, and went on. I knew he would not turn back . . . pretty soon, I heard shooting. When I followed the sound, I found him." José sobbed when he spoke the last words and caught his face in his hands.

Satanta put his arm around the captive's shoulders. "Come, we will leave him to his mother now. Tomorrow we will take Kiowa men and find these buffalo hunters."

Grief absorbed the Kiowa village. They had lost a young man of great promise.

Adrianne helped Woven Blanket wash the body. Together they dressed him in his best clothing and wrapped him in fine blankets and buffalo robes. With each beaded garment, Woven Blanket remembered the love and hope with which it had been made. The men placed his body on a high scaffold with his weapons and saddle. Satanta did not kill his war pony for him to ride in the Land of Many Lodges. Eagle Child had so loved the spotted war pony that the thought of killing the animal would have been horrible to him. He had asked his father, before leaving, to give the horse to Feathered Lance, if he did not return. The little brother held the pony's reins beneath the wrapped body as the old shaman offered prayers on the wind, then Feathered Lance and Hermann led the war pony away. The men burned Eagle Child's lodge at sunset.

Woven Blanket swayed against Adrianne and Satanta as

the flames leaped through the teepee poles into the darkening sky. Grief, loss of blood from her slashed arms and chest, had weakened her. Adrianne helped her to the red teepee and made her comfortable on her bed. A small cry escaped her as the white woman tended the pot, cooking on the fire. Adrianne returned to her side and took her hand.

"He was my sister's son," Woven Blanket said softly through tears. "He was all I had of her. She left him for me to care for and. . . ."

"And you did," Adrianne cut off the words of blame before they came to Woven Blanket's lips. "You did all that any mother can do. You loved him and taught him and gave him the tools he needed. I saw the food you gave José to take for him. I heard you singing prayers at night when he was gone. You gave him so many things, and then you gave him freedom to be himself . . . the greatest gift. I never gave my son that." She looked down through her tears. "I am not a Kiowa and do not understand your way of honor, but I understand your love for Eagle Child." Adrianne felt heavy, unnaturally burdened by the Kiowas' grief and her own. "It's funny the pictures we carry of our sons . . . their first faltering steps, the time they were stung by a bee, their dirty, dirty faces after they had played, so many unmanly things. They would be pretty embarrassed by us, wouldn't they?"

Woven Blanket nodded, then spoke with quivering lip: "He will wander forever between the winds."

Adrianne knew the Kiowas believed that scalped warriors could not find rest. "In my faith, we believe all that is broken and injured is made whole again in the next life. I believe that Eagle Child is, even now, visiting among the People in the Land of Many Lodges, only we say it is a place of many mansions." She leaned forward and wiped the tears from Woven Blanket's cheeks. "He is saying to you . . . 'I am safe and well pleased with this new country. I will wait for you to come to me. Remember me, but do not grieve for me.' "

"Mother . . . ?" Woven Blanket's youngest daughter entered the lodge as cut and bloody as the other women. "Sitting Beside The River is having her baby."

Adrianne gripped Woven Blanket's hand. "You see," she smiled, wiping the tears from her own face with both hands. "Eagle Child has sent you joy in your sorrow."

The women arose and went to birth the new life. When the male child was delivered and cleaned and placed in Woven Blanket's sure hands, Adrianne went to her own lodge. She found Geese Going Moon snoring softly against a backrest. She held Feathered Lance and Hermann Kaltwasser, sleeping, their heads pillowed in her lap.

Satanta and the Kiowas made their war dance the next evening and slipped silently away in the night to gain retribution for Eagle Child and their grief. Satanta rode the spotted war pony treasured by his son. It seemed to Adrianne that the two, man and horse, had united in this vengeance for the beloved boy. When the warriors returned, they carried the scalp owed to the lost boy. Satanta burned it as an offering to him. Adrianne had thought Satanta would kill every white man he saw, but she learned that, among the Indians, excessive retribution was not commended. Even in this case where the son of a war chief had been taken, only one white man's life had made things even again.

After the death of Eagle Child, the People moved restlessly. Adrianne continued the search for Millie and Lottie as the Indians met and parted with their kinsmen and friends. She was burdened by grief for her children and for the Kiowas. She often lay awake with tears on her cheeks as she thought of the lost children and her own lost ability to love. Her heart, she believed, had grown cold over the years with Alexander Doe.

All her warmth had gone to the children, now lost to her. She could not say the words so easily and unafraid as the Kiowa: *I love*. And yet she cared for the Kiowas and, perhaps, for Satanta more than she would admit. Many war parties, another that included Satanta, went out when the grass became green again. They rode for glory and horses as they had for numberless seasons. But they also rode in bitterness and anger for Sand Creek, for the buffalo, for all the lost children like Eagle Child.

Satanta remained troubled even after the revenge of Eagle Child and the following raids. He attempted to take interest in the other children, even welcoming Hermann, treating him like his son, Feathered Lance. He hunted. He worked with a new pony, training it to hunt buffalo. Adrianne and Woven Blanket watched him as he drove the horse away from him with a quick movement of his hand and kept it moving on the end of the line he held, never letting it rest until it was tossing its head and carrying it near the ground. Finally he turned his back and stood facing the women.

"What does he want from the horse?" Adrianne asked with a frown.

"He wants it soft and mellow," Woven Blanket told her.

"Shouldn't a war horse have fire?"

Woven Blanket watched the horse shaking its elegant head up and down. "This horse's fire will be deep and long-burning. When he is through, Satanta can count on this horse. Look, the horse comes to him."

Adrianne watched as the animal dropped its muzzle over the Kiowa's shoulder. He caressed the strong jaw and whispered to it, blowing his breath into its nostrils. "He is very gentle," the white woman observed.

"He is gentle with a woman, too," Woven Blanket said.

Adrianne turned to her, reading the Kiowa woman's face.

"You want me to lie with your husband?"

Woven Blanket's black eyes looked deeply into Adrianne's. "I want you both to heal . . . you and our husband."

Satanta took the new horse with him when a group of men left the camp to raid. Adrianne thought often of Woven Blanket's words as she worked, as she played with the new baby, as she remembered the man's tortured face as he rode away. She and Hermann continued their routine, but soon Adrianne felt that the boy was not reading the words of the fragmented text, but merely repeating them from memory. As they studied, she took the book away, and the boy continued reading.

"I think you've got this, Hermann." Adrianne folded the tattered pages back together.

"Adrianne" — the boy turned his face to her — "I'm tinking of getting married."

The woman's eyebrows lifted as a smile came to her face. "When's the wedding?"

"Aw," the boy blushed. "I mean someday I vill get married, right?"

The woman nodded.

"Vell, if I stay with the Kiowas, I can have two or three vives, maybe more, but, if I go back to the vhite people, I'll only get one. Vich is right?"

Adrianne turned onto her back, running her hands through her cropped hair. "I don't know, Hermann. I can't quite get hold of this myself. Woven Blanket and the others are happy with Satanta. They love him and each other. It's the way things work with them. Our people are not like that. Two women in the same house would kill each other. We couldn't stand it. We'd always be competing, wondering who was getting more time and attention, who was working more."

"You mean vhite people's hearts are so little dey can only love one person?" pushed Hermann.

210

"No. I don't think our hearts are smaller, but our customs are different." Adrianne thought a minute. "I guess plenty of white men have loved and even married two women. Remember Abraham and Jacob and David or, good Lord, King Solomon. He had six hundred wives. But it didn't seem to work out real well for them, did it? They would love one wife more, or the wives would fight. There was so much strife."

The boy shook his head. "Maybe dere's someting wrong with vhite women?" he offered.

"There is nothing wrong with white women, Hermann." Adrianne shoved the boy.

"So vot should I do?" the boy asked.

"I don't know, son," Adrianne answered simply. "In the beginning, God split Adam into two people. He made one man and one woman. Those two halves, rejoined again in marriage, became one again. Our custom holds that in some special way those two should be one undefiled unit even though there's lots of different examples in the old times and lots of carrying on and slipping around since. I guess if I loved someone, I'd try to honor that oneness before God. I don't know how the Kiowa women think about it, but I guess they can be one not just with the man, but with the other women and the children, too. Maybe they don't think so much as individuals, but as a whole, a people, a band, a family." Adrianne sighed at the puzzle. "You know, Hermann, it might be you will find only one Kiowa woman, and she'll be happy with just you."

"I already asked," admitted Hermann. "She said she vouldn't marry me without her sister. There'd be too much vork, and who'd take care of me ven she was busy with the baby." The boy grinned slyly. "For a man, two vives might be kind of pleasant."

Adrianne considered the grin and the boy's meaning behind it. "There you have it. When you smirk like that, you are thinking like a white man, and white people don't think like Indians. We just make something dirty out of the Indians' way." She caught his head in her hands. "Don't do that, Hermann. If you decide to live among the Kiowas, be an honorable man, respect their ways. If you decide to live among the white men, be an honorable man, there, too."

Chapter Twenty-Two

Satanta saw Eagle Child dancing before the fire. His young body whirled in the dancing light to the drum's steady beat. *Whap! whap! whap!* the honor beats struck the head. *"Ya hay lay hay . . . ,"* the voice of the lead drummer sang out vocables as he began the tail, the final phrase of the song. The second and other drummers followed him — *"Way yo hay lay o-oym. . . ." Whap!* When the drum stopped abruptly at the end, the young dancer immediately ended his steps. It was not Eagle Child, but another Kiowa son. Satanta rose, swayed groggily, and headed back toward the white trader's wagon.

The Kiowa picked up the heavy jug and lifted it again to his lips, greedily filling his mouth with the liquid fire. Satanta swayed.

"Why don't you eat something, sleep, and go home? You have been drinking for three days," observed the fearful trader.

Satanta caught the little white man by the throat, staggered, but drew the man to his face. "I decide when I go home, you stupid white maggot." Satanta's knees suddenly gave.

José caught and held him. The gentle Mexican captive helped the Kiowa to his horse. He took Satanta's body home, but his soul still wandered in the darkness.

Adrianne sat in the red teepee, listening to the spring rain, watching the big man in his drunken pain. Sweat covered his bronze body. Sitting up, he swore. José helped the women push him carefully back against his bed. He moaned and thrashed. The white woman dodged his outflung arm,

213

caught it, and held it against his body as Woven Blanket gently wiped his face and body. The Kiowa woman sang softly to the man, her beloved warrior, now riding somewhere far away. Tears ran slowly down her cheeks. Satanta passed into a deep unconsciousness. Unable to watch more, Adrianne left them together and returned to her own small lodge. She missed Hermann's stolid snores. He and Feathered Lance were hunting with Satanta's brother. She stripped off her wet clothes and crawled into the soft bed smelling of sweet grass. The rain outside struck the hide teepee, making it a drum pounded by a thousand drummers, a thousand thoughts and memories.

The sky wept with the Kiowas for three days, until finally the sun, *Pahy,* burst out. The prairie grasses split their soaked seed coverings and pushed slender, white tendrils through the black soil, moving silently, inexorably toward the light. The People came forth again, rested and eager for the new world unfolding. The daily tasks commenced again, renewed as the earth itself. The hides of the teepees began to dry and tighten while the women shook out the sleeping robes. Men went out to see the green miracle that had come with the rain and sun. The long day descended softly, and the People sighed deeply, tired by taking in so much life.

Wrapped with his buffalo robe around his naked shoulders, Satanta watched as the herd slowly ate its way across the new grass in the rain-soft meadow. His eyes were on the spotted war pony, but his thoughts were far away. When he became conscious of another presence, Adrianne stood before him with arms crossed.

"Have you come to taunt me? Are you now pleased that my son, too, is dead?" the warrior asked.

Adrianne did not answer, but continued to study him.

"Your son would have killed you in his weakness."

"Would you not rather die than have your son die?" she asked the man.

"A hundred times." Satanta sighed deeply.

"I would rather have died, too."

Satanta looked at the woman, seeing her as he saw himself — a human being, not a valuable prize of war, not white, not even a woman, but a human being like himself.

"But I did not die, could not die," Adrianne continued. "And neither can you, because there are needs greater than our sorrows. We cannot wallow in our grief, Satanta. We must walk across it wiser and stronger. My granddaughters need me. Your family and people need you."

"It was right to kill your son," Satanta maintained.

"It is never right to take a life before it has time to find its truth." Adrianne drew closer to the confused man.

"Must you always contradict me?" protested the Kiowa.

Adrianne leaned over and kissed him very gently.

Satanta tasted the kiss, then reëmphasized: "Must you always contradict me?"

"Shut up!" the woman said softly, as her kisses continued. She slowly worked her way over his face and back to his mouth.

Satanta surrendered. "I don't even care any more, White Woman."

"Of course, you do," Adrianne answered between kisses, Satanta now sharing their warmth. "It is your nature as it is the sun's to be hot and the winter wind's to be cold."

Satanta's enthusiasm was growing. "But perhaps you will be tempered." Satanta held her more tightly, pressed her more ardently.

The woman pulled away.

"Aagh!" The man slumped back against the rock, again thwarted by the woman.

Adrianne offered him her hand. He looked at it and then into her face. She offered again, and he took her hand. She pulled him tightly to her. "I want to love you," she said gently, then grinned, and whispered against his ear, "not educate the children."

Satanta looked about, caught a brief glimpse of one of the herd boys ducking behind a bush. Holding the woman's hand, he walked beside her toward her lodge. As they neared the teepee, a sudden fear swept over Adrianne.

She turned and spoke earnestly to Satanta, warning him away, lest he, too, reject her. "I'm not very good at this."

This time the Kiowa grinned as he wrapped his arm and robe around her shoulders, drawing her to him, kissing the top of her head, then starting her again toward the lodge. He whispered in her ear: "I am."

Chapter Twenty-Three

Among the Kiowas a marriage lodge was often set up away from the main camp in some place of beauty. There the man and woman spent their first days together, apart from the routine of life. There they learned each other and themselves in new ways, ways that no other would ever know or share. There they found their oneness with each other. There they realized their oneness with life, discovering the heights and depths of the Kiowa affirmation.

Behold, I am alive.
Behold, I stand in good relation to the earth
and its living things.
My senses are quickened.
The earth is warm beneath my body
and the body of my beloved.
The earth itself smells fresh and new.
The ant that moves among the blades of grass
is my brother,
perfect as I am perfect, as we are perfect.
Behold, I stand in good relation to the Sacred.
Earth-maker in His wisdom has made everything.
In His creation, everything flows out of His being
so that nothing is separate from Him,
but everything is Him, all is one with Him.
He has made me and my beloved.
Rising from the water, our bodies sparkle
with the water.

Shining beads anoint our bodies.
Cool wetness dances from our lips into our mouths
as they touch.
Streaming water flows down our bodies,
carrying us with itself into the river again.
We are one with the ever-flowing water.
We are one with each other, with everything.
Behold, I stand in good relation with the beautiful.
My beloved is fair.
In her beauty I see all beauty.
All the beauty around her is more beautiful because
she is there.
Was such beauty always there,
but I did not see because I looked with one eye,
incomplete?
Behold, I stand in good relation with you,
my beloved.
There is no separation between us now.
We are one.
I am whole.
You are whole.
Behold, I am alive.
I am more alive than I had ever dreamed.
I am filled with life and joy and oneness with
my beloved, with everything.
Behold, I am alive.

When Satanta and Adrianne returned to the village, they
had changed. The nuptial time had glazed them with softness,
filled their emptiness. Their sorrows had been absorbed in the
affirmation of life. Part of the village again, they went about
the tasks of living, but remained steeped in each other,
stained, etched, incised with the other's soul. Satanta wore

218

Adrianne as he pulled tight the rawhide strips to mend his saddle, as he studied the young colts, as he talked with the men of war and peace. Adrianne wore Satanta as she lifted the broken branches into bundles for the cooking fire, as she sewed bright beads onto soft buckskin, as she thought of Lottie and Millie.

The Kiowas slowly grazed their way over the season and miles. The great clock of the universe ticked away the days. With each sunrise tick, the People knew something was coming soon. The People looked for it with anticipation. And then it came. One morning, when they awoke, the cottonwood had shed its white down. It touched the women's hair and lips as they washed their children beside the running water. The babies' small, unco-ordinated fingers grasped the drifting down. The men reached out and caught it as it floated on the wind. It whispered to the People: the time was near. It was coming. And then, one day as they tended the ponies as usual, they saw what they had not seen that morning or the night before. The white sage reached to the ponies' knees. The People knew the time had come. They packed their camp and began the journey. In four days' travel they reached the Washita. Here on the peninsula — a broad, sweeping bend of the river — was enough grass, water, land, and trees for the assembled bands of the Kiowas and their guests from among the Comanches, Arapahoes, and Cheyennes to sit down together. Three thousand Indians put up their lodges, awaiting the Getting Ready Days of the yearly *Skaw-dow, Kado.*

Among the peoples of the northern plains the summer festival was called the Sun Dance and known for blood and pain. For the Kiowas, it was a different occasion. It was the time of thanksgiving and renewal. They called it *Skaw-dow,* Cliff or Protection, or *Daw-s'tome,* Procession-entering-the-lodge. Each name showed their debt to Earth-maker who saved the Kiowa maidens from the bear by raising the huge monolith,

Devil's Tower, and who gave them the buffalo. Unlike the tribes of the northern plains, the Kiowas practiced no self-torture. Blood during the *Kado* was considered a bad omen. No cuts were made in their flesh. They did not dangle from ropes attached to pins in their bleeding chests. They did not drag buffalo skulls sewn to their back flesh by long ropes. The Kiowas danced. In the fasting and dancing, the Kiowas became travelers with the Sacred.

As the families set up their lodges and made their meals, Adrianne felt the energy of the assembled People. Excitement ran through her as through the rest of the family. The long-anticipated thanksgiving of the People was beginning. Hermann's excitement knew no bounds. The mere visual stimulation of the clothing and colors of the People and their ponies made the little German frantic. He was here and there, all about the village, returning to Adrianne with gestured reports. Where there had once been a few boys to enjoy, now there were a hundred. The woman smiled and laughed joyfully at Hermann's stories, for she, too, was dazzled by the spectacle of the Kiowas.

At sunrise on the first day of the Getting Ready, the *Tai-may* keeper rode throughout the camp with the sacred object tied on his back. The *Tai-may* was an intermediary for the Kiowas. They spoke through it to *Pahy*, the sun, and *Pahy* spoke for them with Earth-maker. They said to *Pahy:*

The Creator above made you for life.
We do not know Him.
We cannot see Him wherever He is.
But you know Him.
Ask Him to give you power for our life.

The holy man admonished the People as he rode about.

He forbade all quarreling and foolish behavior. No raiding parties, he said, could go out. Behind him rode the chief of one of the alternating warrior societies who would keep order during the *Kado*. When the *Tai-may* keeper had spoken his words to all the People, he rode majestically out onto the prairie and made a circle around the entire assemblage as the People watched. Satisfied with his tour, he returned to his lodge, dismounted, and went inside. The ceremonies were officially opened.

Later in the day, after a sweat-lodge purification, two men went out to find the Sacred Tree, a tall, straight cottonwood with a Y-shaped fork. They reported to the *Tai-may* keeper, when their quest was complete. The holy man gave them water for they had fasted until they had found the tree. Then he called the five bands of soldiers — *Kata, Kogui, Kaigwa, Khe-ate,* and *Soy-hay-talpupl:* Biters, Elks, Kiowa Proper, Big Shields, and Black Boys — they were four mounted groups and one group of foot soldiers. He announced finding the Sacred Tree. The foot soldiers remained to guard the camp, while the *Tai-may* keeper led other medicine men and the tribe to the new campsite. The four bands of mounted warriors followed him and behind them came the women and children. Four times the People halted, and all on horseback dismounted while the *Tai-may* keeper smoked his pipe. After the fourth stop, he pointed to the tree. The young men charged it as if it were an enemy. The first four to strike it counted coup. A stake was placed at the site of the new camp. Young men again raced to count coup on it. The rest of the People returned to the assembly camp and quickly packed to move to the medicine lodge circle camp.

The camp police, the Kiowa foot soldiers, then came to supervise the setting up of the new camp. A portal opening was left to the east and a large opening in the very center for the medicine lodge. The five bands of the Kiowas each had a designated location within the great circle. Satanta's new red teepee graced the Elk, or *Kogui*, band, second to the south from the eastern opening. The *Kogui* were the leaders of the war ceremonies. Among them were famous fighters like Satank, Satanta, Kicking Bird, and Big Bow. Behind the *Kogui* were the *Kaigwa*, or Kiowa Proper. This small, prestigious band was the keeper of the sacred idol, the *Tai-may*. In front of the *Kogui*, beside the opening, were the *Kata*, or Biters, with the principal chief of all the bands, Dohasan. The Biters held the hereditary duty to bring in the buffalo for the *Kado*.

The killing of the buffalo bull on the second Getting Ready day required great care. The hunter and his wife from the Biter band went out with two arrows. The man had to place the arrow directly in the animal's heart, so that there was no bleeding from the mouth and nose as from a shot to the lungs. He must chase the buffalo into its death run until it circled and fell, facing the east as the medicine lodge faced the east. With his wife he carefully removed a strip of hide along its back, from the tail to the head. This was rolled up ceremoniously, placed on sage and dried chips, and then on the warrior's horse, facing east. The warrior prayed:

Sun, look at me.
Let our women and children multiply.
Let buffalo cover the earth.
Let sickness disappear.

Two shots, too much blood, were bad signs.

On the third day of the *Kado*, a sham, or laugh, battle was held. The four mounted societies, dressed in war bonnets and eagle feathers and carrying their shields and guns and lances, attacked the Sacred Tree defended by the foot soldiers. The latter were driven away, and the tree taken. The tree then had to be chopped down, a delicate and dangerous task, for it must be done exactly right. A captive woman often did the work so that no real Kiowa would incur the wrath of the Sacred if something went wrong. She cut the tree, removed the side branches, and painted four red stripes at the bottom of the trunk. A selected warrior and the woman he chose pulled the tree back to camp, stopping four times. There the Calf Old Woman Society had prepared a deep hole. The tree was set into it and secured. The altar for the *Kado* was in place.

During the middle of that afternoon, Geese Going Moon and her friends, the elder women of the tribe, the Calf Old Woman Society, held their dance. Adrianne and Woven Blanket shouted encouragement as the women, some in their eighties, formed their circle around their drumming sisters. The old ones danced with their arms around each other, changed directions, and danced some more. After much serious effort, leading to some shortness of breath, they sat down and puffed on the ceremonial Straight Pipe carried about by the *Tai-may* keeper. Thus they ended the third day.

"Get up, Taukoyma," whispered Satanta against Adrianne's ear. "It is time to get the cottonwood. The medicine lodge is laid out today. All the People will go into the woods and bring the trees to build it. Get up, sleepy head."

Emerging from the lodge, the family joined others, old and young, as they marched toward the grove of cottonwood trees. All along the Washita were trees that suited the People's needs. They called this stream Lodge Pole Creek. As the crowd moved along, men pounded rhythmically on hand drums. The bells and rattle-filled turtle shells around the fur-wrapped calves of the men called out with each step. Tinkle cones on the fringes of the women's dresses answered. Women selected the young trees and cut them. Men tossed ropes and tied them to the logs. There was laughter and song as many hands made quick work of dragging the small trees to the great empty area around the Sacred Tree.

Among the trees, when they had left the others behind, Satanta drew Adrianne to him. Holding her, he began to kiss her ardently.

Catching her breath, Adrianne softly sighed. "You taste good." Her lips moved over the man's cheek and ear. "Are you not afraid that we will be seen?" she whispered.

"This is the time for loving." The Kiowa slid her skirt over bare flesh toward her hips. "There are no chaperones here today. All around us there is loving. A man and woman may do as they choose today. I choose to make love to you, here, in this beautiful place." She returned the kisses, responding to his hunger and her own.

Later, hand in hand, Satanta and his woman returned to the tree-cutting. Amidst the music and dancing around them, they helped pull and drag the logs through the camp. Because it was unmanly for a warrior to get down from his horse, Adrianne dropped to the ground and untied the rope. She smiled up at the shining warrior.

During the Getting Ready Days, the People thus in work and play built the great circular lodge for the Four Dancing Days. Seventeen large trees were set in a circle about the central mast. More trees were laid between them and to the center. The men lifted them with strong arms and lashed them together with rawhide ropes to form the framework. Completed, the lodge spanned sixty feet and rose to twenty feet at the great forked center post to which the seventeen main rafters were attached. Leafy branches were laid halfway up the roof beams to create a shade within for the dancers. But the center remained open to the sun and heavens. Outside, the women tied small cottonwood trees in horizontal rows between the supports. The leaves and branches were left on them. Beyond this screen, they set up more small trees in upright positions, forming a forest of green trees and leaves, providing a cool shade for the spectator women and children.

When the building was completed, soldiers of the tribe gamboled about, stripping each other of clothing, wrestling each other to the ground before adjourning to the creek for a bath. In the evening glow, along the gentle bend of the Washita, the People found time for courting and making love. Returning to camp, they feasted with those they had not seen in the many months of their sojourn upon the plains.

The People strolled about the streets of the village. Adrianne walked with Woven Blanket and the Sisters and the little girls as they visited their friends among the assembled bands. Everywhere among the throng of Kiowas and their friends she looked for Lottie and Millie as she had during the winter and summer travel. There were other captives — children and women. Some were well off. Some lived in utter misery, misused by their cruel masters or their own thoughts.

Satanta's women went to Fat Goose's camp to see a little girl that Flies Far had heard about. Adrianne guarded her heart, wanting the child to be Lottie, fearing the child would not be. The child that hid behind the large Kiowa woman was not the fair, blue-eyed child that Adrianne sought, but she was gentle and loving, unharmed by her captors. The white woman held the little girl, talking to her in the English that was growing strange to both their ears.

"What is your name?" the woman asked.

"Mahala," said the child.

"That's a pretty name." Adrianne stroked the tiny hand, turning it to see the palm. "Do you remember your last

225

name?" The child shook her head. Adrianne kissed her forehead, and she ran off to play with Satanta's daughters, showing them a new doll Fat Goose had given her. That night, beside Satanta, she thought of the white child becoming Indian, of her granddaughters becoming Indian, of herself becoming Indian.

The howling of the Mud Heads, men with mud-smeared buckskin bags over their heads, alerted the People that the time for the Going In Procession was at hand. The disguised men ran through the village. Anything left in the open, they could take. Sometimes an old woman jerked something away from them as they attempted to snatch it. Sometimes they played rough games or imitated members of the band. Before Satanta's lodge a pair of the tricksters grasped each other and kissed fervently through their muddy masks. The large Kiowa laughed as Adrianne blushed crimson, realizing the very public knowledge of their love. The Mud Heads quickly ran on to perform other scenarios, stealing anything left about, ensuring the wide circle around the medicine lodge was clean.

The Going In Procession was the event which gave the name to the Kiowa summer festival. It was a recreation of the buffalo hunt before the People had horses. Rich in symbolism, it required the participation of many households since many buffaloes were required for the procession. Adrianne and Woven Blanket fitted buffalo calf robes over Feathered Lance and Hermann. The boys, as members of the Rabbit Society, were part of the herd that would be driven into the medicine lodge. Throughout the *Kado* they would also carry the Washita's white sand to cover the floor of the medicine lodge.

"Do I really look like a buffalo calf?" asked Hermann, whose freckled face was blacked with charcoal.

"Of course, you do," Adrianne said, tying his chin strap. "Never saw a better-looking buffalo."

"Shoot!" muttered Hermann, turning a bright red beneath his paint. He and Feathered Lance flashed on the same idea at once. They butted heads, then staggered slightly with the pain and impact.

"You two," Woven Blanket said, catching the boys by their arms. "You watch what is going on. You may be little bulls when you are on the hill" — the boys giggled — "but, when you get into the lodge, you must not be foolish or interfere with the men. Do what those around you do." She smiled at the faces half hidden below the shaggy skins. "Go now, little buffaloes." The boys streaked away, kicking and pawing, butting each other and the other boys they met.

The women watched them go. "Let us eat something," said Woven Blanket. "This is a long ceremony." They stooped under the raised sides of the red teepee and sat down before the simmering kettle. The Kiowa woman handed Adrianne a food bowl and began to fill her own. Adrianne looked into the bubbling broth, caught the rich, sweet smell rising in its steam. She quickly covered her mouth and left the lodge.

Woven Blanket found her leaning against a small tree, the back of her hand against her mouth. She cocked her head, studying the white, bewildered face. Then, a smile of realization broke over Woven Blanket's gentle face. *"Aiiyy!"* She went to Adrianne and placed her hand over the white woman's stomach. *"Haw?* Yes?"

Adrianne smiled, softly placing her hand over Woven Blanket's. "Yes," she whispered, nodding.

"Does Satanta know?" asked Woven Blanket.

"How could he?" asked Adrianne. "I just found out myself."

The women laughed, hugging each other.

Woven Blanket sang as they returned, arm in arm, to the teepee.

227

There is a baby coming.
It is swimming in the water.
It is just like a little rabbit.
He's got little rabbit feet.

They finished the preparation for Satanta's guests who were expected after the Going In Ceremony, then the women went to dress. Flies Far and Looking Glass already had the little girls bathed and combed and dressed. Each woman was beautifully clothed in white, fringed buckskin. A cacophony of ornaments hung from their belts and necks and ears. Over their arms they carried folded shawls. The cone-wrapped fringes of their beaded clothing danced with every movement, making a faint music. The Sisters went away with the children, allowing the other women their time of preparation. No one had seen Geese Going Moon for some time as she was busy visiting and maintaining the functions of the Calf Old Woman Society. Throughout the enormous village, every household was in the same stages of putting on their finest clothing for the Going In Procession.

Satanta, magnificent in painted shirt and war bonnet, entered Adrianne's small lodge. "No one ever knocks here," she said, slightly flustered by her complete undress.

Satanta pulled away the dress she held modestly against her. "Ummh," he approved as his eyes ran over her. "I should have arrived earlier."

"But you didn't," she lightly taunted, raising her arms and dropping the soft buckskin dress over her nakedness. The garment fell midway over her calves, covering her high-topped moccasins.

The man reached out, caught her, and kissed her. "One kiss for the Mud Heads," he said as he took the big silver concho belt and fitted it around her waist, drawing her in for another kiss. The belt's ornate drag reached down her right side to the beaded scallops above the deeply fringed hem. He straightened it, gently stroking her body. He sighed. "I am part of the ceremonies, and we have guests tonight, so I will not see you until very late. Poor Satanta."

"Poor, indeed," grinned Adrianne, turning about, arms outstretched to display the fringe for him to see.

Emerging from their lodges, a growing throng of the People followed the processional led by a dozen warriors to the lodge. These men, including Satanta, were brightly painted, dressed in their long shirts and blue breechcloths without leggings. The senior men wore full war bonnets, trailing long, feathered streamers behind. Some of the headdresses had buffalo horns attached. The men were armed with lances and revolvers and ornamented shields. Before them were carried feathered poles, one white, one black. They took up their positions on either side of the lodge door. The musicians stood behind them. Geese Going Moon and the other old women sent up a great cry. The drums and singing started, and the group of warriors began to dance. Adrianne's eyes followed the masculine strength and grace of Satanta.

Slowly the chosen men advanced toward the great center tree. The musicians followed, some beating on a dried sheet of rawhide, others on drums. They shook rattles and, with the women, sang in time with the drums. When the dancing men had nearly reached the sacred pole, they retreated backward, then advanced again, then back again until they were nearly upon the crowd. They drew their revolvers and fired them into the air. The women rushed forward with a shriek and threw their blankets violently upon the ground at the feet of the retreating dancers. Immediately, with the same kind of shriek, they snatched up the blankets and retired, ending this part of the opening ceremony.

Within the camp circle a selected man, called for the occasion The Man Who Drives The Buffalo, emerged from his lodge and entered the medicine lodge. In his left hand was a bow and quiver of arrows, in his right a smoking brand. Inside the lodge, he conferred with the *Tai-may* keeper. Finally The Man Who Drives the Buffalo trotted out to the windward of the grazing herd of one woman and fifty men and boys, including young Hermann Kaltwasser and Feathered Lance, assembled in their buffalo robes on a small hill. Most, tired out from their play, lay resting, but, smelling the smoke, they rose and began to run from him. Now in the doorway of the medicine lodge stood the *Tai-may* keeper. In front of him, a third man, an old Buffalo Medicine Cult Man acting as The Man Who Brings The Buffalo, raised the great Straight Pipe. Four times he pointed the pipe at the confused herd with his left hand. Lowering it, four times he returned to the lodge door. He puffed four times on the pipe, blowing the smoke to the four directions, the earth, and the sky.

Woven Blanket held Adrianne's arm as the old man prayed. She whispered his prayer for the white woman to understand.

O Dom-oye-alm-daw-k'hee, **Creator of the earth,**
Bless my prayer and heal our land,
Increase our food, the buffalo power,
Multiply our people, prolong their lives on earth,
Protect us from troubles and sickness,
That happiness and joy may be ours in life.
The life that we live is so uncertain,
Consider my supplications with kindness,
For I talk to you as one yet living for my people.

At the final signal of The Man Who Brings The Buffalo, standing at the left of the lodge door, the *Tai-may* keeper went inside, and the Kiowa buffaloes came in from the prairie. They came slowly to the ceremonial lodge, imitating the great woolly beasts to whom they owed thanksgiving. Behind, trailed an old scraggly buffalo, falling down and getting up, reeling in his great age, making the children and women laugh. The buffalo circled the lodge four times, at last finding the entry. The crowd who had watched near the edge of the teepee circle ran with a shout. Looking through the walls, they saw the buffaloes circle the altar four times and lie down, huddled together. Collapsed in comic display near the door lay the frayed old buffalo clown. The Man Who Brings The Buffalo, his body painted white and wearing a buffalo robe and shaggy, horned headdress, approached the herd.

Two old men walked with him through the animals, inspecting them, punching them, talking to them. They searched under the robes until they found a warrior who had counted many coups. They loudly called his name as The Man Who Brings The Buffalo touched him with the Straight Pipe. A huge, uvulating shout went up from the women as the deeds of the brave men were extolled. The inspection of the herd continued until four brave men were honored. Finally, The Man Who Brings The Buffalo brought his hands down, ending the ceremony.

The women and children went with their men to wait for sundown. Inside the lodge, the *Tai-may* was carefully taken from its wrappings and decorated for the celebration. The lodge was decorated, and the eight *Tai-may* shields hung above the cedar screen at the west end of the lodge. Cedar, evergreen like the white sage, was considered sacred by the Kiowas and used for prayers and blessings in their homes and on religious occasions. Finally, the *Tai-may* keeper and his assistants emerged just at sunset and circled the lodge with the covered *Tai-may* lifted high on a pole before them. On the final circle, he held the image aloft as the People sang four songs. Then he entered the lodge and placed the *Tai-may* to the left of the Sacred Tree altar, before the cedar screen.

Peering through the revealing wall of branches at the side of the lodge, Adrianne saw that the interior was now transformed. Cedar smoke rose from incense burners fashioned in the white sand carried into the lodge by the Calf Old Woman Society and the little boys' group, the Rabbit Society. Throughout the four days of dancing, these two groups, one the youngest, the other the oldest, would maintain the sand, smoothing and cleaning it each day.

Beside the screen was propped a buffalo skull painted red down one side and black down the other. "The red represents old age," Woven Blanket explained. "The black means success in war."

Adrianne's eyes traveled to the Sacred Tree in the center. A tapering mound of sand had been fashioned around the high altar. The skins of many buffalo calves appeared to be trying to crawl up the tree. In the fork, the buffalo skin taken by the Biters had been draped over a bundle of cottonwood limbs to form an effigy buffalo that faced the east. In the branches above the fork hung strips of cloth, scarves, shawls, and feathers, blowing brightly in the prairie breeze. As the women watched, the procession of men entered who would attempt to fast and dance for the next four days. Ten drummers beside the lodge door began to pound the three-foot drum, the Voice of Thunder. Beside them a small fire burned to tighten the drum head as the nights and days bore on.

"Very few of the men will last the four days," Woven Blanket said to Adrianne as they went back to the red teepee to await their guests. "Most are not able to endure."

"Why do they try it in the first place?" asked Adrianne, brushing a leaf from Speckled Light's hair.

"Oh, they are praying for their families, for health, for children. Many sick children have been healed when they are prayed for in the medicine lodge. Sometimes, even touching the center tree brings healing. The men also ask for success in war and make vows that they will keep in the coming year. On the last day of the dancing, many things will be hung and piled about the tree as offerings. They will return great blessings on their owners."

The four women of Satanta's household busily served Satanta's guests as the important men settled in for their feast. Adrianne had become very careful about looking at any man, except Satanta, since the incident with Bill Cox. Eyes down, she offered a platter of food to the visiting Comanche chief, Silver Broach. The old man caught her wrist, and her blue eyes darted up. He held her tightly, moving her arm back and forth. "Satanta," he said to his host, "a white woman such as this one is worth more than fifty horses, and" — the old chief smiled — "much easier to handle at my age."

"She is my woman," Satanta said abruptly. "I do not intend to sell this woman."

The old man scrutinized Adrianne's face. "I have seen these eyes before."

"Many whites have blue eyes," noted Satanta.

"No." Silver Broach continued to hold Adrianne's wrist. "These eyes. I have seen these eyes before. Where?" The Comanche thought. "The child! The white girl I took to the agency at Council Grove had these same eyes."

Adrianne's heart hesitated, then raced. She looked at Satanta, afraid to speak to the old Comanche herself. Satanta saw the look, but smoothed his shirt casually. "How old was this child, Silver Broach?"

The Comanche considered. "It is hard to tell with white children. They are sometimes bigger than our children at the same age. I would say four or five winter counts."

"How did you come to have her?"

"I traded three blankets and some food to a Cheyenne for the child. But Long Beard Leavenworth at the agency gave me much more. Returning captives makes the white people happy, because they get back their children. They do not want to fight us so much. When we capture their children, it really stirs them up. We should think about that," Silver Broach explained to the other men seated around the fire. "Milky Way has convinced me of the desirability of returning captives. I take Long Beard Leavenworth all the children I can find as I go about, children like that white boy you have in your household, Satanta. He is worth a great deal both in goods and good feelings. Is this woman his mother?"

Satanta shook his head. "The white boy belongs to my woman. If she wants to sell him, she can. That is up to her."

"Pretty one," the old Comanche asked Adrianne in Spanish, "will you sell the boy?"

Adrianne answered the old Comanche by shaking her head. "Does he know the white girl's name?" she whispered, touching Satanta's knee.

"What was the white girl called, Silver Broach?" asked the Kiowa.

The Comanche thought for several moments. "I remember the name because it described her. Her name was Sky Living In Her Eyes."

Adrianne sat back on her heels, looking directly at Satanta.

"You took her to the Kaw Agency?" the warrior asked, watching his woman's face.

"That is right. She is at Council Grove. They are going to return her to her mother in Texas."

The men talked late into the night as the drums continued their insistent rhythm in the medicine lodge. Adrianne lay without sleep upon her bed. Her hand caressed the little Kiowa growing within her, feeling that he, too, was dancing to the music of his people. Her own thoughts danced about the old Comanche's words and their meaning for her, for Satanta. At last, unable to sleep and tired of the tumbled bedding, Adrianne drew her robe about her and walked to the pony herd. From the bluff, she could see the peaceful animals grazing in the wide bend of the river. The moonlight coated them with a silver translucence changing them into magical beasts. Small, golden fires sparkled here and there where the herd boys kept their vigil. The loveliness and serenity of the night and the herd did not quiet Adrianne's soul, but added to its torment. She was overwhelmed with the feeling that all the loveliness of her life with the Kiowas was dying, fading from her eyes as the herd in the moonlight.

Satanta stepped up, unnoticed, beside her. Comfortably, familiarly, he kissed her neck where it joined the shoulder and let his hand caress her body. She turned to him, trying to read his face. Satanta did not want to be read. He wanted to be loved. She surrendered herself to him, but could not stop the dreaded words that escaped her lips: "I have to go back."

He embraced her more tightly. "I will not let you go, Taukoyma. You are my woman, now."

"I must go back. There is no one there for Lottie. She is alone."

Satanta kissed away the words.

Adrianne struggled to say: "Satanta, listen."

But her words were lost on the man. "It is too beautiful to talk here. Be quiet now."

Adrianne suddenly clung to him, attempting to forget what must come with the morning, hoping to capture in this brief moment together every year they would not know. Far away the drum's regular rhythm throbbed for the heart split asunder.

Chapter Twenty-Four

A warm light filled the teepee with morning. "You once said you would let me go," Adrianne whispered as she lay in Satanta's arms.

"I did not love you, then," the man said.

"If you love me, you must let me go." The woman rolled against his chest to look into his face.

Satanta avoided her eyes. "Do not talk to me of this, woman. I will not let you go. Are you not happy with me? Have I not treated you better than any white man?"

Adrianne rested her cheek against his scarred chest. "Yes. You know that. But I cannot leave Lottie alone." The woman's words were soft, but full of decision. She said nothing more as the Indian studied her.

"Are you thinking of going away against my will?"

"Maybe."

"I will come after you, and I will find you, and I will bring you back to the Kiowas."

The woman's head came up defiantly. The blue eyes flashed. "You may try, sir." She pulled the blanket over her nakedness and rolled away from Satanta.

"How would you get to Council Grove?" The Kiowa rose onto his elbows.

"Any way I could. Maybe Silver Broach would take me there."

"He knows I would kill him," Satanta said flatly.

"Must you always threaten to kill someone?" Adrianne rebuked.

236

"I do not threaten," Satanta said simply. "He knows, I will kill him. You know, I will kill him."

Adrianne considered the Kiowa's words. "Then I would get there another way, but I'm going."

"We have been through this before, have you forgotten?" asked the man, catching her arm harshly.

"I have forgotten nothing . . . not you, not Lottie. I am torn in two."

The pain in Adrianne's soft words cut Satanta like a lash. He rubbed his face. "Perhaps I can get her back."

"How?"

"I got you, didn't I?" Satanta smiled.

"You don't know where she is. She may not be at the agency. She may be in some Texas orphanage, or somewhere else. Can you ride into the agency and say . . . 'Hello, folks, I'm the bloodthirsty Kiowa who killed many people on the Brazos and stole a white child. Now I've misplaced her, and I want her back, so I can get her grandmother off my back'? Good God, they'd kill you on the spot and maybe hit this village like the plague, trying to find me."

"You are still not pleasant in the morning, Taukoyma." Satanta put on his clothing and left the lodge.

After he had gone, Adrianne dressed and began to put the lodge in order. Satanta returned with a bowl of mush and waved it under her nose as she worked on the bed.

"Here. Things will look better after you have eaten."

Adrianne gagged and turned away from the offending smell.

"Are you sick?" Satanta asked gently.

"I'm pregnant." Adrianne turned to the man with tears running from her eyes.

Setting the bowl aside, he drew her to him and kissed the wetness from her cheeks. "Do you cry because you do not want my child?"

"No," moaned Adrianne. "I want your baby as I want life."

Satanta held her, gently rubbing her arm. "Can you leave me now, Taukoyma?" His lips brushed the hair above her ear. "I do not think so." He rocked her softly in his arms.

"And Lottie, what of Lottie?" Adrianne sighed in her pain.

"The *Kado* is nearly over," Satanta said. "Many raiding parties will go out from here. I will be going away soon. It may be that José and I can find a way to bring Lottie to you."

Kneeling before him, Adrianne caught his face with her hands. "The soldiers will kill you."

"The soldiers will never know I am around. They are blind and deaf and dumb."

"They found the Cheyennes at Sand Creek."

"They found them because the Cheyennes told them where they were sitting down."

Adrianne stood back. "But they found them, Satanta. Do you remember when you came to me at Sand Creek on the hill above the village?"

The man nodded.

"I was holding a dead child . . . it could have been Lottie or Millie or the child I carry now . . . your child. I don't want that, not ever again, not for another woman's child, not for mine. Can you promise me that? Can you promise me I will never again hold a dead child?"

"You are a warrior's wife, Taukoyma. You share my life. If we die, we will die well. Would you have us grovel before our inevitable deaths? It is our way not to fear death, but to defy it. Ask Woven Blanket if this is not so."

"I think Woven Blanket would rather have her son alive

238

than wasted in a futile fight against an unbeatable enemy." Adrianne spoke softly.

"No enemy is unbeatable," Satanta reflected. "The white man is as vulnerable as any man."

"You may pick off settlers and ranchers, here and there, Satanta, but you cannot stop this tide of determined men bent on opening a country, fulfilling a destiny they believe is theirs."

"Taukoyma, you worry too much," the Kiowa observed. "Kicking Bird and many others believe, as you believe, but what is our choice . . . fight, or lie down and die on a reservation?" He came closer and stroked her hair thoughtfully. "There may be a third choice. I have been thinking of it often since Sand Creek. Good Indians are soon overlooked or killed. Bad Indians are respected and given gifts. If we appear a worthy enemy, the white man is more likely to negotiate with us in ways we can accept. We must be like a difficult woman who appears desirable and wants a union but does not reveal it quickly. If she concedes too soon, she will lose both her honor and the advantages in her marriage."

"I hope you are better at *negotiating* than I have been," Adrianne muttered under her breath.

Satanta looked down at her. "Oh, I don't know," he said. "You held me off pretty well until you had my heart and all that went with it."

Adrianne sighed. "It's a dangerous game you plan, Satanta."

As the *Kado* ended, the ban on raiding was lifted. Every year, following the festival, many war parties went out. The warriors danced the *P'-haw-goon*, the Buffalo Dance, their war dance, claiming the mighty power and strength of the buffalo for their own. In the eerie light of the fire, the drummers sang as the men danced in mock combat with their enemies.

O, Great Father, give me power over my enemies.
Make them blind that I may kill them.
Help me to steal good horses.
Give me health and a long life.

Watching with the other women whose bodies moved softly, almost imperceptibly, with the rhythm, Adrianne shivered. She pulled her blanket shawl more tightly about her and studied the ground, unable to look at the whirling scene before her. In the fire amid the frenzied faces she saw again her burning home, the men wildly looting it, the screams of the children, Susan, lying dead, stripped and scalped, in the yard.

The murmur that came from Woven Blanket's throat made her look up. A man had entered the circle. His face was painted black across the eyes. Black streaks ran down his torso, arms, and thighs. His hands and arms to the elbows and his legs to the knees were also black. Twisting and turning, raising his shield against unseen enemies, thrusting with his lance, he danced and sang.

It was Satanta as Adrianne had first seen him on the Brazos, painted and sinister, an alien being, taking what he wanted.

Woven Blanket whispered the words of his song:

There will be a time,
When my body will be somewhere.
No matter where my enemies may destroy me,
Do not mourn for me,
Because I will not be alive to know it.
There will be a time,
When my body will lie somewhere on a battlefield,
And the wolves shall devour me.
But do not mourn for me,
Because I will not be alive to know it.

240

"Satanta has made his song. He is going away tonight," Woven Blanket said and ducked her head to hide the tears glistening in her black eyes. The Sisters, also, seemed sad as the man concluded his dance. Their children looked up into their faces at the strangeness in their touch.

"Is he saying he will seek to be killed?" asked Adrianne, knowing that many times Kiowa and Comanche men made vows to die in combat rather than live in dishonor or infirmity.

"He is saying he is a man," answered Woven Blanket. "A man does not quake before his death. We are born dead. Death takes us all. We cannot control that, but we can control our fear of death and its power through courage. Choose courage, not fear. That is what Satanta is saying."

"Do you believe that?"

A slight frown came to Woven Blanket's smooth face. "I believe I cannot stop death."

Adrianne stared at the ground.

"And neither can you, Taukoyma."

The white woman crossed her arms tightly over her body, her unborn child. "I believe I must try."

After Satanta and the raiders left the bend of the Washita, the family groups moved onto the plains, migrating along unseen paths in harmony with time and the land and their needs. There was a gentle rest for the People, traveling over the lush grass. Their horses became sleek and fat on the bounty. They themselves ate well from the land and the animals they hunted. They found water and sat down to await the return of the men, to await the fall hunts when the buffalo must be found and killed for winter food and robes.

Woven Blanket opened one hand slowly before Adrianne and Hermann. Inside were the wide, flat seeds of gourds. "I have saved these," the Indian woman said. "If Satanta saw

241

them, he would laugh. He thinks I am silly to want to plant seeds. He says we do not plant. We are Kiowas."

Adrianne raked the dried seeds from the Indian woman's hand into her own. "I am a white person. I can plant," she said. "In fact, Woven Blanket, I will give you a key to the white world as old as anyone can remember. Come on. Hermann, get something to dig with."

The boy shot off as the women walked together toward a clearing in the trees.

"This seed seems dead and lifeless" — Adrianne took a single seed from her hand and held it up as they walked — "but inside it is life, waiting to express itself. If we place it in the earth, if it fall on fertile ground, the life in the earth will go to work on it. It will destroy this dead, dry husk just as it rots a fence post, and life will touch life. The seed will grow into a plant much greater than the seed, bearing far more than the tiny germ we put into the earth. Whatever is in that seed, food or flowers, corn or buffalo grass, will come up. This is a principle of the earth . . . planting and reaping, seed time and harvest, inexorable life even in apparent death."

"Yes," agreed Woven Blanket. "It is so."

"The other night you said neither of us could stop death. But life cannot be stopped, either, Woven Blanket. And, I guess, as seed sowers, white men have believed in nurturing life until it bears fruit just as the Kiowas believe in the power of men to look death in the eye and refuse to be afraid. The visions are different, but there is truth in each."

Hermann reappeared with the broken head from a hoe that a Kiowa at some time had set aside to make arrow points or to scrape hides but had finally discarded in the village garbage heap.

"Dig right in here, Hermann," Adrianne recommended as she squinted, studying the light, shading her eyes with her

242

hand. "This spot will catch the morning sun, Woven Blanket. If we plant the seeds here, next summer, after the *Kado,* when you come again to this place, maybe you will find gourds ready to pick and use."

Hermann worked on his hands and knees, discarding the worthless hoe for the crude knife he wore at his side, ripping away the grass with the other hand, creating a neat, clear circle, deep and loose enough for the seed bed.

"We can put in a couple more hills down here," Adrianne suggested.

"I saw some dead minnows floating on the creek," Hermann said as he wiped the sweat from his brow.

"Good." The white woman fell in with his plan. "Get them, while I dig."

She dug with the boy's knife, as Woven Blanket sat beside her. "You said, when *you* come back next summer, not when *we* come back," said Woven Blanket.

Adrianne stopped digging and looked up into her friend's face. "A sower sows, believing that the seed will come up, believing he will reap the fruit. He doesn't know."

She and the Kiowa woman used their hands to push the loose dirt into little hillocks. Hermann scooted in beside them with the foul-smelling fish glistening in his wet hands. Adrianne scraped aside a shallow in the dirt, and the boy placed the fish.

"Whew, Hermann!" Adrianne gasped as the odor wafted into her nostrils. Looking up she said to Woven Blanket: "The seeds."

Woven Blanket gently laid a half dozen of the seeds among the decaying minnows. The three then pushed the dirt together over the planting and patted it down. They laughed at their earnest efforts and moved on to plant another mound of gourds.

"Soldiers!" screamed Feathered Lance as he ran toward them. "Soldiers!" Behind him ran the little children of Satanta's household and the Sisters. "Get away! Get away!"

Adrianne saw him stop, glancing over his shoulder, while letting the others pass by him, putting his young body between the women and danger. The other children ran on like quail chicks, scattering before a predator. The smallest girl crashed into Adrianne and leaped into her arms. Woven Blanket quickly gathered the others and bent over, trying to quiet them, comfort them.

"Just hold it right there!" The voice was harsh, coming from somewhere in the shadows.

Feathered Lance darted at the man emerging from the trees. The soldier hit him hard with the butt of his rifle. Flipping his weapon instantly, he trained the long gun on the boy, but he lay unconscious. The boy did not move when the soldier kicked him with his boot. Hermann wanted to aid his friend, but Adrianne held him back.

Moving toward them slowly, with the rifle on them, the soldier snarled: "You and the white boy get away from them god-damn' Injuns."

Adrianne did not move away, but turned, carefully handing the child she held to Flies Far. Slowly she stepped in front of the gun, casually sheltering Woven Blanket and the others with her own body. "Put your rifle down, soldier."

"Not likely in this nest of vermin." The man shot a stream of tobacco juice into the fresh dirt hilled over the gourd seeds.

"You are scaring the children," Adrianne said calmly. "Put down the rifle."

"Them squaws has knifes," the man answered, moving forward.

"So do I." Adrianne adjusted the weapon on her hip. "But

244

it's not likely that any of us could reach you before you kill us dead, is it?"

Feathered Lance moaned in the grass. Woven Blanket started toward him.

The soldier fired. "Shit!" he swore as the Kiowa woman fell and struggled on the ground under his sights.

Now Adrianne was running. Hermann was running with her. They both flew into the distracted man, knocking him to the ground, fighting him for the weapon. Even as they struggled, Adrianne brought the knife up under his chin, driving the sharp point into the whiskered skin. The smell of him was strong in her nostrils, as she said: "Put the rifle down, soldier."

He released it into Hermann's determined grip. The boy jerked it away mightily.

"Get up, god damn it. Cover him, Hermann."

The man crawled slowly to his feet.

"If you twitch, I'll cut your heart out," Adrianne swore to him as she backed away toward Woven Blanket. "Put your hands on top of your head."

The man complied, and she knelt beside the woman. Adrianne's eyes ran quickly over Woven Blanket. The Kiowa woman lifted her hand, revealing the wound. Adrianne exhaled quickly and offered a small smile. "It's not bad," she said in Kiowa. Lifting the woman gently toward her to see the exit wound, she said: "It went all the way through your shoulder. You won't even need Buffalo Medicine."

More soldiers broke through the trees along the water. The prisoner jerked his rifle from Hermann's hands. "Get your asses over there," the man growled, and gestured to the women.

Hermann studied the man, then walked deliberately away toward Feathered Lance, who was trying to sit up.

"You little son-of-a-bitch," the man muttered. "Can't you

245

see, I'm trying to save your hide?"

"What's going on here?" a lieutenant, arriving with other soldiers, inquired.

"White woman, sir, and a white boy," the man answered. "They's sidin' in with these god-damn', stinkin' Injuns."

"That'll be enough, Collins . . . quite enough," the officer said more softly, holstering his own drawn weapon. He walked over to Adrianne who was helping Woven Blanket to her feet. "Lieutenant Carter, ma'am, at your service."

Adrianne studied the erect military posture and the young face. "This woman's been shot. And the boy over there was also injured. We'll require the company surgeon." She looked at the other women and children clustered together. The fear born at Sand Creek was in their eyes. She followed their terror to the line of armed men. "It's foolish to go on terrifying these women and children. You can see there are no men in the village, only boys and grandfathers. No one here can hurt you. Please have your men lower their weapons, Lieutenant."

The man barked an order to his sergeant, and the weapons came down to a ready, but discreet, attitude.

"Thank you," whispered Adrianne. She gestured for the Kiowa women and children to come to her side, and, assisting Woven Blanket and Feathered Lance, they went back toward the camp.

Colonel Jesse Leavenworth stood beside Old Man Red Teepee, Satanta's father, with his interpreter, Mr. Jones. He appraised the little party trickling down the creekbank and across the shallow water. He smiled. He would get his captives here. Throughout the summer, the agent had ridden about, scouring the Indian camps in an effort to recover as many of the captives as he could find. Most had been taken the previous summer and fall, following the Cheyennes' outbreak. He was convinced that returning the captives, thus showing the white populace the Indians' willingness to co-operate, would help prevent further bloodshed. Leavenworth realized that he had to control the whites' perceptions as well as the wild tribes' actions. He had already negotiated with the Indians, including Satank, to his satisfaction. This last loop through the plains of Kansas would net him the final captives for the season. He could then turn his thoughts to sending them home.

Adrianne watched as the company surgeon began his work on the wounded Kiowas. Satisfied, she left Hermann with them and let Lieutenant Carter take her to Leavenworth, Superintendent of the Indians of the Upper Arkansas.

The agent noted the woman's Indian clothing and erect bearing as they crossed toward him. He thought to himself — *Nice looking woman* — then caught himself — *but unsuitable now, morally degraded.*

"You are safe, now," the colonel informed the woman. To his amazement, she did not fall on his neck with tears of gratitude. Leavenworth attributed her restraint to the presence of the Indians who, he assumed, had beaten her into submission. The scar on her cheek showed that she had undergone a harsh servitude. The man also figured she was too ashamed of whoring with the Kiowas to look a white man in the eye. He had seen it before. This one, like most of the other women he'd found, was pregnant. The Kiowa men wasted no time. The agent glanced at the soldiers around the periphery of the camp. He knew the lascivious thoughts in their minds as they considered this woman, as they jested about her, some other poor bastard's wife or sister. She'd end up in a saloon, catering to their lust and contempt, if her husband wouldn't have her back. Pity, but true. "What's your name, ma'am?"

"Chastain," Adrianne answered, looking directly, almost defiantly, into his eyes.

"Very well, Missus Chastain. If you have any possessions, get them now. We need to pull out and put some distance between us and this village before nightfall."

"What if I want to stay?" the woman asked.

"You do not have to be afraid of the Indians, Missus Chastain. If I so much as suspect they are holding you by threats or coercion, I have the authority, and the will, to destroy this entire village."

"But if it is my desire to stay . . . my wish?" Adrianne tried again.

"I can't let you do that, Missus Chastain. You are white. It is my job . . . these troopers' job . . . to return all white prisoners like you and the boy. Surely, you can't want him to grow up a savage, separated from his own family forever."

"No." Adrianne looked at the ground. "No, I don't want Hermann to be separated from his family. But me . . . I'd like to stay, if you can help me get my granddaughter, Lottie Doogan, back from the Kaw Agency. Silver Broach brought her in."

"What you do after I take you in and clear up the records, I do not care. But, raise a little white girl as a Kiowa, ma'am? I don't think so. In five . . . at most ten years . . . these people will all be dead or on a reservation. If you think anything of the child, you wouldn't put her through what's coming. If you care anything for these people, you wouldn't want them to be caught with a white woman and child in their camp, when the trouble starts. And you, Missus Chastain, you don't have to be ashamed to go back, ma'am. There are lots of white women like you. I've brought them in myself. There are naturally problems. . . ." Leavenworth's glance fell to her waist. "But the Quakers at Council Grove will assist you in putting your life back together. Besides, ma'am, your husband and children love you and need you . . . in spite of everything."

Adrianne's brow knit into a frown as her eyes ran over the now familiar faces of the Kiowas and the strange and hostile faces of the soldiers. "My children?"

"Yes, ma'am. You owe it to your children to go home and make them a life."

"And the Kiowas?"

"The Kiowas will never be able to come after you or harm you again. The Army is turning its full attention to the West, now that the war is over. Returning prisoners, such as yourself, may stop the coming fire for some, but the Indians' old ways are doomed, over, even as we speak. These little children here . . ." — the agent scanned the village circle — "will never know the old free life. It's all over, but the dying. I'm afraid they'll only know fear and starvation, until their elders have the sense to surrender and settle down on the reservations." Leavenworth was assuring the woman who searched his face for the undeniable truth of his words.

"And then what?" Adrianne asked, seeing the Kiowas through her tears, seeing visions of their struggle and suffering and defeat.

"Then, we'll civilize 'em. We'll teach 'em to read and write and to farm and practice trades." Leavenworth warmed to the prospect of progress for the untutored savages and clapped his hands together enthusiastically. "Why, ma'am, we'll make white men out of them."

"In many ways, Colonel Leavenworth," the woman said with tears running down her cheeks, "in *many* ways, that will be a crime and a waste."

"You best get your things, Missus Chastain. It's time to move on," Leavenworth said impatiently.

Adrianne stopped beside Woven Blanket, whose wound had been cleaned and dressed. Even Feathered Lance had a bandage wrapped around his head. Hermann stood behind

249

him with arms crossed, making sure that his friend was well treated by the white men.

"It's time to get your things, Hermann. We are going back," Adrianne said softly. She answered the boy's questioning look with a small smile. "It's time, Hermann."

The boy hesitated, then trotted toward the small, faded red teepee. Adrianne stood looking down at Woven Blanket, then knelt beside her friend. Looking into the Kiowa woman's black eyes, she gently put her hand on her shoulder. Woven Blanket placed her own bloody hand over it. Adrianne started to speak, but stopped, unable to force words through the constriction in her throat. She very gently bent her head forward, touching Woven Blanket's forehead. "You are the sister I never had," she finally managed. "Closer than blood, deep as love. I am going to get Lottie now. I won't be back. I won't be going East. I'll be on the Brazos . . . rebuilding my place. You'll always be welcome there, and safe."

"Missus Chastain, it's time to move on," Lieutenant Carter reminded.

Adrianne obediently went into the red lodge and returned, dressed in her white clothes, torn and tattered, but well-mended. The young officer noted that the boots had originally been expensive. Adrianne now showed no sign of her captivity, except for the white scar that ran down her cheek to her chin and the hair trimmed just above her shoulders. From her ears dangled Mexican silver crosses, and a bright blanket was wrapped over one shoulder and around her waist, concealing the child she carried. Hermann clasped Feathered Lance's hand and forearm and lifted his bundle to move off with Adrianne.

"We have arranged for you to have a horse," Leavenworth said.

Adrianne picked up the reins held by Geese Going Moon.

250

The old Kiowa woman looked into her blue eyes. "I said once you might not have to stay with us too long. I didn't know, then, how much we would go through together, how much I would love you, how much it would hurt an old woman, when you went away."

Adrianne's hand went to the woman's wrinkled cheek. She touched it softly as Geese Going Moon's lips brushed her palm. She then bent and kissed the old one, before mounting quickly, astride, and turning the horse toward the column. Hermann trotted behind on his shaggy pony.

Adrianne came to a stop beside Leavenworth. "Did you pay them for the boy and me?"

"Didn't seem they wanted money," the agent said.

"You have the money?"

The man nodded.

"I'm not going, until you pay them the going rate, Colonel," Adrianne stated.

"They didn't seem to want it," Leavenworth repeated.

"It's theirs to do with as they choose, isn't it?" asked the woman.

"Lieutenant," Leavenworth sighed, "have Mister Jones deliver this to Old Man Red Teepee." He handed a small bag to the young officer.

Adrianne caught Carter's sleeve. "Ask Mister Jones to tell them the money is for the horses you are taking. They may take it for horses."

As the party of soldiers and captives rode out of the village, Old Man Red Teepee tossed the sack of gold coins in the dirt beside the teepee and went inside. When the Kiowa village prepared to move on, away from this place of sadness, the coins still lay untouched, scattered on the ground as the People walked over them while taking down the lodge. When one of the little girls squatted in fascination and picked up some of

251

the glistening gold, Flies Far gently took the coins from her hand and dropped them again on the ground. She dusted the child's fingers as if they had held something dirty. Then, leading the child, she returned to her own work. Even as the last Kiowa travois disappeared in the distance, the prairie wind began to cover the unwanted ransom with the refuse of the village and the eternal red sand of the plains.

Chapter Twenty-Five

"Get quiet back there," Sergeant Henry barked, rising and turning in his stirrups, scrutinizing the men who were making low whistles and calls. "There will be none of that." The men sobered from their open appraisals of the white squaw, but the sergeant could not control their thoughts. "They're a woolly bunch, ma'am," he apologized without enthusiasm.

"Can you keep them off of me?" inquired the woman.

"They are soldiers, ma'am," the sergeant affirmed.

"I saw what the soldiers did to the women and children at Sand Creek," Adrianne said. "I saw one woman split open with her unborn baby lying beside her. The soldiers stretched women's private parts over their saddle cantles and hats."

"*Pfft*. That was Colorado volunteers . . . trash . . . not soldiers." The sergeant rubbed his mouth.

"Can you keep them off of me?" Adrianne asked again. "I can't fight them now. I might lose the child."

Sergeant Henry glanced at the woman's hand, resting over the developing baby. "I'll make a point of it, ma'am. Personally." The sergeant rode silently for several moments, then added: "Might be a mercy, though . . . for you and the kid. A 'breed ain't welcome nowhere, nor his mother. You'll never be able to pass over this Indian shame, dragging a Kiowa kid around with you."

"That is your thought, Sergeant, not mine."

"I stand corrected, Missus Chastain." Sergeant Henry shifted his tobacco, set his stained hat, and followed the woman back toward civilization.

253

The arrival of the two new captives at Council Grove did not lighten the heart of Agent Henry Farnsworth. His hands were already full. He had been given the order to "care for the captives," and he intended to do so. But his quarters were overrun. Besides the Indian children who boarded at the mission school, he now had a growing number of captives. The Kaws, to whom he had been sent, received less of his time than the ever-increasing number of women and children taken from Texas.

Colonel Leavenworth offered his assistance to Mrs. Chastain as she dismounted. She ignored him, but entered the door he swung open before her.

Friend Farnsworth offered his hand and name, then introduced the woman to his wife.

"Missus Chastain has come to get her granddaughter," Leavenworth explained.

For a moment Farnsworth's face lit up at the thought that someone was going to leave.

"Her name is Lottie Doogan. She is just six," Adrianne continued Leavenworth's statement.

A frown clouded the Quaker's plain face. "Lottie Doogan was sent back to Texas."

Adrianne turned to see Leavenworth's face.

"Are you sure?" Leavenworth asked.

"Quite sure," Farnsworth answered. "She is blonde, blue-eyed, about five or six."

"To whom was she sent?" pushed Adrianne.

"Well, she went with a black woman and her children . . . ," explained Farnsworth.

"Mary Johnson," interrupted Adrianne.

"Yes, that's right. I didn't think that was quite appropriate, but the child knew her and her children. The Negro woman said there was a lawyer, Charlie Morehouse, who knew the family's affairs and would take care of things. We had no idea someone would come for her."

Adrianne sat down, suddenly weak, holding onto Hermann's scrawny shoulder.

"Missus Chastain has been among the Indians herself," Leavenworth informed the agent.

Susan Farnsworth, the agent's wife, came quickly to Adrianne's side. "Art thou not well?"

"I'm tired," Adrianne said, touching the beads of sweat that coated her face.

"I will take thee to thy room. I'm afraid that it is very crowded here. It's a small room, and Missus MacFee and her baby already occupy it." The Quaker woman helped her rise. "And thou come, too." She caught Hermann Kaltwasser by the sleeve. "There are several white boys here."

At the door Adrianne turned to the two men — Indian agent and missionary. "When can we leave for Texas?"

The men looked at each other. "We are gathering a group to return to Texas now, Missus Chastain," said Leavenworth. "As soon as the funds arrive, we will start you south. Of course, we will have to wait until you and Missus MacFee are in a condition to travel."

Adrianne and Hermann joined Mrs. Caroline MacFee, her infant, and four nephews in the crowded eight-room stone building of the Kaw Mission. The beds were tumbled and un-made, the floors littered with clothing and refuse. The nearly naked children ran wild. Hermann shoved one as he darted past. Adrianne sat down on a jumbled bed, considering the recent turn of events that once again put Lottie just beyond her reach.

"It ain't too bad here," Caroline MacFee offered. "There's food. It ain't bad, even if a fat-assed Injun woman

255

cooks it. At least, it's a house with a roof and floor, dirty as it is."

Adrianne looked at the refuse-covered floor, then at the other woman. "Whose camp were you in?"

"Satank's, a mean, old, horny bastard. He's the one got me in this state." She glanced at her distended abdomen. "At least, I reckon it was him, but there was plenty of others doin' me, too. Ain't nobody but you and me knows what a woman really goes through among them savages." Caroline MacFee spit out the words so hard she jerked her ample breast from the nursing white infant. "Ain't nobody, and I sure ain't a-tellin' them, neither."

"That baby is white," observed Adrianne.

"Sure she is. I's a-carryin' her, when I was took," said Mrs. MacFee.

"The Kiowas let you keep her?" asked Adrianne softly.

MacFee nodded.

"They say they don't do that. Doesn't seem they were too bad to you."

"Hell, that old man just wanted to keep me wet, so he'd have hisself a cow. Injun don't never do nothin' fer nothin'."

Adrianne sighed, dreading the coarse company that she had joined at the mission. "I guess we'll be going back soon now." She rubbed Hermann's back reassuringly.

"Don't count on it. They're always trying to get money. Besides, I ain't fit to travel, carrying this god-damn' Injun baby. Shit, losin' it wouldn't be no bad deal. But these dainty-assed Quakers is so careful, I could puke." MacFee shifted the baby, exposing her other breast.

Adrianne rose, turned Hermann toward the window, and walked with him to look out through the glass panes. It had started to rain. "I can't hear the rain, Hermann."

"Sometimes a house ain't nearly as friendly as a teepee,"

the child perceived. "You suppose dis rain is vatering the gourd seeds ve planted?"

Adrianne patted his shoulder. "It's said God allows it to rain on the just and the unjust. That pretty well covers it, so I imagine it is raining on those seeds."

"Good, I hope Voven Blanket finds 'em next summer and remembers us." Hermann looked back at the filthy woman on the filthy bed with disgust. "Hell, Injuns don't live like dis."

Adrianne stared at the black sky and sheeting rain. She took a deep breath. "By God, neither do I. Go get a broom, Hermann. We'll need a bucket of hot water, soap, and some rags, too." As the boy left the room, Adrianne began to pick up the mess from the floor. She stripped the bed. "Are there clean sheets?" she asked Caroline MacFee.

"Ain't you delicate for a Kiowa whore?" the woman asked contemptuously.

"I'm not a whore." Adrianne faced the woman, drilling the words into her.

When she turned back to the bed-making, Mrs. MacFee muttered: "You ain't no better'n me. Don't matter what airs you put on, Missus Chastain. Your belly proves you ain't no better'n me."

In a short time Adrianne Chastain had the room in order and had moved on to the littered hallway. With Hermann's help, she corralled the running boys and sat them down to play. The mission was little different from her own inn, although sorely in need of management. When Mr. Farnsworth arrived at his wife's insistence, the change in the upstairs rooms was striking. On the spot Farnsworth offered her three dollars a week to nurse the sick, sew clothing for the nearly naked children, and help cook and care for the growing number of Texas captives. Mrs. Chastain accepted.

Over the weeks Adrianne sewed and scrubbed floors and nursed the sick. She rearranged the upstairs, placing the boys in one room and the small children in another. She still shared quarters with Mrs. MacFee who seemed fascinated by work, but never participated in it. Once when Adrianne was supervising the boys, cutting wood for the small stove upstairs, Mrs. MacFee pointed out that a good limb could be put in the stove or fireplace and shoved in as it burned away over several days. This arrangement required a minimum of effort and was highly economical in terms of time and trips to and fro, cutting and carrying wood.

"And does thou not stumble over the limb protruding from the fire into thy room?" asked Mrs. Farnsworth earnestly.

"Hell, no," said Mrs. MacFee. "You just pick up yer god-damn' feet."

Suddenly Adrianne broke into such laughter that she had to sit on the cutting block. Tears ran from her eyes. Hermann patted her back to aid her spluttering efforts at recovery. Caroline MacFee and Mrs. Farnsworth joined in the laughter, pounding their legs and leaning against the building. When Friend Farnsworth stepped out and looked at them quizzically, his wife shooed him away, still unable to speak. The women returned to the house, wiping their eyes and attempting to display a dignity they did not feel.

The housekeeping tip, however, was not followed by Adrianne, who, according to Caroline MacFee, was just "wearin' herself to a nub." Indeed, Adrianne did work hard, so hard that she would fall asleep immediately when sitting in a chair or when she hit the bed. She did not want to think or dream. The night was a dangerous, unguarded time, when her thoughts could spin away out of control.

"You know," Mrs. MacFee's voice came once across the darkness into Adrianne's departing consciousness, "some of

258

them Kiowa men could work a woman up real good. My old man never done nothing like that. I weren't nothin' more to him than a convenience, like a slop jar in the winter. Fucking me weren't no more to him than takin' a leak or a crap. Yes, sir, some of them Kiowa men could work up a woman real good. I bet that big 'un of yours could do it. Reckon we won't get no more of that."

"Shut up." Adrianne covered her head with the pillow and turned to the wall. "Shut up. Just shut up," she said softly to the darkness.

As the summer slipped into fall, a flurry of official letters flew back and forth to Washington, requesting money for the upkeep of the Texans and money for their transport. Adrianne also began her own campaign. When she could not sleep, she wrote letters. She wrote to Charlie Morehouse, asking where and how Lottie was. She requested that funds be sent immediately to the Kaw Agency for her own passage back to Texas. And she wrote to the family of Hermann Kaltwasser, informing them that their boy was alive and well and being cared for. She wrote that she could not give them a date for his return, but assured them that she would bring him home as soon as her health and other arrangements permitted.

The weather was cold when Wilhelm Kaltwasser arrived at the Kaw Mission. Adrianne saw the tall, angular German from the stairway where she was scrubbing away on the raw boards. Hermann lay on his back, reading aloud, with both feet straight in the air against a wall. "Hermann, do you know that man? Do you think he could be from Washington?" she asked.

The boy righted himself, slowly observing the man shaking hands with Henry Farnsworth. "Papa?" Hermann said to himself in disbelief. He looked at Adrianne. She smiled. "By Gott

259

. . . is Papa! What do I do, Adrianne?" The young German was suddenly shy and cautious.

"Well, you might go down and say hello," the woman said, resting on her heels so that she could see the boy's face. "Or even give him a hug. He's ridden a long way in cold weather to get you and take you home. Your pa sure wasn't trusting luck or waiting till I could get you there. I guess that old German loves you, Hermann."

Throwing the book down, the boy descended the stairs like a tornado and whirled into his father's arms. "Papa, Papa!" the boy said over and over.

The German lifted the boy and walked about with him, holding him, kissing him. "I thought you vas dead, Hermann. Your mama and me, ve thought you vas dead. But you ain't. My boy is alive!"

Adrianne tossed the scrub brush in the bucket of water and wiped her hands on her apron. She came awkwardly down the stairs as Wilhelm Kaltwasser made a turn with Hermann in his arms.

"That's Adrianne, Papa," said the boy.

In two strides the man was across the floor. He set Hermann on his feet and took the scrub bucket from Adrianne's hand. "Missus, you shouldn't carry such a ting."

Adrianne smiled, thinking now even strangers were compelled by her condition.

"Thank you, Mister Kaltwasser."

"Name is Vilhelm." The man offered a hand that swallowed her own and pumped her hand enthusiastically. "You give me back my son, Missus. My vife and I and Hermann, ve is grateful."

"Hermann has been solace and joy to me, Wilhelm. He saved my life as much as I ever saved his. Besides, I don't think the Kiowas were going to kill him."

260

"They's gonna put me out of business pretty damn' fast," Hermann spluttered. "By Gott, Papa, they had their knives out and vas after my pants."

Adrianne looked down with a smile. "It wasn't me that saved him. Satanta bought him from the men who took him." The words came so quickly, so comfortably, to her lips that she heard them as they were spoken. Realizing what she had said, the pain it brought, she turned away from the man and boy.

"Satanta?" asked Wilhelm. "Ain't he a bad Injun?"

Adrianne braced herself and turned back to Wilhelm. "Well, he was not a bad Injun to Hermann and me. If you'll excuse me, I think I saw you were carrying a mailbag. I'm expecting a letter about my granddaughter."

"*Ja*," Wilhelm Kaltwasser affirmed. "A man give me the mail to bring. He vas pretty cold and vanted to git home, instead of comin' out *hier*. I give it to dat Farnsworth."

As Adrianne walked away, she heard Hermann take up the story of their captivity with Satanta. "That's right, Papa," Hermann explained, leading his father. "I lived with Satanta himself and his family. His son, Feathered Lance, vas my friend. I had a horse, and I hunted, and. . . ."

"Anything for me, Mister Farnsworth?" Adrianne asked of the missionary who stood nearby.

Farnsworth drew a letter from the small stack of envelopes. "It's from Texas, Missus Chastain."

Adrianne's hand trembled as she reached for the letter. She took it quickly and opened it as she walked to the stairs. Leaning against the newel, she read:

Dear Madam:
With regard to your letter of the 21st Sept., I am
unable to make a reply at this time. In the interest

of protecting my minor client, I cannot divulge information regarding her whereabouts, and certainly not any money for your travel without proper identification of yourself. It has been reported to us by knowledgeable parties that Mrs. Chastain and her son are both dead, killed by Kiowa Indians. If you continue to pursue this matter without proper identification, I must assume that you are attempting to perpetrate a crime, and I assure you that you will be punished to the full extent of the law, as you deserve.

Sincerely,
Charles Morehouse
Guardian and Administrator

"That snake, that everlasting snake!" Adrianne fumed to herself as she paced. "What are you up to now, Charlie? Why don't you want me in Texas?" She stopped suddenly. "Money, of course. It's always money, isn't it, Charlie? Just a few more days with my money. Oh, I'm going to kick your ass, you thieving son-of. . . ."

"You got bad news, Missus?" Wilhelm asked.

Adrianne was startled by the man's concerned voice. "Well, yes. The man who has my granddaughter and my money refuses to accept me without identification."

"Vot kind of identification?"

"I don't know that . . . a paper, someone who knows me," Adrianne thought aloud.

"Hermann knows you."

For a moment Adrianne brightened. "No," she corrected herself. "Hermann only knows I told him I am Adrianne Chastain. The same is true for Leavenworth and Farnsworth.

262

Charlie Morehouse will never accept that. I have to find someone who knows me from the Brazos and is known to Charlie . . . a neighbor, a friend . . . someone irrefutable, unimpeachable." She sank slowly into a chair. "That could take months. I would have to go home to get any proof at all." She sighed. "So long again. So long without knowing about Lottie."

Adrianne had to make an effort at listening during supper, her thoughts were so far away. Hermann sat very close to his father, eating vigorously as usual, talking continually. Finally, a light filled the boy's eyes. "Papa," he asked, "vas heifer?"

"*Ja, ja,*" his father said of the spotted calf that had kept Hermann remembering his home, had in a way kept him alive.

Adrianne smiled as tears filled her eyes. She wondered if Lottie was old enough to have some remembrance of her, some dream to keep her alive in the cold, dark world of Charlie Morehouse.

Before the man and boy started back for Texas the following morning, Wilhelm Kaltwasser came to thank her. "I vould like to have time to know you better and tank you better, Missus Chastain. But Hermann's mama don't know vot is happening. I don't vant her to have to vorry and vait too long. The sooner ve get home, the sooner she be satisfied."

"I can understand that," Adrianne agreed in her pain at the parting. "I shall miss you, Hermann."

Hermann clung to her, sobbing. "I'll be an honorable man. I vill."

"Of course, you will." Adrianne held the boy away from her to see his face. "Hermann, I'm going back to Texas, too. Not just yet, but soon. I will see you."

The boy wailed and grabbed her again.

"Say, Missus," Wilhelm said, observing the woman's condition, remembering the letter. "You ever need someting, you got friends ven you get to Texas."

"That's a comfort to me," she said, trying not to cry out as the man took Hermann's hand from hers. "God," she gasped as the man and boy walked away down the front steps.

Hermann looked back as he rode out of the yard on his shaggy pony beside his father. Adrianne forced herself to smile and wave. The weight of her separation from everyone and everything she had come to love settled over her. When they were gone, she walked blindly to the barn and cried against the horse she had ridden from the Brazos. At last, exhausted of tears, she wiped her eyes and stroked the horse affectionately for its gracious tolerance, if not understanding. She gently pressed her hand against her waist and went back to the house. For now, she and the unborn baby were trapped in the stone mission with Mrs. MacFee.

Chapter Twenty-Six

Adrianne continued the work for which Farnsworth paid her, although she would have worked for nothing. Only when her mind was at some task could she forget that Hermann was headed home to Texas. Only when her mind was otherwise occupied could she forget the Kiowa. Even then, her mind would occasionally wander back to him. It was very late as she sat beside one of the mission boys who was feverish, wiping his forehead with a wet towel.

"Thou art tired," whispered Susan Farnsworth, gently pushing her from the bedside chair. "Go and sleep. I will sit here or get one of the other women."

"I do not wish to sleep. I need to think of a way to get home," Adrianne said, rubbing her neck and stretching her back, now weary with the weight of Satanta's child.

" 'Tis a pity what that Texas man is doing to thee, but tomorrow is another day." The gentle woman spoke assuringly.

"There have been so many tomorrows here." Adrianne rubbed the back of her folded arms. "Is there ever a now with these men? I must get home to Lottie."

"Thou couldst not travel anyway . . . now. Thou art too far along."

Adrianne gently touched her swollen stomach. She sighed.

"Does thou dread thy child?"

"Dread him?" asked Adrianne.

The Quaker woman looked down. "Thou cannot know his father or desire a child made under such circumstances. Missus MacFee is plain about that."

"I'm not Missus MacFee. This is my child, Missus Farnsworth. I know his father. I do not dread his son."

Susan Farnsworth leaned back, somewhat shocked by this woman's words. "I am sorry to have misspoken. I spoke worldly thoughts. I am afraid I have become used to women here, who do not want the children begotten upon them by the Indians. Some are even grateful when the child dies. Our Society thinks all children deserve a life. I was going to offer to raise thy child, here, at the school, or send him to a family in the East."

"Not this child," Adrianne said. "He will be born, and he will live."

"Thou hast considered the difficulty for thee and for thy child?" Mrs. Farnsworth looked down, studying her hands.

"I will manage," replied Adrianne.

"Thou will manage, but will thy child?"

Pains woke Adrianne. She moaned, catching her stomach. *Well, my little Kiowa dancer. Our time has come. There is a baby coming. He is swimming in the water.* Adrianne struggled out of the bed, knocking over a small glass.

"What's happening?" inquired Caroline MacFee.

"The hard pains have started," responded Adrianne.

"Mercy," said the country woman, throwing her feet out from under the covers and onto the floor. "Let me help you."

"I'm fine."

"Missus Farnsworth and I will be the judge of that." Mrs. MacFee helped Adrianne into a chair. "I'll be right back with her."

As the woman departed in her nightgown, Adrianne looked at the room of her confinement. It was simple and now clean, but nothing like the Kiowa lodge where she had helped with

266

the birth of Woven Blanket's grandchild. She felt she wanted to go out somewhere in the open where the air could cool her sweating body, where the child could fall gently from her onto the earth. But before she realized it, Caroline MacFee was back with Susan Farnsworth, and they were lifting her onto the bed.

"Please," Adrianne said. "Let me deliver, kneeling."

"Thou are not a wild Indian," Susan said. "Thou will have thy child like a civilized woman."

The hours passed, but the pain did not. Susan and Caroline remained by the bed, wiping her face and arms with towels wet in icy water. "What is taking so long?" Adrianne asked Mrs. MacFee as Susan went for more water.

"You ain't no chick, dear."

"You are deceived," Adrianne answered. "I'm just starting."

Mrs. MacFee patted her face gently with a damp cloth.

"Your mouth is a cesspool . . . your underwear is dingy . . . and I would be afraid to eat anything you cooked, but your hands are gentle and full of kindness, Caroline."

The other woman smiled tiredly. "Whatever you say, Missus Chastain . . . Adrianne."

Adrianne suddenly caught Caroline's hand. "If I die . . . no, I will not die, but I will tell you the truth nonetheless, Caroline."

Mrs. MacFee leaned closer, holding the laboring woman's hand tightly.

"I do miss him in every way. And I do regret that I will not share his bed again."

"Ha," chortled MacFee. "You do not regret what brought you to this?"

Adrianne smiled weakly as the pain began again. "I can't say that, no." She breathed harder as Susan Farnsworth again appeared at the bedside. Adrianne fought the pain. Exhausted, she fell asleep as it passed.

Caroline MacFee studied Adrianne. "She's a lady," she said. "She'd die before she'd lie. Drag this Injun brat the rest of her life and never back water to nobody. Me, I was glad when you give mine away to that Injun woman to raise. Nobody will ever know but us that Caroline MacFee couldn't stand to face her sorry old man with an Injun kid. Folks can whisper I whored with the Kiowas, but nobody'll have living proof." She considered Adrianne's face. "Waste about her, ain't it?"

"Yes, a waste for them both," said Susan contemplatively. "Do thou think we should fetch the doctor? She's gone on far too long."

Adrianne woke suddenly. "Dear God, help me," she begged, writhing in pain.

"Go get the doctor, Caroline," Susan decided. "I will handle this."

By the time Caroline returned with the doctor from Council Grove, Susan Farnsworth was carrying away the bundled child of Adrianne Chastain.

"It's gone, Doctor," she said, leaving the room, accompanied by the physician.

Caroline MacFee went to the bedside and sat down heavily, waiting for Adrianne to awake again. She dozed as she waited.

"I want to see my baby," Adrianne said weakly, arousing Caroline several minutes later.

Caroline fought herself to full waking and leaned over the ashen woman who had become her friend. "It's gone, sugar."

"I heard him cry," whispered Adrianne frantically. "I heard."

"Well," Caroline answered, "I reckon something happened, Adrianne. It ain't a perfect world."

"Did you see him?"

"Missus Farnsworth took it away."

Adrianne attempted to rise, to get out of the trap that held her. "Help me, Caroline."

Susan Farnsworth, who had now returned with the physician, pushed her back gently. "Doctor Harris is going to give you something to help you rest."

"I don't want to rest," protested Adrianne. "I want to get up. I want my baby."

"Easy now, Missus Chastain," said Doctor Harris, forcing medication between her lips as Susan Farnsworth and Caroline held her. "What's done is done. No going back, now."

"No," shouted Adrianne, spitting too late, fighting weakly. "No."

The man and the two women held her against the bed until the medicine and sheer exhaustion felled her protests. Susan Farnsworth cried quietly beside the bed throughout the night, weeping for Adrianne and the child of Satanta.

Someone had put up the shade, and sunlight struck Adrianne Chastain, burning through her eyelids until she awoke. She lay for moments, trying to remember where she was. A house, she knew, but not her own. And then she knew and closed her eyes again. A small moan escaped her throat.

Caroline MacFee's head came up. "Are you awake?" Not waiting for the answer, she called out loudly: "She's awake. Thank God, she's awake."

Susan Farnsworth scurried into the room. She bent over Adrianne who opened her eyes and said softly: "I want to see the baby . . . his body."

"Mercy, child," Susan whispered, sitting on the bed, grasping Adrianne's hand. "Thou hast slept for four days. We despaired of thee and held its funeral yesterday."

"Oh," choked Adrianne. "I cannot bear this . . . not this."

Adrianne did not know when winter began to change into spring. She sat in the upstairs bedroom at the window where she had stood with Hermann Kaltwasser and watched the rain that watered the gourd seeds, but she did not see. The food set before her went untouched, until Susan Farnsworth and Caroline MacFee fed it to her slowly, forcing in some nourishment. She chewed and swallowed, but did not know she ate. By turns the women sat with her or stood for long moments, watching her, adjusting the bright quilt across her lap. She slept sitting in the chair at night, awaking in the darkness that was indiscernible from the darkness within her soul.

"Britt Johnson can read," Adrianne Chastain whispered between parched lips.

"What?" asked Caroline from her bed. "Did you speak, Adrianne?"

"Britt Johnson can read," the woman said again.

Caroline went to her and knelt beside the chair. "Adrianne, do you know where you are?"

Adrianne turned at the sound of the words and looked into Caroline MacFee's face. She considered the words for a long moment as she looked about the room. "I'm at the Kaw Mission."

"Hallelujah!" shouted Caroline, catching Adrianne's face in her hands. "Great God Almighty! Set still, now. Don't move." Caroline ran from the room and galloped down the stairs to find Susan Farnsworth outside, where she was hanging clothes. "Adrianne's to herself!" she exclaimed.

The women ran together back into the house and up to the bedroom. Adrianne stood at the dresser, scooping water from

270

a basin onto her face and throat. They came slowly, cautiously, into the room, suddenly shy in their hope and joy.

She turned, seeing them in the mirror, and wiped her face with a small towel. "I can write Britt," she said. "He can read. He can tell me where Lottie is." She sagged slightly in her weakness, and the women rushed to her, crying and hugging her. Within the hour, Adrianne Chastain had written her letter, and Henry Farnsworth had posted it in Council Grove.

Adrianne worked to regain her strength as she worked at everything else. The small hope, or perhaps the duty, of finding Lottie had led her out of the darkness as the tiniest light of a distant fire may lead a lost man across the blackest night. Britt Johnson's reply came in less than two months. He told Adrianne that all was well, and that he had been successful in negotiating with the Indians for the return of Mary and the children. Lottie was with his family in Weatherford, away from the danger of the Brazos frontier, away from Charlie Morehouse. The child was in good health, but was quiet now, as might be expected after her captivity and long separation from her family. She did, however, enjoy the bulldog pups, Britt said, and seemed better than at first.

Adrianne folded the letter neatly and stuck it into her skirt waist. She went directly to Jesse Leavenworth's office. The agent looked up, startled by her unannounced presence. He noted that her eyes were no longer glazed and unseeing, but danced with fire and purpose.

"By God, Leavenworth, I want to know what is going on here. Are you completely incompetent? My granddaughter, Millie, is somewhere out on the prairie, shivering in the wind, and you are sitting in front of the fire, writing letters. Find her, and let me go home. I can travel now, and I have work to do." Mrs. Chastain had had enough.

271

"You know I have sent out time and time again. We were told on good authority . . . I have told you repeatedly . . . the child is dead."

"She is not dead."

"Don't be obstinate, Missus Chastain." Leavenworth leaned on the desk. "Think about the other little girl . . . what was her name? . . . Lottie."

"I am thinking about her. The sooner I find Millie, the sooner we can go home to Lottie," Adrianne explained. "I want to go look for her."

"Missus Chastain, you have an exaggerated view of your abilities . . . and mine," spluttered Jesse Leavenworth in growing anger. "We don't want to expose you to the dangers of traveling across Indian country, let alone allow you back among the Kiowas. A thousand miles across open country? Ridiculous! I've told them that in Washington. Ridiculous! They must give us money for a water route. I will personally take you to Fort Smith, and you can return home through civilized country."

"Not without Millie," said Adrianne resolutely.

Leavenworth threw his papers at the desk. "The Kiowas say she is dead. We have asked repeatedly. You have been told repeatedly. Now let me ask you something. Could you find her, when you were on the plains? Could Satanta himself find her?"

Adrianne looked down. "No."

"Then, how in God's name can you expect a white man to find her? I suggest you turn your attention to your living granddaughter. We'll keep looking. That's the best I can do for now."

"Very well," agreed Adrianne. "If I cannot go and look for Millie, I will go home. I want to leave tomorrow."

Leavenworth dropped his head into his hands and ran his

fingers in exasperation through his hair. "There is no money, Missus Chastain. There are no arrangements. You cannot leave tomorrow or for that matter perhaps for weeks or months. It may be fall before we hear anything from Washington. You must wait."

"I'm through waiting, Colonel Leavenworth. I'm going home," Adrianne Chastain said softly.

"You can't do that," blustered Leavenworth.

"Watch me." Mrs. Adrianne Chastain closed the door of the Indian Agency.

Without identification, without more cash than her earnings at the mission, Adrianne Chastain hired on her word and her father-in-law's business reputation among the freighters what she needed to make the journey — teams, three teamsters, and five wagons. She filled them with supplies and spoke to the Texas women and their children held at the Kaw Mission.

The following morning she mounted one of the wagons, cracked the bullwhip in her hand, and headed the captives for Texas. Across the thousand miles she drove the creaking wagon, listening to the love song of Caroline MacFee as she spewed profanities over the backs of the second team. By the time the women reached Weatherford, their families had received word of their arrival and waited expectantly. Adrianne slipped from her wagon unnoticed in the confusion and passed through the crowd to the big, black man who held a small, white girl in his strong arms. The woman stopped a few paces away from the child, afraid to rush at her in her own hunger.

"There's Marn," Britt Johnson whispered softly to the child. Seeing the woman, the child buried her head against the black man's neck.

Adrianne waited.

"It's all right, Lottie," added Mary Johnson, standing at her husband's side. "Marn's come to take you home to the Brazos."

"She's come fer you," said Britt again. "What's you gonna do, baby? What'd you tell me you was goin' to do, when you seen her?" There was a long hesitation, and then Lottie Doogan released the neck of Britt Johnson and reached out toward Adrianne Chastain.

The woman ran to the little girl and took her in her arms. Mingling her own tears with her kisses, she spoke the child's name over and over. "Lottie. Oh, Lottie." She turned about on the sidewalk, trying not to crush the child in her need. She sat with her on the weathered steps and rocked her. *After all . . . after all,* Adrianne thought to herself, *I have Lottie. Yes, after all, I have Lottie.* "We're going home, Lottie. You and I are going home."

Britt Johnson and his family sat around the woman and child, watching the crowd clear from the street. At last the man spoke: "When you leavin', Adrianne?"

"Just as soon as I can arrange for money to be sent to Kansas. Just as soon as I can see a lawyer about a crook," the woman said, rocking the contented child.

"Charlie Morehouse?"

"Charlie Morehouse."

Driving up Elm Creek, Adrianne Chastain passed the homes of her neighbors. They came out to watch her pass by. Thornton Hamby removed his hat and shook her hand. His new bride, Gracella, offered the woman and child water and a roof for the night, but they moved on, wanting to reach home. Just before twilight, Adrianne drew the team to a stop in the yard of the burned-out ranch. She sat on the box, looking about. Had she expected that Susan's body would still be in

274

front of the steps or Jule Johnson's on the charred porch? She did not know. She knew only that she and Lottie were home.

The men Britt Johnson had hired for her arrived over the next days and weeks. They pulled down the remains of the house and started a new structure of stone, just as the woman had visualized, lying in the Kiowa teepee, trying to keep her sanity. The barns were repaired, the garden plowed and planted, new linens and furniture bought, and Charlie Morehouse discharged. Over time, she reopened the freight business and the inn. But every evening, when moonlight poured over the valley of the Brazos, after everyone was fed and every chore completed and all slept beneath her clean blankets, she stood on the new porch of the new house, looking at the high hill across the creek.

Finally, one night when the cottonwoods shed their down and the white sage almost touched the grazing horses' knees, Adrianne crossed the creek and climbed the hill above her home. She needed the perspective, she told herself. She wanted to see how the ranch looked now, rebuilt. Near the top, she turned back to see the place. *It is good,* she thought of the neat buildings, sitting comfortably on the land. *There is harmony here.* She smiled at the Kiowa thought. A few more steps and she topped the hill to stand, overlooking the ranch. She turned at last slowly to see the spacious land beyond stretching over the curving earth, running beneath her feet out onto the distant prairie where the Kiowas were. A movement in the shadows startled her reverie. The soft whicker of a horse drew her attention. One of the herd must have gotten tangled in something. Adrianne forgot her meditation and went to set the animal free. When she saw it clearly, she stopped frozen. The colt she had saved from the bear, the colt Satanta had given her, was tied to a feathered lance. Around its neck and down its mane were wreaths and garlands of flowers and sage. Feathers danced in its forelock as it tossed its lovely head. "Oh," Adrianne Chastain gasped. She went quickly to the horse, stroking it, whispering to it, smelling its wonderful earth smell. Then Adrianne Chastain began to dance. As she danced, spreading her shawl, dipping to the beats of unheard drums, she sang:

Behold, I am alive.
Behold, I stand in good relation to the earth
and its creatures.
Behold, I stand in good relation to the Sacred.
Behold, I stand in good relation to the beautiful.
Behold, I stand in good relation to you.
Behold, I am alive. I am alive!

"So you remember the Kiowas," a voice said from the shadows.

Adrianne turned. Satanta stood, waiting.

Epilogue

"I'll have the other stone ready for you tomorrow afternoon," the stone cutter said, looking at the black-clad woman. "I never had nobody before buy two stones exactly alike. Whatever'd you want two for?"

The woman looked up. "I'm taking one home to put on a hill above my place. His body may be here, but his spirit is there . . . *free.*" She said the last word very softly to herself.

"Seems kind of wasteful. But, I reckon, it's your money. Besides, the tombstones ain't for the dead, but for the living. Are you satisfied with it, all right? Can I go home now? My wife is waiting supper."

Her eyes were not on him. She did not hear him.

Adrianne Chastain nodded. "Yes, you have done a good job. I will pick up the other marker before I leave tomorrow." She handed the man who had a boy with him a handful of coins for their work.

As their wagon crunched away over the sandy road, Adrianne walked over the cemetery. She bent to wipe dirt from the face of the new marker.

Satanta, Chief of the Kiowas, she read as her finger moved over the deeply cut letters. *Tibi Venebo.* She looked up at the massive prison walls beyond the graves. So many years, so much sorrow had come since the time she and the Kiowa had ridden together over the plains. Now it was over, all the battles, the trial that had put him there, and the war

277

that had sent him there for good. Somehow she felt he was safe now. Not somewhere on the plains, his body eaten by wolves, as he had sung long ago, but safe in the Land of Many Lodges, waiting. She touched her lips with her fingertips, and then the chiseled words as she whispered: "*Tibi venebo,* my beloved. I will come to you."

"Hunnh," a man cleared his throat. "I'm Thomas Goree, the warden. I saw you from the prison."

"I intended to call upon you tomorrow and thank you for your efforts on Satanta's behalf. But how did you know I was here?" asked Adrianne Chastain.

"Ma'am, every eye on this side of the building has been on you, since you got here. I was bound to hear. May I see you to your buggy? It's kind of lonely out here, isn't it?"

"Yes," the woman agreed, lowering the black veil over her face.

As they walked across the porous soil back to the hired buggy, Thomas Goree continued: "I wrote to you, when I saw that he was failing. I hope his death did not come as too great a shock."

Adrianne shook her head. "No. I had expected it for a long time."

"It was a brave thing you did, speaking up at the trial. You probably saved many lives. The Kiowas might have burned the whole frontier, if Satanta had been hung. It took a lot of courage to defend a man so thoroughly hated."

"Courage?" asked Adrianne.

"Yes, ma'am, it couldn't have been easy for you . . . knowing what people expected, . . . knowing what they would say, if you spoke up for the man. You could have lived quietly without adding any further to the dirty speculations." The man ducked his head, knowing that his words were wrong, wanting to add comfort, instead of pain. "But for a few hours on the

Brazos, your life would have been quite different."

"My life was made complete in those hours," Adrianne contradicted the man. "Of course, I did not know that then. You are the superintendent of a great prison for men convicted of crimes, or perhaps the lusts for money and power and revenge that lead to crimes. But until that October afternoon on the Brazos, I, too, was a prisoner, as tightly bound as any of them. Then I lost everything that was important . . . my home, my children, my dignity, my freedom, even my honor. When I had spent the last coin of my life and virtue, when I was completely bankrupt and had nothing more to give, I fell into the boundless and abundant love of God. Satanta was the portal. I shall always be grateful to him and love him."

"Well, then, ma'am, you know he wasn't a man for a prison. He just could not adjust, when they sent him back the second time after his release and the Anadarko outbreak. I guess, when he realized General Sherman would never relent again, he gave up. He was just steadily slipping away."

"Yes," the woman said thoughtfully, "steadily slipping away."

The warden spoke as they walked. "How long had it been since you'd seen him?"

"July Fourth, Eighteen Seventy-One," Adrianne answered. "Right after the trial. That was the last time I spoke with Satanta. July Fourth, Eighteen Seventy-One."

The man offered her his hand as she stepped into the black rig. She paused for a long moment, looking back at the cemetery, the new gravestone, and the prison beyond.

Adrianne Chastain saw the lantern bobbing before her again, leading her through the wet-smelling stone laundry back to the cell where Satanta and Adoltay, the young chief accused with him in the wagon train raid that resulted in the murder of seven teamsters,

279

were being held. The soldier stepped aside to allow her to look into the room.

"What have you done?" Adrianne asked, holding an iron bar of the small window, pressing her body against the heavy wooden door that stood between her and Satanta.

"I have fought my enemies," the Kiowa said.

"They were just common, ordinary men, no threat to you, no match for you." The woman spoke with sadness.

"They were taking corn to soldiers," Satanta stated.

"And you were trying to show you were a better chief than Kicking Bird. And then you were bragging about it before the white men, throwing it in the face of William Tecumseh Sherman himself."

"You always speak too frankly." Satanta gently placed his hand over hers. "Let's go home, Taukoyma."

Adrianne looked into his eyes, trying to read their blackness in the shadows. "You know . . ." — as she began the sentence, the weight of realization settled over her — "we can't do that . . . not in this life. You've fallen into their hands, Satanta. They are making an example of you."

Satanta nodded and sighed deeply.

Adrianne tried to shrug off the feeling that the man was slipping away, slowly receding from her. "Joe Woolfolk and I spoke for you. You will not be hanged. You will go to prison. He thinks that you have a good chance of being released when the general's point is made."

Satanta seemed uninterested. "Ha! I am a hostage again! But the boy will be glad to hear that. I hate white men's ways. I hate how they nearly ruined you. But now you are a Kiowa woman. You are Satanta's woman."

Adrianne nodded, forgetting the intricacies of the justice system, the foolishness of temporality, realizing beyond the inessential circumstances of their lives the meaning.

"I will come to you on that high hill above your house," Satanta said. *"One day I will come to you."*

"Tibi venebo," Adrianne Chastain whispered as she took the reins and turned the sorrel horse toward home. "I will come to you."

About the Author

CYNTHIA HASELOFF was born in Vernon, Texas and was named after Cynthia Ann Parker, perhaps the best-known of 19th-Century white female Indian captives. The history and legends of the West were part of her upbringing in Arkansas where her family settled shortly after she was born. She wrote her first novel, RIDE SOUTH!, with the encouragement of her parents. Published in 1980, the back cover of the novel proclaimed Haseloff as "one of today's most striking new Western writers." It is an unusual book with a mother as the protagonist, searching for her children out of love and a sense of responsibility, rather than from a desire for revenge or fame. Haseloff went on to write four more novels in the early 1980s. Two focused on unusual female protagonists. Of the two, MARAUDER was Haseloff's most historical and finest novel among her early books. As one review put it: "MARAUDER has humor and hope and history." It was written to inspire pride in Arkansans, including the students she had known when she taught high school while trying to get her first book published. Haseloff's characters embody the fundamental values — honor, duty, courage, and family — that prevailed on the American frontier and were instilled in the young Haseloff by her own "heroes," her mother and her grandmother. Haseloff's stories, in a sense, dramatize how these values endure when challenged by the adversities and cruelties of frontier existence. Her talent rests in her ability to tell a story with an economy of words and in the seemingly effortless way she uses language. Haseloff, whose previous novels include THE

CHAINS OF SARAI STONE, MAN WITHOUT MEDI-CINE, and THE KIOWA VERDICT, this last the winner of the WWA Spur Award for Best Western Novel in 1997, once said: "I love the West, perhaps not all of its reality, for much of it was cruel and hard, but certainly its dream and hope, and the damned courage of people trying to live within its demands." THE PRAIRIE QUEEN will be her next **Five Star Western.**